OPEN YOUR HEART

A MATT BOLSTER YOGA MYSTERY

OPEN YOUR HEART

A MATT BOLSTER YOGA MYSTERY

NEAL POLLACK

Text copyright © 2013 Neal Pollack
All rights reserved.

Printed in the United States of America.

Published by Thomas & Mercer, Seattle

ISBN-10: 1477848444
ISBN-13: 9781477848449

Library of Congress Control Number: 2013910651

Originally released as a Kindle Serial, July 2013

For Dido Nydick, Charles McInerney,
and Dara Susini, the Austin teachers

PROLOGUE

At sunrise on Monday, Rogelio Suarez found the million-aire's head wrapped in a yoga mat.

Rogelio, the gardener, had come early to trim the palms, which was much easier in the morning than in the afternoon. He didn't enjoy the dawn patrol more than anyone else, but he was used to getting up at 5:00 a.m. for work. Besides, even this close to the coast, it got hot above the frond line around midday, so it was better to get going, especially given the relatively high quality of the job. Rogelio had friends who, by now, were already blowing dust around the parking lot of their day's second Gardena minimall. By comparison, Rogelio felt like a yachtsman. At least it was quiet and private here in lawn-land. He could stop to drink a Red Bull on ice if he wanted and no one would bother him. He could even have a Monster Energy, which, when he drank it, made his heart feel like it was going to blow out of his chest. It felt like freedom.

As Rogelio dragged along his ladder and machete, he saw the mat in the middle of the back lawn, like a soft, oblong, bright-purple egg left by the Yoga Bunny. That was curious. Sometimes he'd find a plastic champagne glass left over from a weekend fundraiser or Bat Mitzvah party, but usually the owners kept their lawn as immaculate as a Beverly Hills cemetery. Which, Rogelio was about to find out, the lawn now somewhat resembled.

Rogelio had a lot of survival rules in his life, which was why he'd been relatively successful for so long in such a brutal city, but one of his most steadfast was *Never touch the gabachos' exercise equipment.* In particular, he'd learned to walk a wide path around anything yoga-related, like mats, blocks, or blankets. The *gabachos* took that shit seriously, like they were religious artifacts. They often placed them next to statues of the Buddha and that weird Indian monkey god. Rogelio didn't practice yoga himself—by the end of the workday, he was too tired to do anything but drink a beer and watch Los Doyers—and he wasn't particularly interested in it or curious about it. But he respected spiritual beliefs, even those he didn't understand. If someone had come into his house and messed with his wife's Virgin of Guadalupe altar, either on purpose or by accident, they'd be walking funny the next day.

But on this day, Rogelio needed it out of the way. The *gabachos* didn't like their stupid rubber mats sullied by lawn trimmings, and he was worried that his severed palm fronds would float down. Rogelio dropped his work gear, went to the mat, and touched it. There was a bulge in the middle, and a few sticky red droplets along the edge. Rogelio knew then there was trouble and should have called the police immediately. Instead, he flipped the mat open.

His boss's head tumbled out. It had been chopped at the neck, poorly. Bits of gristle and trachea hung down like so much exposed wall cable. The bald head, which had been as shiny and blemish-free as a custom-polished wooden bedknob when Rogelio had last seen it, now looked gray and puffy. The mouth was barely open, and the eyes had rolled back in a death-moan. No amount of detox-spa scalp exfoliation was going to save him now.

Rogelio shrieked, loudly, *como una niña*.

The day had begun.

Six hours later, LAPD homicide detective Esmail Martinez stood in the yoga room of that same Beverly Hills mansion. Martinez had dismissed the gardener, innocence determined, to drown his morning terrors in a lunchtime *michelada*. Inside the yoga room, responding officers had found three other mats holding equally gruesome parcels. One enveloped a bloated, hairy naked torso; another held two arms and two legs bound together with yoga straps like corded wood. The third and vilest contained a variety pack of viscera, a horrible rubber burrito of guts and bile that made a huge stinky mess when the mat unrolled. At least one officer blew his breakfast.

"A yoga room," Martinez said. "A goddamn yoga room."

Such houses used to have billiard rooms, indoor swimming pools, bowling alleys, or even a second living area. But now that extra leisure space was all waxed bamboo flooring, red flowing silk, and Hindu iconography. You weren't a proper West Side doyenne unless you kept a handcrafted harmonium in the corner under an imported Krishna tapestry.

Martinez had done yoga. It was hard to avoid yoga in L.A. He'd felt pretty mellow for hours afterward, too, but he'd soon decided that his evenings were better spent drinking tequila and beer, and watching *Gladiator*. Having Russell Crowe at full volume on his custom-installed home-theater system made him seriously feel like a man.

Still, even with his limited experience, Martinez knew something had gone sour here. Wasn't yoga supposed to be about calming down the mind and loving your fellow humans? For a discipline that preached peace, love, and relaxation, it sure seemed like yoga made a lot of people who practiced it totally crazy. And sometimes dead.

The dismembered man wrapped in the yoga mat had used his considerable Hollywood power to bring a couple of Kate Hudson comedies into the world, which in turn had paid for his wife's Eastern-tinted spiritual fetish. And now look at him. His head had been sealed in a bag and taken somewhere cold, to rot more slowly.

Martinez didn't quite understand. But he knew someone who claimed to.

That someone entered the room.

Matt Bolster stood about six-two, with sandy-blond hair— slightly receding, close to shoulder length—and three days of graying stubble. His body was fit, though certainly nothing special in this Hollywood era of four-hour prelunch workouts. Walking through the average American airport, this guy would have been a relative Hercules, but in L.A., he was just another pretty-good-looking middle-aged dude with a casual style. He wore light-brown pants crafted from the finest hemp, brown flip-flops, and a T-shirt depicting Dr. Bruce Banner meditating in lotus posture. The words "Hulk Relax" were written underneath. There was some red in his eyes. He looked like he'd just rolled out of bed, not necessarily his own.

Matt Bolster was a man with few attachments.

"Hey, Bolster," said Martinez. "Nice of you to show."

"I got here as fast as I could."

"I called you four hours ago."

"Like I said."

"I don't know. You showed up pretty fast after Ajoy Chaterjee was murdered."

"I really needed the money then."

"You need the money now, too."

"Not quite as much."

Of course, Bolster still needed it pretty badly, but he didn't want Martinez, his former partner, to know that.

Make him think you're flush, Bolster, he thought. *Don't show weakness.*

Matt Bolster had once been an LAPD homicide detective just like Martinez. But one day a girl took Bolster to the Hollywood YMCA for a yoga class. Within months, he'd quit the force, cashed in his modest pension, and moved to a small apartment just off Venice Beach. Now Bolster was a certified instructor with five hundred hours of study tucked into his stretchy shorts.

Suddenly, his given name became very ironic. How could his parents have known, back in 1968, that their son's name would someday represent two popular yoga props? Back then, there was no Lululemon, or Bikram, or 4:00 p.m. Core Power Vinyasa Flow. Yoga was something the Beatles did in India, not something that encompassed the physical and spiritual lifeblood of every upper-middle-class person from Encinitas up to the Sonoma Coast.

Bolster quickly realized that yoga wasn't going to pay for anything other than a coffee after class. So he'd hung out a P.I. shingle. Just about any cozy could stake out a motel room or do online document searches. But Bolster was the only one who could do that while also knowing how to adjust someone trying to get into revolved triangle. He had expertise.

"You solve one major homicide, and you think you're a hot-shit yoga detective," Martinez said.

"I don't think I'm anything," Bolster said. "Besides, it's not like I'm batting a thousand. I couldn't do anything for you when that acupuncturist got it in Koreatown."

"That one was rough," said Martinez. "Six needles in each eye."

"Talk about pressure points," Bolster said.

"They caught the guy, though."

"Yeah," Bolster said. "In Korea. And not because of me. I didn't speak the language."

But he did speak a little Sanskrit. It was part of his training, and it served him well. He took off his shoes and stepped inside.

"I wish I could afford a yoga room," he said to Martinez.

"Yeah, well, you can't have everything in life," Martinez said.

"Actually, if you practice yoga right, anywhere can be a yoga room."

"Is that so?"

"Yes. You do yoga in a *shala*. People think that means 'sacred space' or temple, but it's actually a Sanskrit word for 'barn.' Very subtle."

"Very," Martinez said. "Get to work, Bolster."

"Time to activate my powers," Bolster said.

Such as they are, he thought.

Bolster didn't actually have any special deductive skills, but he was pretty good at sussing out the vibe of a situation. Yoga taught him to work his edge, and he'd found his edge in buckets. It wasn't about being the best detective in the world; it was about living in the moment and loving himself despite his extreme limitations as a human being. Matt Bolster definitely had limitations. But he also had lots of self-love to give.

He looked around.

The yoga room had one wall that was fully glass. This overlooked the sloping lawn, a "cocktail pool," a two-bedroom guesthouse, and an impenetrable border of eucalyptus trees that marked the back of the property. The rest of the room's walls were painted a soothing shade of ochre, a double-coated veneer that exuded warmth and mellowness. But the perfectly waxed floors had been sullied by red-yellow splotches, and the room smelled faintly of rotten meat. Someone had danced with his shadow self in here. The shadow had won.

Sacred space, my ass, Bolster thought.

Over in the corner, a police tech was dusting an altar, maybe ten feet by twelve, covered with an exquisite red lace tapestry. On top of that sat an incense burner and a statue of Ganesha that had a wilty-looking garland of flowers around its neck. The flowers looked at least three days old. There was also an iPod docking station, but no speakers. Bolster looked up. The speakers had been built into the wall, in all four corners. This was high-end.

Bolster looked at the altar. There was a photo of a good-looking blonde, midforties or so.

The yoga wife, he thought, ruefully. *There's always a yoga wife.* He knew the type well. In the photo she had her arm around a handsome, tanned guy who was wearing shorts, a tank top, and a hoop earring. *The guru.* They both grinned toothfully in a way that indicated their relationship involved a lot of complex positions that could only be practiced with a partner.

For every dozen hotshot yoga teachers swinging their cocks around Manhattan Beach at twenty bucks an *asana* pop, there was someone who offered privates to the lonely rich, making real American coin. As with anything else vaguely shady, a lower profile combined with genuine skill tended to lead to higher profits. The trouble was that sometimes the grift worked both ways. Yoga had a vengeful side.

"Find him," Bolster said.

"Find who?" said Martinez.

"The teacher."

Bolster pointed at the picture.

"He and the wife did it together."

"How do you know?"

"I know."

"And how am I supposed to find him?" Martinez said. "Everyone in L.A. looks like that."

"His name is Todd Lovelace. He trained with Patthabi Jois in Mysore in the early '80s, and then he went and lived in an ashram for a while. When he came back to Los Angeles, he used to walk around Santa Monica wearing pink robes, like a *hare krishna*, but that didn't get him any followers. So he kept the shaved head but worked on his tan and started playing loud music during his classes. That worked the ladies up into a frenzy. In 1999, he opened a studio on LaBrea, and on Friday nights he plays the harmonium and chants for like four hours. He gets more ass than 1979 Mick Jagger."

"I'm guessing you have an address for me, too," Martinez said.

"Yeah, he lives in a condo complex just down the block. But he's also got a pad up in San Luis Obispo. That's where he takes his special clients. I'm guessing that's where they split. Unless they went down to Mexico, which makes sense. Anyway, that's not my priority. I don't do manhunts."

"You got a motive for me?"

"Sex? Money?" Bolster said. "Who knows? Yoga distorts the passions."

"Of course it does," Martinez said.

"When you catch them, you can hold a press conference," Bolster said."I know how much you love to do that."

"Fuck you, Bolster," Martinez said. "Are you sure about this?"

"Absolutely," Bolster said, tapping his right temple. "Yoga can drive you nuts."

He held out his hand.

"Pay up, Martinez," he said.

Martinez handed him a thick envelope.

"Two thousand bucks," Martinez said. "Mostly hundreds and about twenty twenties."

Bolster peeked into the envelope, looking pleased.

"Nice," he said.

He headed toward the door, looking distracted.

"Gotta jet," he said. "I'm subbing a four o'clock at the Santa Monica Zen Center. A favor for a friend."

"Good for you," Martinez said.

"They think they're going to get a huge workout, but I'm going to have them do legs up the wall for twenty minutes. They'll never know what hit them."

And then he was out the door.

"What was that?" the tech said.

"That was Bolster," said Martinez. "I used to work with him."

"You pay him to solve crimes for you?" the tech asked.

"Sometimes," Martinez said. "But that wasn't payment. It's poker money from Saturday night."

It had been rough. Bolster had just worn Martinez down, hand by hand. A lot of the guys at the game were drunk before midnight. Martinez had started to fade around 2:00 a.m. But not Bolster. He went almost until dawn, drinking nothing but water, blinking only when necessary, until every other player was completely exhausted, heading toward an all-day hangover. Their cards started flopping around like fish on the dock, while Bolster raked in the chips.

That guy could sit calmly forever.

CHAPTER ONE

So tell me, Matt Bolster," Suzie Hahn asked, "have you solved any awesome cases lately?"

Suzie stuck her little microphone right up in Bolster's grill. She was across from him on his couch in the living room of his one-bedroom Venice Beach apartment, looking excited to be alive. Bolster's cat, Charlemagne, sat between them, sullenly watching *Finding Bigfoot*. The cat seemed to find the green tint of the night camera scenes soothing. Because of the ongoing interview, Charlemagne had to watch it on mute, and he didn't look pleased. Charlemagne seemed to really enjoy swatting at the screen when the protagonists imitated the Bigfoot call. Bolster had never known an animal that liked TV so much.

"Mwroooooowr!"

"Cut the crap, Charlemagne!" Bolster said.

"I can edit that out," said Suzie. "We don't want audio of you being mean to your cat."

Suzie Hahn kept a blog about the L.A. yoga scene, which she covered with surprising thoroughness. She attended up to five classes a day, getting there either via bike, public bus, or ride-mooch. She never had a negative thing to say about any class or any teacher, which may have contributed to her blog's rising popularity. Bolster wasn't sure how, but she seemed to make a living doing this sort of work, bless her heart.

In the last few months, Suzie had added a podcast to her media mix. After Bolster solved the Ajoy Chaterjee murder, she'd pestered him for an interview. He'd agreed, mostly to get her to stop texting him. Besides, he figured, no one would ever hear it. But he was wrong. Suzie Hahn had thousands of listeners all over North America. And they were loyal. She had her niche.

Her first question was "What's it like to be a yoga detective?"

"It's like being a regular detective," Bolster said. "Only a lot more relaxing."

That was the phrase that launched a thousand ships. Or at least a dozen ten-session passes. After Suzie's first interview with Bolster, more people started showing up at his yoga classes. She'd advertised them pretty prominently and kept doing so. Bolster couldn't figure out why. Suzie didn't seem to have a crush on him. She didn't seem to have a crush on anyone. Finally, one day, he just asked her.

"Why?" he said.

"Because you're my friend, and I think you're awesome," she said.

Well, at least someone did. Bolster was grateful. After he became a regular on Suzie's podcast, his status in the yoga world perceptibly changed. He wasn't the guy with a hundred students and a headset, at least not yet, but he could draw fifteen people at noon and on evenings and weekends a couple dozen. Guaranteed. One Saturday morning at ten thirty, Bolster counted forty bodies. He had followers. This was actually starting to pay some bills.

But with benefit came struggle. Yoga was supposed to be about authentic connection, with yourself, and with others. That seemed easy enough to Bolster when it was just him and five overweight Iraq veterans rolling around in the back room of a West L.A. addiction center, but he found it harder to keep it real when trendy yoga people actually started to pay attention to him. More people meant more chance for dysfunction in the room. Still, it was all just part of the practice, and Bolster thought he could handle it.

"So tell me about the producer who was murdered in Beverly Hills," Suzie asked. "The wife ran away with Todd Lovelace?"

"Apparently," Bolster said.

"I can't believe Todd would kill someone," Suzie said. "I took a class from him once, and he was a really nice guy."

Soledad O'Brien, she was not.

"Were the guts *everywhere*?" she asked.

"They were mostly cleaned up by the time I got there."

"OK, let's change gears. I love to ask all my guests this, but you've been so fascinating every time I've talked to you that I keep forgetting. Do you mind answering a really basic question?"

"Those are the best kind," Bolster said.

"Cool," she said, leaning in, smiling. "So, Matt Bolster, what's your favorite yoga pose?"

Bolster had answered this question before.

"Headstand, definitely," he said. "I like it so much better than shoulder stand. Of course, they're complementary poses, and you can't master one without understanding the other . . ."

This went on for a couple of minutes. Like most yogis, Bolster had a pedantic side. Suzie stopped recording.

"Great!" she said. "I might edit out the stuff about the shoulder stand."

"You want a beer?" Bolster asked.

Suzie looked thoughtful.

"Hmm," she said. "I don't drink before taking a class."

"You're always taking a class," Bolster said.

"I know, right? So I don't drink. I was thinking about biking over to a 6:00 p.m. flow at Hacienda de Paz."

"OK," Bolster said.

"But I *am* thirsty," she said. "Have you got any kombucha?"

"There's a jar in the fridge," he said.

"Excellent!" she said.

Bolster hung out with a lot of yoga people. He liked to be hospitable to them, even if that involved home-growing a fermented symbiotic bacteria that smelled like old socks soaked in white vinegar. Fresh kombucha always made him friends.

While Suzie was in the kitchen filling her reusable BPA-free bottle with magic sour kombucha juice, Bolster checked his e-mail for little shots of joy. A West Hollywood studio was offering a "Find Your Mind Meditation Flow" weekend workshop for $225. *Pass.* A lecture on "The Secret History of Asana in Pre-Colonial India" at Loyola Marymount. *Snore.* Another Netflix offer. He was already sharing a subscription with three other people. *No.*

But one gem shone out from the coal.

Dear Matt Bolster, the e-mail read. *This is Kimberly Wharton. I'm the Media and Entertainment Director of The Hart Yoga Federation™, which was started by Tom Hart back in 1996. Through Hart Yoga™, Tom has trained hundreds if not thousands of teachers around the world and is widely recognized as one of the leading authorities on the yogic body and the spiritual qualities of asana flow.*

Sometimes Bolster had to admire yoga entrepreneurs for their devotion to PR bullshit. He usually deleted stuff like this immediately, but the second paragraph flipped the formula.

So I'm writing you with an offer, Kimberly Wharton wrote. *I've been listening to Suzie Hahn's podcast and like what you're serving up down there in Venice. How would you like a teaching spot at the next Gathering up at the Hart Center™ in Ojai next month? Your stories and experience and teaching style would really appeal to our Gathering crowd. You'd probably just get a small class in the early afternoon, Saturday and Sunday, because you're new. But we can offer you $200 plus meals and a private bedroom in the teacher's dorm.*

Bolster was familiar with Hart Yoga. He knew some really talented teachers who'd come through the lineage. But there were problems with the practice. Every time he did a Hart Flow, he felt good afterward, almost too good, like his chest was about to explode with happiness and goodwill. It was nice to have some degree of that in your life, sure, but Bolster's life goal wasn't to float around grinning like an idiot. Yoga was supposed to simultaneously lift you up *and* ground you. You need to balance hyper *prana* energy with its earthy, downward-flowing counterpart, *apana*. Hart Yoga didn't have enough *apana*, Bolster thought. The people who practiced it didn't always make the most skillful life choices. They were doing yoga, but their practice was a little too trendy for Bolster's taste.

On the other hand, the hardcore Hart Yoginis looked damn good in stretchy pants. This was L.A., after all, one of the few places where the commercial stereotype of the gorgeous yoga babe was actually true. Of course, ordinary people of all shapes and sizes practiced here, but they didn't do Hart Yoga, at least not more than once. It was too physically demanding, too expensive, and too flaky, qualities that tend to attract a certain clientele. Namely, the type that could afford to attend expensive weekend resort parties in Ojai.

The Hart Gathering had been going on for a few years. Getting invited to teach there, whether you were Hart-trained or not, was a rite of passage for the L.A. yoga teacher, not one that many got to experience. In a world that was supposed to exist without status, it was nonetheless a total status symbol—not a career clincher, by any means, but a real boost, kind of like an Independent Spirit Award. As people liked to say around this town, it was an honor just to be nominated.

"Weird," Bolster said, as Suzie came back into the room.

"What?" said Suzie.

"I got invited to teach at the Hart Gathering next month."

"Oh, I know," she said. "I'm on their media advisory board. I help plan the Gathering. I recommended you."

"Really?"

"It wouldn't be a yoga festival without the great Matt Bolster."

"Stop trying to boost my ego," Bolster said. "Too much ego is bad for a yoga teacher."

"Don't be such a nerd," Suzie said. "Just go and have fun!"

She was right, of course. Someone was offering Bolster money to spend a private weekend with a large group of young, sexy, emotionally unstable yoga women, and also some dudes, who would hang on his every word. It wouldn't be healthy, but it sure would be fresh.

Hey, Kimberly, Bolster typed. *Thanks for the flattering offer. I guess I could fit it into my schedule. Do you need me to send you an invoice?*

CHAPTER TWO

On the Friday morning of the Hart Gathering, Bolster woke up early for him, a bit after 8:00 a.m., and strolled down the boardwalk to a little stand for a double shot of espresso. He didn't usually drink coffee, preferring tea's milder buzz, but some days required a little extra brain-jacking. The espresso jolted him so much that he ripped off his shirt, charged toward the ocean, and threw himself into a cold oncoming wave. Fully awake, he went home, smoked a bowl of *indica* to blunt the coffee's edge, and took a shower.

Bolster had his travel backpack on his bed, which at the moment contained nothing but the splayed form of Charlemagne. *Sorry, fat-ass*, Bolster thought. *No weekend away for you.*

Bolster wondered what he should wear to teach at a yoga conference. For the daytime hours, the answer was obvious: a pair of decent exercise shorts, a variety of semi-ironic super-hero T-shirts, and a pair of long hemp pants for after class, along with optional hoodie in case it got chilly. For the nights, he wasn't so sure. Maybe a pair of jeans, a pair of cords, a pair of closed-toe shoes, and a couple of collared shirts.

Also, a bathing suit. Yoga people liked to sit in hot tubs. It was an all-inclusive privilege of their membership in America's surprisingly large Eastern-spiritual-tinted bourgeois leisure class.

Bolster wanted to fit in with them, at least clotheswise. He knew that desire was kind of shallow, but there it sat, and he had to accept it as such. He wasn't going to show up in Ojai looking like just another hippie yoga bum.

Next, he packed a handful of condoms (just in case something intriguing presented itself), a dozen or so off-brand ibuprofen, a full sheet of Lactaid, and a little pill bottle full of fine *sativa* to go with his pipe, his lighter, and the little silver-plated pick he used to clean gunk out of recalcitrant bowls. He was set.

Road trip.

There was a knock at Bolster's door. He opened it. Lora Powell stood there, looking calm. She was Bolster's meditation teacher, and she really walked the Zen path. Lora had no possessions, other than an old Honda Civic and a few pieces of Tibetan artwork she'd picked up on a retreat. She lived at a small *zendo* tucked up in the folds of Mount Washington, teaching classes, cooking, cleaning, and otherwise living communally with a couple of guys who weren't technically monks but still practiced celibacy and preached the eightfold path. It wasn't ideal, but, as Lora always said, "It's hard to get a good gig in the Zen world."

Lora had been Charlemagne's original owner but had to give him up when one of the fake-monks developed an allergy. Bolster had agreed to take the cat but thought it would only be temporary. Now Lora was Charlemagne's babysitter whenever Bolster went out of town.

"Hey, Bolster," Lora said, giving him a kiss on the cheek.

"Howdy."

Charlemagne yowled hysterically.

"Your friend missed you," Bolster said.

Lora put down her bag and ran over to the couch.

"Hiiiiiiiiii, baaaaaaaaby!" she shouted.

The cat immediately turned on his back and started squirming around, clearly desperate for a tummy rub. She gave him what he wanted, and he purred ecstatically.

"He never does that for me," Bolster said.

"You should be nicer to him," she said.

"It goes both ways."

"When was the last time you cleaned his litter box, Bolster?"

"Five, six days ago?"

"How'd you like to poop in a toilet that hadn't been flushed for five days?"

"Point taken."

"He's such a sweetie," Lora said, as Charlemagne nuzzled her.

"I dispute that," Bolster said. "Are you sure you don't want to come along instead of staying with him? I'm allowed to bring an assistant."

"Thanks for the offer," Lora said. "But those aren't my kind of people."

"Mine either," Bolster said.

"They invited you and you accepted. That means that you belong to them."

"No attachments," Bolster said.

"Right," Lora replied.

An hour later, Bolster was cruising the 101, though "cruising" might have been a misnomer, since he was in 30 mph traffic through Calabasas. He drove Whitey, his 1998 Nissan Sentra, which had ceased being stylish the day it left the production line but now just looked like a battered old shoe, trying to find its way among thousands of bigger, stronger, and better-looking cars. It was a feeling that most cars (and people, for that matter) in L.A. knew well. Whitey hadn't given Bolster much trouble, other than a weird midlife electrical malfunction that had fried its automatic locks and rendered the front driver's-side window inoperable. But it was worn and ugly and not much fun to drive, even on a sunny day heading toward the coast.

Suzie Hahn sat in the passenger seat, headphones on, listening to something sunny and spiritual while gleefully promoting the Gathering with her phone's Twitter app. She was happy and drug-free all the time. Her body was clean and healthy, her thoughts unsullied, her sleep calm, her diet sensible and steady.

Not for me, Bolster thought, as he sucked on a joint, passing it to the backseat.

In the three-hole, barely fitting, sprawled Bolster's buddy Slim. In the absence of legitimate yoga help, Slim would serve as Bolster's assistant for his Gathering classes. Slim had no particular yoga skills other than a preternaturally innate sense of how to live in the moment, but he had his uses. He was a skilled martial artist and could claim constant access to the best weed south of Eureka.

He took the joint from Bolster and gave it a good long drag, filling the car with smoke from his exhale. Suzie coughed and rolled down her window. The one on her side actually worked.

"I barely fit back here with my didge," Slim said.

Slim played the didgeridoo, and played it well, as far as anyone could gauge such a thing. He claimed to have toured with a band that once was the opening act for Nine Inch Nails. Though Slim offered no proof of this in the form of posters or photos or anything else, Bolster believed him. Slim's stories often had at least a remote basis in fact. If you Googled "didgeridoo" and "Widespread Panic," you could always find at least a couple pictures of Slim.

"Sorry, dude," Bolster said. "Whitey's meant for speed, not comfort."

"Luxury living," said Slim.

Slim was wearing an American-flag bandana and a black T-shirt depicting a cartoon pig being loaded into a sausage grinder, with the caption ENJOY YOUR BACON! Bolster congratulated Slim on making a bold political statement. Slim responded by saying he'd found the T-shirt at Goodwill and just thought it was funny.

The traffic cleared before they hit Thousand Oaks. It took them eighty-seven minutes to get to Ojai, total, a good day on the road. They turned north onto the 33 at Emma Wood State Beach and crawled upward. The first few miles through the foothills were hot and dusty; there hadn't been a real rain in months, and the landscape was all rusting front-yard boats and firecracker stands and convenience stores that had too many customers hanging around the parking lot for that time of day. But at a certain point, the trees turned green, the air turned crisp, and the architecture turned rustic genteel. Mohammed had come to the mountain.

"I love it up here," Suzie Hahn said.

Ojai had been a go-to destination for Southern California's seeker class for nearly a hundred years. In 1922, the great thinker J. Krishnamurti took up residence at a retreat in the heart of the verdant valley, saying, "It is essential sometimes to go into retreat, to stop everything that you have been doing, to stop your experiences completely and look at them anew, not keep on repeating them like machines. You would then let fresh air into your mind. Wouldn't you? This place must be of great beauty with trees, birds, and quietness, for beauty is truth and truth is goodness and love."

Such clarity and simple wisdom appealed to a certain kind of Western luminary, and Krishnamurti catered to them for more than sixty years, playing host to the world's humblest salon. He sat in a state of blissful critical inquiry with Dr. Jonas Salk, Jackson Pollock, Igor Stravinsky, Greta Garbo, D. H. Lawrence, and Aldous Huxley, among many other lights famous and obscure. Though Krishnamurti had been dead for nearly thirty years, and no one nearly as intelligent as his guests had existed since—with the possible exceptions of Neil DeGrasse Tyson and the guy who created *Mad Men*—Ojai's spiritual tradition lived on in the form of yoga studios, natural-healing centers, and shops selling candles made with natural ingredients. It was a functional, prosperous town, not showily megacommercial, nestled among high chaparral and pines and orange groves, and the occasional trickling waterfall. The real estate wasn't cheap, but it wasn't coastal price, either.

That's why, barely ten miles away from where Krishnamurti had once quietly reigned, Tom Hart was able to build his Hart Center, a perfect glade for elven yoga princesses. But compared with Krishnamurti's humble spiritual stroll, Tom Hart was leading a caravan of party buses. When his followers opened their hearts, there wasn't much room left for the content of their heads.

As Bolster approached the Hart Center, three of Whitey's four windows rolled down, he could hear the tinkling of bells, chirping, the steady trickle of a dozen fountains, and the unmistakable rhythm, from somewhere in the gut of the resort, of a Michael Franti song. Bolster's tastes didn't run toward pop yoga music, but the Hart people loved it.

Someday, Franti, he thought, ruefully, *you will face your reckoning.*

They parked the car in a roped-off area marked with a sign reading TEACHERS' LOT and walked their stuff a short distance up to the main lodge. It was low-lying, with a gabled roof, brightly painted shutters, and wood siding that looked so fresh that it might have been cut the day before. Neatly mani-cured patches of native-style landscaping framed the entrance; these cultured arrangements of brush and aloe and decorative succulents, accented with shiny rock, were a sure indication that you were about to enter Yoga Land. The sign above the entrance, reading THE HART CENTER FOR HEALING AND DEVO-TION™, was another giveaway.

Slim stood at the entrance, held his didge to his lips, and gave it a ceremonial-style blow. It sounded like geese mating. Bolster gave him a look.

"I felt moved by the moment," Slim said, shrugging.

They went inside. Suzie didn't get two steps inside the door before she unleashed a squeal.

"Oh my God!" she shouted. "Hiiiiiiiiii!"

A registration table had been set up in the foyer. Behind it sat a woman, not thin, not tall, but perfectly sculpted, a Botticelli in yoga pants and knit pashmina. She practically glowed with health. Her hair waved perfectly, the tawny color of red-panda fur. She was Bolster's type, pretty much exactly, especially when you figured in her wry, noncommittal eyes. She stood up.

"Suzie Hahn!" she shouted.

They hugged, jumping around like soccer players who've just teamed up for a goal. When they extricated, the fox-like lady turned her attention.

"You must be the great Matt Bolster." She held out her hand, which Bolster gladly took. "I'm Kimberly Wharton. We e-mailed."

"Oh," he said.

Bolster didn't know why he was surprised when people he corresponded with turned out to be hot. This was Yoga Land, after all. If he wanted ugly, he could always go back to dealing with bail bondsmen.

"Suzie has been talking about you. We're really psyched to have you at the Gathering."

"I'm psyched to be here," Bolster said, adding, in his thoughts, *but not so psyched to be using the word "psyched."*

"It's so awesome," Suzie said.

Kimberly said, "I'd really like to take your class, but Tom is giving Level Three teacher-certification seminars at the same time."

"That's fine."

"It's the Air Module," she said. "He doesn't offer it very often."

"No problem," Bolster said, though he had no idea what an Air Module was. He hadn't seen that mentioned in *Light on Yoga*.

"So today you can take a class or two if you want or just kick back and enjoy the scenery."

She winked at him.

"There's a lot to look at."

Slim was off to the side, playing with his instrument.

"Hey man," Kimberly Wharton said. "I like your didge."

"You know what they say about the size of a man's didgeridoo . . ." Slim said.

"I don't," Kimberly replied, looking sincere. "What do they say?"

Hart Yogis weren't particularly known for their senses of humor.

Bolster and Slim took their stuff to the "teacher's dorm," essentially a bunkhouse with a common TV room and a snack vending machine. Except, instead of TV, there was an electric fountain. And instead of a vending machine, there was a glass container filled with ice water and sliced cucumber, as well as dishes full of dried berries and nuts. Their room had bunk beds, a simple dresser, and an attached toilet and shower. The Hart Center saved the fancy accommodations for paying customers, though the teacher's bunkhouse did have free wireless.

Bolster and Slim changed into their bathing suits, smoked a bowl, and walked to the pool area. It was a quiet afternoon, but a dozen women lounged near the water, along with a couple of dudes with manicured dreadlocks and catalog bodies. Bolster watched as one of them, his skin nut-tan, practiced crow pose at the pool's edge, then rose up slowly and carefully into a perfect handstand. He held it for at least a minute, raised up one hand, then the other, and finally flipped himself into the water. Everyone applauded as he emerged from the pool with a little headshake.

A woman came up to Bolster and Slim.

"That's Hanuman," she said. "Isn't he amazing?"

"His name is *Hanuman*?" Bolster said.

A certain kind of American yoga practitioner—Craigs and Lizzies all hopped up on an *asana* high—had a tendency to adopt spiritual names to signify their ascension to a higher plane of mental reality. Hanuman was one of the most important Hindu gods, the loyal monkey-servant of Rama, a great trickster and fierce warrior. It takes big stones to take the name of a deity.

Hanuman emerged from the pool, dripping. The yoga sylphs surrounded him, with happy smiles. This was not the home, it appeared, of *bramacharya*, the ancient Tantric art of sexual self-restraint.

"The Force is strong in that one," Slim said.

"Yeah," Bolster replied. "Too strong."

Bolster couldn't help it. He felt his alpha-male hackles rising. If he'd had feces to throw at Hanuman just then, he would have. Hanuman walked by him, toward the towels.

"Hey," he said.

"Hey," Bolster said.

"I'm Hanuman."

"Matt Bolster," said Bolster. "This is Slim."

Hanuman shook Bolster's hand and leaned in. His grip was taut. His breath smelled faintly of mint and apples.

"You're teaching this weekend," he said. "I saw your name on the flier."

"Yeah," Bolster said.

"Don't expect too many students the first session. You need to build a reputation."

Some reputations are better left unbuilt, Bolster thought.

"I just want to make sure no one gets hurt," he said.

Hanuman laughed, almost dismissively.

"No one gets hurt doing yoga," he said.

People get hurt doing yoga all the time, Bolster thought. *In so many ways.*

"What time's your class?" asked Hanuman.

Bolster told him.

"That's when Tom's teaching an Air Module. It's very rare that he offers it up. So I can't make yours."

"No problem," Bolster said.

"It's all good," said Hanuman.

Why do people say that, Bolster thought. *It's not all good. Sometimes it's very bad.*

"I like your sleeve, dude," Hanuman said to Slim, pointing to Slim's left arm, which was covered in fiery tats from wrist to shoulder.

"Thanks," Slim said. "It's temporary."

"It doesn't look temporary," Hanuman said.

"According to the *Yoga Sutras*, everything is temporary," said Bolster.

Slim and Hanuman looked at Bolster quizzically. All around them, damp women paraded shamelessly in front of a verdant backdrop, like a yoga-themed revival of *Temptation Island*. Philosophical arcana had no place in such a setting. It was a good day to clench your *mula*.

"Let's have ourselves a weekend," Slim said, and he cannonballed into the pool.

"You ready to hang out, Bolster?" Hanuman said. "It can get wild at the Gathering."

Bolster was pretty sure he didn't have a choice.

CHAPTER THREE

Tom Hart entered our earthly realm in Glendale, Arizona, in 1966, during the height of a tire-melting summer. Unlike his hero the Buddha, who he'd often misquote later in life, Tom began in humble circumstances. His parents brought him home from the hospital to a four-room cinder-block house painted Pepto-Bismol pink, which sat in the middle of an unincorporated lot. It was a habitat fit only for desert scrub and scorpions. It had as many water beds as it had windows, plus a swamp cooler, allowing the house's interior to somehow feel simultaneously scorched and moldy.

His dad owned a dumpy bar on Sixteenth Avenue, east of Glendale Boulevard, one of the least reputable streets in an already sketchy town. Dad's tastes ran toward fringed leather jackets, big sunglasses with brown lenses, pencil mustaches, and cheap whiskey. Mom didn't have her own car, so when Old Man Hart was at work—which he was most of the time—she breast-fed, stranded on a concrete raft in the middle of the desert. Three years later, a little brother joined the happy party, and six months after that, Mom walked in on Dad making water bed waves with a cocktail waitress. Dad was quickly dispatched, and though he'd occasionally drift into view on weekends or Christmas, he was less a man than a cigarette-smoking specter with bad taste in clothes and music. Mom raised the Hart boys alone.

She got a job at the phone company, back when doing such a thing meant job security and steady income. Gradually houses went up around them, and the roads got paved, and Tom and his brother went to school. Tom spent his childhood babysitting, more or less, making breakfasts and lunches by age eight and vacuuming by age ten. Sometimes Tom would watch *Wallace and Ladmo*, the local morning cartoon-host heroes, imagining a different childhood for himself, a life with some comedy, or at least a whiff of whimsy. He'd look in disgust at the nice Phoenix children with their curls and blond crew cuts and their pretty, indulged faces. To his mind, they might as well have been Martians. It was always the other kids who got the Ladmo bags.

But Tom Hart didn't need Ladmo, because he had God. His mother got him started young. Mrs. Hart (who never called herself anything else, even, strangely, when she remarried in the early '90s) raised her boys on a steady diet of Jesus and Whataburger. On Sundays after church, Tom got used to downing two thin brown patties coated with neon-yellow mustard. As he ate, his mother told him, "Jesus is watching over us, all of us, even your bastard of a father. No matter how hard times may get, he's with you, always. You have love inside your heart. Jesus is that love."

The idea that someone was with him always scared Tom more than a little. But it became the framing principle of his life. Mrs. Hart didn't worship a vengeful God. Her guiding Jesus was forgiving, accepting, and nonpunitive. So Tom believed. Thinking of Him brought serenity to Tom's childhood, a time that very easily could have belonged to the devil. And soon, thanks to God, Tom would learn that he had a special gift: he could persuade people to give him lots of money to help promote putatively spiritual causes.

Tom was one of the Christian kids, a very good boy. He had no time for teen fandom. MTV rose and he barely noticed. He'd already lost a father to drink, so he ignored alcohol of all kinds. Drugs weren't even mentioned in his circles. Occasionally, he'd steal a chaste kiss with someone under a pine-scented Young Life weekend retreat moon, but it never led anywhere. His heart was full of Jesus, and there was little room for girls. After school clubs, summer camps, church car washes: everything existed to make Tom a purer fund-raising vessel for the Lord.

In his senior year, Tom gave a speech to an international association of high-school believers in Topeka as a representative of his church, which raised hundreds of dollars to send them there. In his speech, he told the story of how his mother had raised him and his brother up from the depths, harnessing Christianity's mighty power to save his family from ruin. He said, with all sincerity, "I truly believe that Jesus radiates from all our hearts and into the hearts of all who need him. We exist as living testaments to God's holy love." And he'd believed it, obviously, because the auditorium thundered. Two months later, the Christian scholarship offers began to arrive.

He settled on a small school in the southeastern foothills of Southern California, about thirty miles from downtown Los Angeles. In 1986, the city was entering one of its most decadent periods. But they lived clean up at Central Pacific Christian, which was so buttoned-up and well mannered it might as well have been a genteel retirement village. Tom's life was suddenly very different. Whereas he'd come of age in the spiritual soup—down with the seekers who'd lost jobs and homes and even, in tragic cases, children, people who really needed the Lord—suddenly he found himself being trained for Christian *leadership*. These were kids, like him, who'd taken charge of Christian communities in high school. Many of them came from far more privileged backgrounds, and they showed it, driving up to their dorms in brand-new Corvettes and BMWs. Tom only had a used bicycle, which he rode to the convenience store to get Oreos and Slim Jims. Tom had always known poverty, but he'd never *felt* poor until now. He was a scholarship kid. His classmates weren't just holier than thou. They were holier than *everyone*.

He participated in classes, and in prayer meetings, and occasionally would throw a Frisbee on the lawn with his roommates, but slowly, he could feel the Lord leaving his heart, and he began to despair. At night, he would drop to his knees and beg for help. "Please, Lord," he'd say, "help me keep my faith in you." But his soul was heavy. When he was done praying, he'd cry for half an hour. Sometimes, he'd eat out of an ice-cream tub with a spoon, and then he'd stay up and watch ESPN, in the days when ESPN was showing lawn bowling at 2:00 a.m. It was the mid-'80s, and late-night media options were limited for sad young American men. Like another of God's favorite angels, Tom Hart was heading for a fall.

One afternoon midway through his junior year, as he was sitting down to write a thirty-page paper for his seminar on the secret diaries of Saint Francis of Assisi, Tom got sick. At first, it was just a mild headache, then a bit of a fever, and then chills. He assumed that he'd caught a cold and took a couple of Bayer aspirin. But the headache got worse, and eventually he had to lie down. A couple of hours later, the tremors started. Tom found himself shivering uncontrollably, but also sweating. His right leg started to spasm. His lungs ached. He could feel them filling up with fluid. And then he realized:

I need to go to the hospital right now, or I'm going to die.

Unfortunately, Tom had chosen to live alone that year in a singles dorm dotted with lonely, rough-carpeted "common areas" that the residents never used.

"Help me," he moaned.

But no one could hear him.

Tom pushed himself up. His arms were shaking and his eyes were leaking fluid. He lurched toward his dorm-room door and stumbled into the hall, falling to his knees. His legs weren't working right. His mouth was the only part of him that felt dry. The rest of him was soaked. He lay down, gasping.

But he didn't die that day, because his room was only two doors down from the rear exit, which happened to open onto a reasonably well-traveled sidewalk between buildings. Tom dragged himself toward the door, clawing the synthetic carpet with his half-bitten nails, feeling the spirit leaving his body like shampoo foam going down the shower drain. Somehow he pulled himself up enough to push open the bar to the back exit and down three concrete steps, the lower half of his body useless and numb. The last thing he remembered, for days, was lying on his back on the grass, the Southern California sun warm on his face, as he drooled and flopped around like a hooked fish.

A week later, Tom Hart woke up in a hospital room, feeling spectral. There was an IV in his arm, which seemed to have lost half its mass. His sainted mother was there, stroking his hair. His little brother sat in the corner, looking worried.

"What happened?" he said.

"You had a bacterial infection in your spine," his mother said. "You were in a coma for several days. But everything's all right now."

And she began to cry. Because, of course, everything was *not* all right. The virus had caused nerve damage to Tom Hart's spine, leaving him mostly useless from the waist down. Not exactly paralyzed, but weak and dysfunctional.

Fortunately for Tom, though he didn't realize it at the time, he'd been hospitalized in Pomona, California, which, in addition to being a prosperous college town, was also home to Dr. Mitchell Cohen's Pranic Healing Institute. PHI was an alternative health center of the type that tends to take root in places with large populations of wacky progressives who have a reasonable amount of disposable income. But the PHI was no mere repository of hippie quackery. Yes, it preached *ayurvedic* nutrition and sometimes prescribed herbal remedies for anxiety disorders, but those treatments had been making people feel better for thousands of years. These were real doctors who practiced real medicine, and they all had real degrees. Except for the likable *reiki* guy, whose background was a little sketchy.

Tom Hart's doctor at the hospital didn't moonlight at the PHI. But he had taken many hours of classes there. Tom may have ended up assigned to the only spinal specialist in North America whose first thought didn't immediately turn to surgery and massive doses of painkillers. One afternoon, while he was looking at Tom's chart, he turned to Tom and said,

"Have you ever heard of yoga?"

From such innocent questions, wicked empires rise.

On Friday evening, after a predictably bland dinner of steamed vegetables, mushy grain, and overtart hibiscus iced tea, Bolster and Slim went back to their bunks, took a couple of hits off a portable vaporizer, and chowed down on some beef jerky from Slim's backpack.

"Why is the food at these things always so fucking horrible?" Bolster asked.

"I don't know," said Slim. "I don't go to these things, usually."

But Slim had been having fun. He'd shown off some martial-arts moves by the pool and spent a good forty-five minutes of the afternoon giving an impromptu didgeridoo concert on the lawn, which attracted a half-dozen mellow dancing ladies, far more than his usual audience of zero.

"The worst part," Bolster said, taking a drag, "was how everyone was talking about how blessed they were to be eating. I understand that we're supposed to be grateful for everything we have. But these people weren't just glad that they were being nourished for another day. They were acting like this food was *amazing*. Just because you do yoga doesn't mean you have to turn into a fucking idiot. You're supposed to practice discernment."

"Right," Slim said, though he hadn't been listening. "So you want to head back?"

"I guess," Bolster said, grabbing his mat bag.

"Relax, buddy," Slim said. "This is yoga. This is *fun*."

Slim was cool, but he had all the intellectual acuity of a duck. Bolster was definitely capable of having fun in a yoga crowd, but not, at the moment, this one. Part of that might have just been insecurity. Bolster felt off. He wasn't used to being in the crowd's bottom third, percentile-wise, when it came to looks.

It was time for the weekend's opening convocation, or, as it was known in the Hart world, The First Gathering. They held it in the main room of the great hall in the main lodge, a vaulted space that could legally hold three hundred. The space was blond wood all around, with big windows to let in abundant natural light, plenty of top-rate ceiling fans, and a low stage equipped with professional-quality sound equipment and spot gels. This was the big stage where the big yogis played.

By the time Bolster and Slim got there, the room was already three-quarters full. Bolster was glad he'd brought his mat, because that appeared to be the seat of choice. Running a yoga conference wasn't cheap, but you could always skimp on chair rental. Bolster and Slim found spots toward the back, pretty far from the stage but at least away from the doorways. It gave Bolster a decent observational vantage point.

All around the room, a beach of gamine yoga monkeys— mostly but not all female—had unrolled their mats, upon which they were doing unimaginable things. Some of them had their legs behind their heads. Others were bending backwards from a straight stand. There were many swooping, one-legged *chaturangas*, and various peacocks and folded trees, poses that most yoga practitioners took a decade or a lifetime to master. These were poses that Bolster wouldn't even consider trying, and they were doing them as warm-ups. Worst of all were five guys, smack in the middle of the room, who were shirtless, perfectly sculpted, and standing on their hands. Every now and then, one of them would swoop out of handstand and through a *vinyasa*, never even touching down his feet until hitting a perfect upward dog. Then he'd push back into down dog, immediately drift forward into crow, and then lift back up into handstand. It was an impressive, unworldly, and totally annoying display.

Bolster could stand on his hands, too, and it was fine to do in private or in a certain class context. But to do it in public only fed narcissism, and narcissism was the enemy of all true yoga.

"Enough with the fucking handstands already," Bolster said to Slim, who was busy trying to push himself into a handstand.

"Cut that out," Bolster said.

"Why?" Slim said. "It's fun. Quit being such a grandpa."

The lights dimmed. Music played, harmonium mostly, accompanied by lyrics that, if spelled out, would look something like "Ahhhhh-ai-ai-ai-ai-waaaaaaahhhhh." It was a sound meant to invoke higher feelings, a sign that a spiritual being would soon appear.

Tom Hart appeared on stage, smiling and waving like a politician who'd just won on primary night, pointing at people in the crowd, pumping his fist. Bolster had been prepared for the preternatural cheeriness, but he wasn't ready for how *powerful* Hart would appear. He wasn't tall, but he was thick and looked like a massive tree among his willowy followers.

This was how it always went at the Gathering: Friday was to arrive, relax, and see old friends, to take things casual and build community. There were workshops and seminars, but it stayed low-key and friendly. By the evening, the students were ready, so, as the proverb goes, the teacher appeared.

"Hello!" Hart said, happy and friendly.

"Hello!" said everyone in the room, except Bolster. They replied with a frightening uniformity of tone.

"How are you all liking the Gathering so far?" Hart asked.

There followed fifteen seconds of whooping and whistling that Bolster found obnoxious. When Hart said, "Are you all remembering to *take it easy*?" everyone but Bolster said "Yes!" He was having a hard time relaxing.

"All right," Hart said. "Now, you're going to have a lot of time to hear me talk this weekend, because, you know, I talk *a lot*."

"Too much!" shouted someone from the front, where the favorites and the most fervent sat.

Hart laughed. "Maybe so," he said. "But tonight isn't about talking. It's about *flowing*, about feeling our bodies and our hearts and opening ourselves to the sky. About finding the devotional part of ourselves and giving just a little bit to the people around us. About connecting to the universal divine."

Oh, brother, Bolster thought.

"So let's sit up straight on our mats," said the guru, signaling that the flow was about to begin. "Feel your sitz bones evenly distributing weight underneath you. Close your eyes and take in the sounds around you. Listen to the birds and the breath. Good. Now breathe in for a count of five. One . . ."

And, just like that, the room snapped into silent attention. No one moved a twitch. This was a well-practiced bunch of yogis.

They flowed solid for forty-five minutes. It was a night class, candlelight style, so everything was soft and slow and relaxing. It was all back-bending and heart-opening, but it lacked grounding. Hart's flow was all pretty by-the-book, but his people took it as writ, and they began to improvise, twirling and whooshing like belly dancers, celebrating everything that their young and supple bodies could do. At the height of the flow, Hart stepped aside and said, "Ladies and gentlemen, I present to you Hanuman. And his Hanumaniacs."

Bolster had never before seen a yoga class get interrupted for a featured performance. But this was Hart's Gathering. He wrote the rules.

Hanuman came out on stage with three other dudes, all of them dreadlocked and shirtless, wearing the same long tan hemp yoga pants that Bolster favored. This embarrassed Bolster a little, but what could he do? Comfortable and attractive yoga clothing for men was hard to come by.

The Hanumaniacs, who Bolster realized were the guys from the center of the room at the start of the class, started doing the most athletic sun salutations that Bolster had ever seen, one-legged chair poses that jumped perilously back to *chaturanga dandasana*, and extended side angles that extended longer than they should and then wrapped around and then bound. Their spines were like perfectly aligned, brilliantly calibrated rubber bands, with just enough tension to stretch but not enough to snap. These guys had *trained*.

"Whoa," said Slim, next to Bolster. "They're good."

"Don't get sucked in," Bolster said. "Being good at yoga does not mean—"

"Shhh," said Slim, who was clearly feeling the Hart Yoga vibe.

Hanuman planted his palms and rose into handstand. His Hanumaniacs joined their leader, but, Bolster noted from his far-off perch, Tom Hart did not. He was not one of the gapers. He stood off in the shadows, where it was impossible to see his facial expression. But Bolster could see that Hanuman was truly popular. Judging by the sizable number of women who wore T-shirts bearing the image of his Indian monkey-god namesake, there were more Hanumaniacs in the crowd. Bolster couldn't imagine Tom Hart liked that much.

Hart took control again after about five minutes and began the cooldown leading up to a *savasana* during which he recited the names of 128 colors. It sounded like he was reading them off a Crayola box, but even Bolster couldn't resist the trancelike powers of Hart's invocation. He drifted off somewhere between "periwinkle" and "rosé."

Speaking of rosé, Bolster awoke to an announcement that there would shortly be a "limited pour" of boutique wines in the restaurant pavilion. Suzie Hahn came bounding over.

"Wasn't that amazing?" she said.

"I do feel pretty good," Bolster said. "The guy knows what he's doing."

"Right?" Suzie said, shaking her head. "*Right?*"

"Let's not get too enthusiastic," Bolster said.

"I can't help it," said Suzie. "I love the Gathering!"

"Me too!" said Slim, who had wandered back after taking an ogle-tour around the room.

"Bolster," Suzie said, "there's someone here who wants to see you."

Suzie stepped aside. Someone deadly was walking toward Bolster, someone whose very existence spelled trouble, and whose presence in a room spelled almost *immediate* trouble. Especially for Bolster. He couldn't think of anyone else on Earth he wanted to see less. Yet here she was, standing right in front of him, looking better than ever and smelling so very good.

What is she doing here? Bolster thought. *And why is she doing this to* me?

"Hello, Matt," said Chelsea Shell.

CHAPTER FOUR

"Where have you been?" Bolster hissed.

Matt Bolster and Chelsea Shell had a tragic history, at least from Bolster's perspective. She had been a key member of millionaire yoga guru Ajoy Chaterjee's inner circle. A rising seductive yoga force. Chelsea never had to teach in the Valley or on the Eastside; her clientele had been drawn strictly from the flats, from the ocean up to about La Brea. At her height, just the mention of her name would draw forty people at two thirty on a Wednesday.

Things went sour in Ajoy-land. Ajoy pulled his Circle in too close, and one morning he turned up dead in his studio on San Vicente. Chelsea didn't kill him, but she and the rest of the Circle had watched Ajoy torture himself to death, and they'd done nothing. The tree had rotted, from the roots to the branches.

Bolster entered the scene, to investigate. He took one of Chelsea's classes, and they went to In-N-Out Burger together. Then they drove up to a house in the hills where she was staying without the knowledge of the owner and fucked on a rug. After that, Chelsea slipped Bolster a roofie and stole his wallet, which she later returned. But things didn't improve. She kept showing up at his apartment, and sometimes he'd let her come inside and rub on him a little bit. It was bad for his investigation. Bolster rarely struggled with attachment, but Chelsea turned his guts to clay. Her unpredictable nature drew him, like swirling matter getting sucked into the maw of an imploding star. She inspired him to melodramatic thoughts.

The investigation ended, and Chelsea split. Since she didn't have a steady address, few real possessions, and no bank account, it was easy for her to disappear. Her classes were left unfilled, her phone went unanswered. There were no updates to her website, her Facebook feed, or her Twitter account. She didn't have a Pinterest, but if she had, it would have gone unpinned upon. Bolster hadn't heard from her in eleven months, and neither had anyone else.

"It's cool, Matt," she said. "I'm a Hart Yogini now."

"That doesn't explain anything," he said.

Chelsea touched Bolster's arm and took him to a quiet corner, where they could lean against a wall. He didn't even try to pull away. Twenty seconds in and she already had Bolster halfway to supine. Typical.

"Look," said Chelsea, "I know I was weird and shitty to you back in L.A. You were doing a tough job, and I made it much worse."

"That's for sure," he said.

"But you know as well as I do how fucked up that situation was with Ajoy. I didn't know what I was doing. When he died, it was like I'd just woken up from three years of hypnosis."

"You *poisoned* me," Bolster said.

"I know, right?" she said. "I was so bad."

Bolster sighed.

"So what happened to you?" he said.

"Well, I went up north to chill out a little bit. I know this Ashtanga couple that lives in Bali half the year, so they let me crash at their place in San Francisco."

There were few worse places to escape the madness of yoga culture than San Francisco, which had a well-developed scene buttressed by decades of spiritual lunacy. It was the place where tender American souls went to die. Or sometimes thrive.

"I was there for a couple of weeks," she said, "just chilling out, writing poetry, but I started to get restless. A body has to move, you know?"

"Yes," Bolster said.

Chelsea had seen a poster at a coffeehouse that said Tom Hart was giving a workshop at a studio in Marin. She'd always been curious about his yoga and had wanted to try it, but Ajoy Chaterjee was threatened by Hart's growing movement. He had forbidden his Circle from going near the practice, calling it "yoga for teenage sex monkeys." The newly liberated Chelsea Shell called the studio. They said the workshop had been sold out for months, and there was a one-hundred-person wait list. That Friday, the day the workshop started, she went down to the studio, without shame.

"It's been a really hard time for me," she said to the desk person, who apologized nicely and told her, again, that it was full.

Tom Hart had stepped out from behind a curtain, the smell of steamy eucalyptus trailing behind him. It was a vapor trail, a signature scent. He wore an unadorned white tank top and black workout shorts. His eyes shone with clarity and purpose.

"What's going on?" he said.

The desk clerk told him. Tom Hart nodded. He looked at Chelsea, up and down, and smiled. She smiled back, tucking her chin just a little.

"Let her in," he said.

Tom was teaching the Water Module, Part Two, that weekend. Chelsea Shell drank it up. Even though she'd missed Part One, she didn't care. She instantly understood everything that Tom was trying to say. She was wearing a half shirt and folding her legs behind her head in the middle of the room. Tom Hart definitely noticed the beauty and sincerity of her devotion.

"He made my heart feel like a balloon," Chelsea said to Bolster. "The grief I was carrying around with me for all those years with Ajoy, it just instantly lifted."

She had come to Tom Hart. *And probably for him as well*, Bolster thought ruefully. But he didn't say that.

"Well, that's great," Bolster said, instead.

Chelsea kissed Bolster on the cheek and hugged him, hard.

"Isn't it, though?" she said. "I'm so happy you could join us this weekend."

"Sure you are."

"Seriously, I missed you. You should come to the after-party tonight."

"There's an after-party?" he said.

"There's *always* an after-party."

Bolster was never one to turn down an after-party, but something about this scene was cramping his *bandhas*. He felt good, but he also knew that good feelings could be a trap. Yoga was nice to you right up until the moment it hit you on the back of the head with a rock. He would resist for now.

"I'd better not," Bolster said. "I have to teach tomorrow."

She laughed.

"Life is the teacher!" she said. "We're going to dance!"

And she twirled out the door.

Bolster was *not* going to let the Gathering's—and Chelsea's—weirdness affect him. Nothing she said could be trusted, but it didn't matter. The world around was a swirl of sound and sensation, but he could master it; he could view even his greatest temptations with a neutral mind and an open—but not stupid—heart. He was going to teach his class, do his work, collect his check, and get out. Bolster closed his eyes and took a deep breath. He counted in for ten seconds, and then out for ten seconds.

When he opened his eyes, Slim was standing there.

"What's up?" Bolster said.

"I've been talking to the people here," Slim said, "deeper than I've ever talked with any people before. They have beautiful souls."

"It's not their souls you're seeing. It's their tits."

"Life is chemistry," Slim said. "Through our hearts, we're bound together to the divine."

"I see."

"At least that's what Tom says."

Bolster was officially the last skeptic at the Gathering.

"Are you going to the after-party?" Slim asked.

CHAPTER FIVE

Bolster woke early with a clear mind and taut muscles. It was like someone had scrubbed his *nadis*—the energy channels that run through your body as part of the *chakra* system—overnight, allowing him to tap some previously unforeseen wellspring of fresh energy. He was suspicious. Usually he started the day feeling like his head was being crushed in a waffle press.

The window was open. Bolster had left it that way overnight. He breathed in, deeply. The air almost shocked him with its clarity. In L.A., even near the beach, the atmosphere was 75 percent leafblower fumes. This smelled natural, with a hint of pine, the Earth's cologne.

In the bunk above, Slim was snoring, his left arm flopping over the rail like a corpse's limb. He'd staggered in around two thirty, reeking of wine and weed, humming happily to himself. Slim moved through the world untroubled, a big unprepossessing baby—albeit one with dangerous kung fu skills. Even when his world was going to shit, which it almost always was, Slim never had a bad day.

Bolster, on the other hand, always had at least a light cloud cover in his mind at all times. The gloom never dissipated. He'd seen too much of the world's pain and unhappiness and had also probably smoked too much pot. His mind dripped with suspicions of conspiracy and betrayal.

But not today. Today Matt Bolster felt sharply joyful, something he hadn't experienced in quite a long time. He was beginning to taste Hart Yoga's sweet, sweet nectar. *Just drop your head back*, Tom Hart said, *and feel the flow. It tastes like honey wine in heaven.*

Bolster rolled off the bunk, slipped on a pair of yoga shorts, and walked shirtless into the hall. He heard wind chimes and, more distantly, the classically soothing sounds of recorded sitar music. In the bathroom, he splashed some water on his face, deodorized, peed, and scraped his tongue, not necessarily in that order.

Bolster looked in the mirror and saw an abstraction of himself. Was he a slightly tired middle-aged man in reasonably good physical condition, all things taken into account? Or was he an immortal child of the universe who lived, whether he knew it or not, in continual union with the divine mysteries of all creation? Or maybe both?

Either way, he thought, *I'm walking the path.*

And either way, Hart Yoga was slowly turning him into an idiot. He knew it. But he couldn't resist.

Bolster left Slim asleep and headed to breakfast. It was being served on a large patio, off the second story of the main building, which overlooked a little forest, a lot of mountain, and a relatively unpolluted stream. As bad as dinner had been—soggy vegetables and cold quinoa—the breakfast was outstanding. Bolster would have liked some vacation bacon, but this was Yoga Land, a strictly no-meat zone. But there *was* an incredible array of sweet fruits and fresh eggs, both scrambled and hard-boiled, as well as several different kinds of hard and soft cheeses, fresh-baked bread, homemade jams and jellies, and orange juice squeezed from the adjacent vineyard's sacred bounty. No matter how much people abused it with chemicals and over-tilling, California's magnificent loam just kept producing wondrous edible treasures. Bolster chowed down.

He was so into his breakfast that he didn't see Hanuman approaching.

"Hey man?" Hanuman said. "Mind if I join you?"

Bolster had a mouthful of fresh goat cheese. He took a sip of juice and pointed to the bench across from him.

"Please," Bolster said, though he didn't really mean it.

"Thanks," Hanuman said. "I don't think I saw you at the after-party."

"I skipped it," Bolster said. "I was tired."

"You didn't miss much," Hanuman said. "Everyone gets really excited at the beginning. It's almost too crazy. They dance around like puppies off their leashes. I bailed around midnight myself."

"Glad I made the right call," Bolster said.

"The *real* fun happens on the second night," Hanuman said, winking.

"What does that mean?" Bolster said.

"You'll get an invite," Hanuman said, tucking into his granola with soy milk and berries. "All the teachers do."

Bolster *still* wasn't sure what that meant.

"You're teaching today?" Hanuman said.

"Yeah."

"Sorry I can't make your class," Hanuman said.

"No worries," said Bolster.

"I've got to do handstands for Tom during his Air Module. You know how it is."

"How?" Bolster said.

Bolster was, unwittingly, entering Detective Mode. If you just listened, eventually people would tell you something.

"Well, when you're the assistant, you've got to assist," Hanuman said. "It doesn't really matter whether or not you know as much or more as the teacher. You need to wait your turn."

A crack in the china, Bolster thought.

"You know what I mean, right?" Hanuman said.

"Sure," said Bolster.

Go on.

"It just reminds you," Hanuman continued, "that no matter how much you give your spirit or body to something, it's not really yours. We all have to remember that we're just renting space in the universe."

The weird thing, Bolster thought, was that even though Hanuman's words should have dripped with bitterness and regret, he sounded so happy and matter-of-fact saying them. It was as though Hart Yoga shut off all internal controls, leaving its practitioners spouting raw, unpacked inner dialogue. They practiced total honesty with a complete lack of self-awareness. Whoever learned to harness that power could control quite a team of horses. Or get stampeded by them.

"I'll admit it, Matt, I feel adrift, sometimes," Hanuman said, unnerving Bolster with the sudden and random mention of his name. Bolster hated it when people did that.

"Yeah?" Bolster said.

"Sure," said Hanuman. "Don't we all? But at least I have Hart Yoga. I just need to practice for two hours, maybe three, and I'll feel whole again. All is bliss."

Just like that, the glaze reappeared, the other side of Tom Hart's magic formula. The higher up you climbed, the more your personality bisected. You could be simultaneously vulnerable and impenetrable.

"Bliss is good," Bolster said.

Hanuman's face lit with joy, and he began waving frantically.

"I see a friend," he said. "Excuse me."

He got up and ran toward a group of women, shouting, "WHAT UP, BABY DOLL?"

Bolster took another sip of juice. By the time Hanuman returned, he'd be done eating and long gone. Which was fine.

It had been a productive breakfast.

Bolster's class was scheduled from 11:15 to 12:30 in Shakti Room A, which, not surprisingly, was right next to Shakti Room B, in the back far corner of the main lodge. He accidentally opened up the door to Shakti Room B, connected to his room by a sliding canvas wall. In there, a stern older woman was leading two students through a series of grim standing poses using props. They looked at Bolster severely, like he'd just barged in while they were bathing.

"Sorry," he said, and closed the door.

Bolster looked down the hall. It was empty, except for a staff person who was pushing around a little portable dust-gatherer. The cucumber water on the marble-top hall table had barely been touched. You'd find more traffic in a Hardee's drive-thru at midnight on a Tuesday. This is what happens, Bolster guessed, when you get scheduled opposite an Air Module.

Slim stumbled up, carrying Bolster's gear. Since Slim didn't actually have anything to offer, yoga-wise, Bolster had decided to employ him as a kind of caddy.

"Where is everybody?" Slim said.

"We've still got ten minutes," Bolster said. "People could show."

He sat down in lotus position and closed his eyes. Ten minutes passed. No one showed. Bolster had prepared a special flow, to be accompanied by a brief explanation of the heart *chakra*, because people here seemed interested in that sort of thing. He'd also done a short, scripted reminder about the importance of keeping things grounded, which he'd anticipated in advance would be a problem. But it didn't matter. Bolster unfolded his legs and looked at the clock. It was 11:22. He nudged Slim, who had fallen asleep a few feet away, with his foot. Slim shot up, looking frightened.

"Mama?" he said.

"No, it's Bolster," said Bolster. "Get up. No one's coming."

"Oh, bummer for you."

Bolster tried to remain neutral under such circumstances. Sometimes people came to class and sometimes they didn't. But this was an even easier situation for his ego to handle. The good thing about teaching at conferences was that you got a flat fee whether you drew in clients or not. You could afford to be nonchalant when you weren't headhunting.

"It's no big deal," Bolster said. "We'll get people tomorrow."

It was silent, save for the endless soothing whir of the lodge's filtered solar-powered HVAC system.

"Would you mind if I went to the Air Module instead?" Slim said.

"That's fine," Bolster said. "I'll come with you."

He wanted to see the big boss at work.

Bolster and Slim arrived in the big room a couple minutes after the Air Module had started. The room was full to capacity, with only an inch or two between mats. Tom Hart's sexy followers packed in nose-to-tail, yoga lambs to the slaughter. Slim scanned the room. A couple of gamine things in the middle waved at him and blew him kisses. He tiptoed through the crowd with the grace of a circus performer and sat behind one of them, immediately starting to give her a neck rub. When you enter a situation ready to party, anything can happen.

Bolster didn't immediately spot anyone he knew, other than Suzie Hahn, who was sitting in the front row, smartphone held out in front of her, acting like the main hall at the Hart Center™ was the Press Briefing Room at the White House. She smiled gently. Bolster couldn't figure out if Suzie had bitten from the Hart apple or not, because she had the same look at every yoga event.

Bolster leaned against the wall in the back of the room, where people sat as raptly as those in the front. Tom Hart was on the stage, less than a hundred yards away. Bolster found himself squinting a little; he was, despite all the yoga, still a man in his midforties. He didn't have any trouble hearing, though; Hart was wearing a microphone headset, the rightful inheritance of any guru who'd proved his ability to consistently attract triple-digit, festival-sized crowds. The mic was clear-colored. From the back, it appeared almost invisible. Tom Hart liked to give the illusion that his voice could project across continents.

He was saying, somewhat obviously, "Air is all around us. We breathe it, we walk through it, we alter it, but nothing can change the fact that *we are air*. I want you all to take a nice deep inhale, for a count of five. Imagine that you're breathing from the base of your spine, up through the central core of your body, filling and inflating your lungs, and then letting the air travel upwards and to the side. Fill your belly, your chest, and your throat with air. Make it a long count. And go . . ."

The room sucked air in, as one. It sounded like a big gust of wind and smelled like organic breath mints. Bolster joined them. He liked breathing, and he especially liked breathing in unison. He was cynical, but also a yogi, and therefore believed that the breath united everyone under a cosmic energy field. That was undeniably true; what distinguished one yoga teacher from another was how they *harnessed* that energy. Tom Hart had figured out a system. He thought he was a master. But to Bolster, he just seemed like a kid doing a dangerous science experiment outdoors during a lightning storm.

"One . . ." Hart said.

The room kept breathing; Bolster did too, up to the count of five.

"Now hold on to that breath," Tom Hart said. "Just for a second. Maybe a second longer. And a little longer . . ."

Bolster did that. He could feel himself becoming light-headed.

"And release, for the count of five . . ."

The room deflated, like a plastic inner tube.

"Now, normally," Hart said, "I only exhale like that when I'm practicing yoga, and also doing one other thing that's medically necessary."

The room laughed. *He's a stoner!* Bolster thought, excitedly. Iyengar Yoga, this was not.

"But you should exhale like that *all the time*," Hart continued, "because air is everything and we are air. When you realize that, you can do anything."

Hart inhaled, and, from standing pose, threw back his head, arched his spine, folded back, and landed on his hands, his spine bending as quickly and easily as cheap plastic. His students applauded. Bolster could see Hart's face visibly reddened, even from the back of the room. But the laid-back guru just grinned.

"See," he said. "Not a problem. The air offered no resistance. If you just *take it easy*, if you just *feel* around you, your body can do anything."

Just as effortlessly, Hart moved himself back up to standing. Some of the students gasped. Bolster had to admit that Hart's form really was quite elegant and natural. By comparison, Bolster's poses made him look like a grouchy troll.

"Who wants to flow?"

Hoots and whistles.

"So let's flow!"

The room reverberated with recorded sound: *wooooooo-weeeeee-waaaaaa-wooooo ommmmmmmmmmmm!* This was accompanied by a tabla and blocks knocking together and the faintest hint of Auto-Tune. Tom Hart placed his palms together at the heart and chanted, in a sonorous, beautiful voice:

"*Vande Gurunam.*"

"*Vande Gurunam,*" his students chanted back.

This was the Invocation To Patañjali, the patron saint of Ashtanga Yoga and the mythical author of the *Yoga Sutras*, a harsh, dry, and arcane book of cryptic aphorisms that somehow became the intellectual basis for most Western yoga practice. But despite its somewhat severe source material, the Invocation had a kind of dark, incantatory beauty to it, giving yoga a bit of a sinister edge. It was mostly about powerlessness, as its words placed the student prostrate before a benevolent guru.

Way back in the day, Patañjali appeared in myth to be an ordinary, mild-mannered scholar, but, like a cheesy Marvel Comics character, he had the power to sprout an infinite number of cobra heads. He could transform into the living incarnation of Ananta, the divine Lord of Serpents and ruler of the mysterious serpent race called *nagas,* which hide deep within the earth, guarding mysterious treasures. Bolster bet that Tom Hart's disciples didn't know that when they chanted *samsara hala,* and that Hart probably didn't, either.

The Invocation included the words *jangalikayamane,* which loosely translated as "jungle physician," to describe Patañjali. Bolster found this amusingly anachronistic. But judging by the fact that he once referred to the phrase during class as the "title to an obscure Kool & The Gang song" and no one laughed, other people weren't in on the joke. He wondered if Tom Hart would get up with the get down. Right now, though, Hart was busy turning the Invocation into something that sounded more like an Enya song.

"*Caranaravinde*," he chanted, too melodically for words that were supposed to defy melody. Madonna had once recorded the Invocation, back in the height of her yoga-Nazi days. This version sounded better, superficially, Bolster thought, but it was just as dumb.

"*Caranaravinde*," the crowd chanted back.

They worked their way through the chant, filtering the spirit of the ancient snake scholar through their willfully naive, well-dressed sensibility while Tom Hart glowed on the stage in front of them. Hart bowed his head, then raised it, opened his eyes and said, calmly and simply: "Let's flow. Hard."

Bolster found a far corner and unrolled his mat. If he was going to be critical of the Hart Flow™, Air Module edition, then he was going to have to practice it. Watching other people do yoga was as boring as watching other people praying.

Hart skipped the warm-up. His students didn't need one, he always claimed. If their alignment were right, they'd be fine. And it was true that he had excellent alignment. It was one of his calling cards. His Hart Aligned™ DVD had helped establish his national reputation.

Bolster felt his bones stacking perfectly. He contracted his quads and breathed, jacking back into reverse warrior earlier than usual in practice, and holding it *way* longer, by at least ten beats. That was what Tom Hart did, seemingly all day long. He took any pose that involved backbending or turning one's gaze to the sky and tripled it, both in length and intensity. Chests opened to the sky, infinitely (shoulders close to the ears, shoulder blades together), in a sign of openness and devotion.

"Feel the air," he said. "Mingle with it until it surrounds and becomes you."

Twenty minutes in, Bolster had his T-shirt off and was sopping his forehead with it. The windows were open and the fans on, but all those bodies were generating *tapas*, heat-energy that burns away your sense impressions. Bolster felt a fuzz settle over his brain. A few rows in front of him, Slim was deep in some sort of almighty trance. At the front of the room, Suzie

Hahn filmed the whole thing on her iPad, smiling, not sweating at all. By not practicing, she was automatically the smartest person in there.

They bent and thrust and leaped and twisted, held downward dog until their calves felt like they were going to burst. Then they "flipped" their dog, keeping both feet planted and one hand while they twisted their bodies open, extending one hand toward the front and their chins toward the ceiling.

"This is rock star pose," Tom Hart said, "and you are all rock stars! Looking good, rock stars! Rock 'n' roll!"

Bolster wanted to see Hart take a stage dive right there. Or vomit into a toilet. That would have been very "rock star." Also, a guitar solo might be nice.

Instead, it was time to invert. Hart announced this, simply, by shouting "INVERT!" This was a cue for Hanuman and his handstand boys to start doing their work in the middle of the room. Some of them chose to do handstands for five minutes. Others drifted in and out of different poses as the mood caught them, their shoulder muscles buttressed by daily kettlebell workouts. Around the room, women in sports bras floated into forearm stand without effort. There were a few shoulder stands and more than a few headstands, but no basic headstand versions; the *least* experienced people were in tripod, their eyes softly focused, empty of content. Senior students, meaning people who'd been practicing Hart Yoga™ more than a year, were doing all kinds of arcane iterations, including a frightening one where they stood on their heads—and only on their heads—arms crossed at their chest, in a pose that must have had spinal surgeons across North American licking their lips in anticipation of future business. Chelsea Shell, in the far left front corner of the room, balanced on *one* forearm while also touching her feet to the back of her head. And she did it smoothly, with no seeming exertion at all. How was that even possible?

Bolster couldn't hack it. He did a regular headstand for fifteen breaths—normally he could hold for five minutes or so, but not after a practice *this* tough—before dropping into child's pose. While down there, he felt something undefined, simultaneously ephemeral and thick, but it was there, in the hum of the room's sound system, in the hot rasp of all the breath around him, in the taste of the saliva on his lips and the dampness gathering on his mat. Heat traveled from the top of his head and down through his throat, penetrating his core with a savage ecstasy. His whole body tingled.

He was seconds away from getting a serious boner.

Then everyone was down on their mats, panting like dogs in the noonday sun.

"Can you feel the Hart Vibe™ in your blood?" Tom Hart asked. "It is inside you. Always."

Bolster did feel it.

He *did*.

"Don't worry," Hart said. "It will go away."

This got a laugh. Gradually, everyone sat up.

"All right, I think you got your workout," Hart said. "You've earned whatever you've got coming the rest of the day. Take a bath. Go swimming. Read a book. Smoke 'em if you got 'em. Do some more yoga, if you can still walk after this. Most of all, *relax. Take it easy.* That should be the first rule of yoga, after 'look sexy.' Just kidding. We all work too hard."

The room was quiet, and rank with sweat.

"Now repeat after me," Hart said. "We are all lighter than air!"

"We are all lighter than air!"

"We can float!"

"We can float!"

"We can soar!"

"We can soar!"

Bolster hated this kind of pop New Age call-and-response stuff, but he was doing it too. His body was suffused with a flood of tingly warmth. Tom Hart had power. Everyone chanted together.

"We are alive!"

"We are alive!"

"We are alive!"

And they all were.

For now.

CHAPTER SIX

In April of 1986, almost exactly twenty-seven years before something much more serious would happen to him, Tom Hart spent two weeks in the hospital. He left in a wheelchair. Though he was walking again, he needed help. The virus had made him weak below the waist, a quivering, confused mass of nerves and shriveled, twitching muscles. His eyes had lost their confident Christian clarity, replaced by the confused fog of a fallen angel. He had no strength, no balance, and no faith in the Lord. It was time to mend.

Dr. Mitchell Cohen's Pranic Healing Institute was just five rooms plus a quiet courtyard with a fountain inhabited by little floating bells, in a low-lying office complex in central Pomona, framed by nondescript dark-brown wood shingles, with Bermuda grass all around, plus fringes of Cleveland sage and coffeeberry. The entrance smelled tender and inviting, like perpetual spring.

Tom met with Dr. Cohen, a short, unprepossessing guy with curly gray hair and glasses. He wore a white coat, just like a real doctor, which he was. Dr. Cohen had reviewed the specifics of Tom's case.

"How are you feeling now?" he asked.

"Pretty bad," Tom said, guilelessly.

"I bet," said the doctor.

Dr. Cohen helped Tom out of the exam room, which was mostly generic, other than a chart that talked about something called the *chakra* system, which Tom had never heard of before.

He was on the verge of receiving a lot of new information.

Dr. Cohen took Tom into another, brighter room. It had a view of the courtyard and contained little more than a chair and a couch. The doctor put a cassette into a player and turned it on. Sounds of waves and chirping birds came out of the speakers. He told Tom to lie on the couch, face down, and Tom did.

"Now," Dr. Cohen said, "I want you to say to yourself, 'I am healthy; I am well.' Do this consciously. Not, 'I will *get* healthy, or I will *get* well, but say it as an objective fact, like it's already happened."

"But I'm not well," Tom said.

"This is about setting an intention," said the doctor. "It's an important step. Just give it a try."

"OK," Tom said.

He thought to himself, *I am healthy. I am well.*

"Now," said the doctor. "I want you to breathe. Consciously. Imagine your breath filling your belly, and count it twenty-seven times. I am breathing in twenty-seven; I am breathing out twenty-seven. I am breathing in twenty-six; I am breathing out twenty-six . . ."

Tom did that. By the time he reached twenty-two, he could feel his consciousness receding, or so he thought. He couldn't quite tell. While he lay there, Dr. Cohen continued taking him through the drill. Tom breathed into his chest, and then his throat, and then through his nose, all consciously (or subconsciously) for the count of twenty-seven. When that was over, the doctor had Tom visualize every part of his body, from his toes up to his temples, running through them very quickly, not giving Tom's attention time to linger. This was, the doctor said, "full body awareness."

All session, Tom drifted in and out; sometimes he'd hear Dr. Cohen giving instructions, while other times everything, including his mind, seemed far away. Occasionally he'd come to and realize that he was making a purring sound, like a half-asleep cat licking its fur. Phrases would come and go: "warm hot red triangle at the center of your pelvis"; "coffin by the graveside"; "verdant forest"; and Tom had no idea what was going on. He'd descended deep. Thoughts, emotions, pain, sickness, wellness, sounds, smells: all melded into one reality, bigger than he could have imagined yet also containable on a pinhead. Tom Hart drifted in an unknowable universe, face down on a couch.

He couldn't have possibly known that Dr. Cohen was, in fact, reciting a pretty standard script for the *Yoga Nidra*, the ancient Indian "yogic sleep," the most profound vehicle for self-exploration and transcendence ever designed by humans. It was actually a simple exercise in creative visualization, but something about the order in which it was presented gave it a kind of incantatory power. The *nidra* started shallow but soon went deeper, from asking the practitioner to visualize a babbling brook to asking him to remember a time in his life when he felt happy and fulfilled. And then he had to visualize a time when he felt unhappy and unfulfilled. All of these feelings and memories were valid, and he just had to sit with them on an equal plane, even, or especially, if he was just a naive college student coming off a strange bout with a crippling spinal disease.

"Now," Dr. Cohen said, "tell yourself again: I am healthy. I am well."

I am healthy, Tom Hart thought.

I am well.

"OK?" said the doctor.

"OK," said Tom.

"You can sit up and open your eyes."

Tom did. He looked at the clock. Fifty minutes had passed since he'd gone under, but it could have been five minutes. Or five hours. Time had compressed, or expanded, to the point where he wasn't aware of it. For the first time ever, he had disembodied.

"How do you feel?" asked the doctor.

"I feel . . . good," Tom said, almost surprising himself with his answer.

"That's good," said Dr. Cohen. "It's good to feel good. We've opened up some neural pathways to healing. And we'll keep doing that, with your permission, over the next few weeks, as long as the student health service is covering it for you."

This was the '80s, after all. Affordable health care was easier to find, though not necessarily with an Eastern tint. You still had to manipulate the paperwork to cover that stuff.

"Sure," said Tom.

"We'll expand the practice out," said Dr. Cohen. "You've got to get some strength back in those legs. You need to do some good old-fashioned physical yoga. It'll be 90 percent exercises."

Tom went outside to wait for his mother to pick him up. She'd rented an apartment, month to month, so he could live with her while he healed. His head felt clearer than it had in years, perhaps ever. The sun was warmer, the smells sharper. Everything was full, *actual*. He took a breath in and was stunned at how delightful it was to breathe. In the present moment, he realized, no matter what pain lay behind him, everything was perfect and beautiful. His shattered faith had already begun to repair itself. In a world this full of natural magic, he thought, how can you not believe in something?

Tom was better already.

He was healthy.

He was well.

And he hadn't even started doing the poses yet.

But the poses were what stuck. Tom Hart started doing yoga therapy once a week and kept getting better and stronger. His therapist gave him home exercises, and he did them twice a day, even though he was only supposed to do them once. The ground was solid beneath his feet again. Dr. Cohen had assigned him some simple meditations, too, which made him feel quieter and happier. Slowly, Tom felt happiness, like he had in high school, when he'd always worn a secret smile on his face.

By September, his mother had gone back to Phoenix, leaving Tom to catch up on the school he'd missed. But Tom rarely went to class. He couldn't even begin to feign interest in his studies. Though he still felt love in his heart, he no longer professed it for Jesus. It was a similar kind of bliss, but from a different source. He felt like he was developing secret powers.

Tom leapt and hopped and flung himself around his dorm, unfettered by fear, or by anything else. His body had transformed, and he played it like a first-chair symphony violinist.

Though he didn't really need the sessions anymore, Tom kept meeting with Dr. Cohen.

"Everything just feels so . . . clear," he said one day.

The doctor smiled.

"That means the yoga is working," he said. "Things that used to bother you suddenly don't bother you so much."

"I want to know more," Tom said.

Tom's desire to seek the truth had come during a yogic lull in the West. The ecstasies of Transcendental Meditation had long since been buried. A brief mid-'70s housewife hatha craze had fizzled with the rise of aerobics. People weren't doing yoga in the park or in glass-walled rooms on major urban blocks. You had to really be listening hard to hear Mother India's spiritual call. Somehow, Tom Hart had tuned into the frequency.

"There's a place you can go," Dr. Cohen said.

In January, one semester short of undistinguished graduation, Tom Hart left his Christian self behind. His mother begged him not to, but he told her he felt it in his heart. His faith had changed. She couldn't protest; she'd always raised her boys to follow their inner spirit. Who was she to dictate what form it would take? Her God was a tolerant one.

Tom cashed in what was left of his work-study money and bought a nonstop one-way coach class seat from L.A. to Bombay. From there, it was only a two-hour train ride to Ganeshpuri, where Tom, with nothing but a backpack and $200 in his pocket, staggered through the streets, having eaten or drunk almost nothing in two days. He wandered dazedly past cows, and children playing marbles, and old men squatting, chewing *chaat*, and spitting in the gutter. His mind was fogged by jet lag and thirst. The ashram sat up on a hill, at the end of a dirt road shaded by *banyan* trees and vines that seemed to reach to the sun. Tom staggered through the front door, his T-shirt soaked in sweat. There was no one at the desk in the unadorned foyer, but another door sat beyond. Tom opened it and went through.

There, in a dark, cobwebby room, sat three middle-aged men, peacefully meditating atop a rickety wooden platform that dated to the Raj. The room appeared to have no special spiritual qualities. It was, in fact, little better than a barn.

One of the men looked up.

"May I help you?" he asked.

"I'm here to learn about yoga," Tom said.

"What do you know already?" asked another of the men.

Tom Hart knew basically nothing. But he had been practicing physical poses up to three hours a day. He was young, and it was warm out, so he didn't need much of a jump.

He threw down his backpack, took a breath, and folded forward. Within seconds, he was standing on his forearms, his stomach pulled in tautly, his feet overhead, everything perfectly aligned. From their platform, the yogis watched placidly. Then Tom folded his legs into a perfect lotus, barely moving his folded upper body. His mouth curled into a little smile; his eyes were clear, as though he were gazing into an invisible halo of light. He was ready. And so, clearly, was the ashram.

The yogis looked at one another. They'd been looking for ways to keep the lights on. India had grown weary of its mystical traditions. People respected yoga there but saw it as a relic of the past, kind of how Pennsylvanians looked at the Amish. But for Americans, the secrets of the heart *chakra* were as fresh as morning flowers. Someone like Tom Hart—young, good-looking, basically clean-cut, and white as the Cliffs of Dover—could really bring in the crowds they needed. They could tell him just about anything, and he'd believe. One of them said:

"We'll take you in. How much money have you got?"

After the Air Module, and a laconic lunch, Bolster lay on a raft in the pool for a long time. He could feel his skin crisping; he knew the exposure wasn't good for him, but he needed the warmth on his muscles. Every so often, he'd slide off into the water, dunking his head underneath and slithering over to the deck where his iced tea, cubes long since melted, awaited him. He was utterly wrecked. Tom Hart had flowed all the anxiety out of him.

Bolster took a sip and put his head on the deck, which felt appealingly warm. He looked up. Chelsea Shell was standing in front of him, looking really good in a royal-blue one-piece, her hair done up in a bun.

"Hi," she said.

"Hey," said Bolster.

"Do you need company?"

"Why not?"

Chelsea lowered herself into the water next to Bolster. She gave a little intake of breath as, Bolster imagined, the water hit the sensitive bits.

"Feels nice," she said.

"It does," said Bolster.

She ran a toe over Bolster's left calf. He didn't protest. But he did look up at the sun for a second. Judging by the position, it was maybe three thirty. There were a lot of hours left before bed.

"You're looking pretty red, Bolster," she said to him. "Maybe we should get you into the shade."

"That sounds good."

"I have some lotion."

"That doesn't surprise me."

Bolster hoisted himself out of the pool and was on a lounger while Chelsea Shell rubbed lotion on his back. Around the world, millions—no, billions—of people worked for fewer than three bucks a day, living in almost unimaginably deprived surroundings. And he was getting paid for *this*. Bolster felt something way deeper than guilt, so intense that it pretty much just cycled back around to pleasure. Chelsea had smooth, warm hands. Bolster was pretty sure she'd taken serious massage training. Almost all of them did. Massage could be a pretty decent income stream once you had clients in pocket. You could pass off anything as spiritual growth if it felt good.

"So has Hart Yoga fulfilled all your hopes and fantasies?" Chelsea asked.

"Not all of them," said Bolster. "I can't quite process it. My brain feels like glue."

"You're just afraid to be happy."

"I'm not afraid," Bolster said. "I'm just skeptical."

Chelsea dug a sharp elbow into Bolster's trapezoids, which made him wince.

"Skepticism is just a pose," she said. "It covers up deeper fears."

"When I see three hundred half-naked people bowing before a guy on stage, I get nervous," Bolster said. "You should, too. Look at what happened with Ajoy."

"This is different," she said.

"Why?"

"Because Ajoy was dark, and Tom is made of light."

Bolster rolled over and looked at her.

"Is he?" Bolster said.

"Of course," she said. "He's genuine."

Bolster didn't know if Tom Hart was genuine or not. He didn't care. The sun had pounded him. He was sleepy.

"Made of light?" Bolster said. "Listen to yourself."

"We all need to stop living in the shadows," Chelsea said. "To stop being so sad all the time."

"So Hart Yoga forces everyone who practices it to speak only in motivational clichés?"

"You're a jerk," she said. "Come with me."

Chelsea took Bolster by the arm, across the decking, and through a wood-slatted door. There were a few people around the pool, but no one seemed to notice or care, as though this kind of thing happened all the time at the Hart Center™. Maybe it did. Bolster's resistance was low. It was almost as though he were walking in someone else's skin. Part of it was Chelsea Shell, and part of it was that the day's activities had ground his inhibitions to dust. He couldn't begin to care about his privacy.

"Is this your first time in a ladies' locker room?" she asked.

"Hardly," Bolster said.

Chelsea grabbed a couple of thick towels off a folded stack. She opened a glass door, and Bolster felt a hot wafty wave of scented steam. He saw blue and white tile and heard the telltale hiss. But this smelled a lot better than the Korean spa on Wilshire that he frequented from time to time.

"Are we gonna have a *shvitz*?" he said.

"You're already sweating," she said.

"That's true," Bolster said.

They slipped inside and the door closed behind them. Bolster pressed against the wall, which was warm and dewy. Chelsea slipped off her straps. Her bathing suit dropped to her waist. Her skin was alabaster, her elbows just a little bony. She pressed her breasts against him, flesh on flesh. They were small but firm.

"What's your game, Shell?" Bolster asked.

"I don't have a game," she said.

"You can't really believe this Hart Yoga bullshit."

"It works for now," she said.

"Or maybe you were just waiting for me to show up."

"I wasn't," she said. "But I'm glad you did."

"You're just using me," Bolster said.

"I am," she said. "Bolster equals sexy."

Not everyone in the world would agree, but he certainly worked for her.

Chelsea's lips parted, and they kissed, sweetly at first. Bolster was tender to the touch, like boiled meat. But he didn't mind this kind of touch. Chelsea tasted like sweet, warm, fresh syrup. She draped a couple of towels on a hard tile bench and settled Bolster down like a baby. Bolster was hard without even thinking about it. The thought of what was about to happen made him feel hot and wasted. Chelsea folded a towel. She got on her knees in front of him. Then she slithered, face first, planting her lips on his neck. Bolster breathed in sharply, realizing that he was about to experience the *Kama Sutra*, live. His hands slid down Chelsea's back, toward her ass. He steeled himself for the ride.

A half hour later, Bolster was back asleep on his lounge chair. Then felt himself return to consciousness, with a little snort, but didn't really want to wake up yet. He felt satisfied, but also guilty. Mentally, he needed to be stronger. It wasn't as though women were his weakness, exactly. Because of his line of work, he knew plenty of beautiful, intelligent, thoughtful women, none of whom he ever thought about. His attachment lay elsewhere, with danger. He'd had the same problem when he'd been a cop, always the first one through the door or to open the car trunk, never looking around. Bolster had liked to slam his fist on the table just to get a reaction, to stay at the bar thirty minutes longer for that extra drink, to ask just one more question, not because it was necessary, but because he loved getting a reaction. When he'd started practicing yoga, that had abated. And, finally, almost stopped. His tendency toward the extreme had just been another form of ego food, and yoga sought to eradicate ego. But Chelsea Shell tickled that dirty corner of his heart. His ego spread like a plumed bird around her. And he loved the feeling. He needed to fight harder.

Bolster opened his eyes. The sun was lower, the air a little cooler. Also, Chelsea was gone. Instead, Suzie Hahn sat next to him, happily slapping away at her laptop.

"Hey, sleepyhead!" she said. "Have you been having fun?"

"I think so," Bolster said.

"I know, it's awesome, right? I'm blogging all about it right now."

Bolster moaned. His head throbbed. Chelsea Shell had struck again. Every time he hooked up with that woman, he passed out, though this time she hadn't used drugs. At least he didn't think she had.

Bolster needed water.

"Hey, you're really sunburned!" Suzie said.

He closed his eyes again, hoping that the afternoon would rewind, and he could undo his actions.

But he couldn't.

When he sat up, Suzie was still there, typing, making herself laugh.

CHAPTER SEVEN

Slim spent the afternoon playing volleyball, the only dude on a team with five A-level Hart Yoga instructors, none of whom could possibly have been older than thirty-two. The ladies liked him up front, because he was tall and good at blocking, but he preferred his time behind the line. The rule was that you got to keep your joint in your mouth as long as you held your serve. In the second game, he scored seven straight aces and smoked that fat hash-oil-laced sucker down to the roach. By the time the game ended, he was more stoned than he'd been for at least a week, or maybe a month. It was, without much question, one of the finest times of his life.

Slim had no bank account, no driver's license, and no permanent address. He got his mail at a P.O. box on Pico, which he checked twice a year, and got his e-mail whenever he was around someone else's computer. Whereas Matt Bolster struggled constantly to live in the moment, Slim faced no such challenges. For instance, when he hosted his monthly Monday night poetry jam at the International Theosophy Society at

Sunset and Western and nobody showed, not even the featured poet, did Slim suffer self-pity? Of course not. He just locked the door, rode his bike to the Tiki Ti, and drank three Doctor Funks before making his way to the Burrito King for dinner. Or if his borrowed Jeep broke down on the road to Hana, which it invariably did, he just stuck out his thumb and ended up spending a month trimming stems at an underground weed collective.

He flowed. Sometimes that flow landed him asleep at a bus station or in jail, but it was constant. If you're not going anywhere in particular, Slim figured, you'll always end up there eventually.

After the volleyball game ended, Slim said his see-you-laters and wandered off through the compound. That was another difference between him and Bolster; he could easily spend two hours with a half-dozen women whose bodies made Misty May-Treanor look like Terry Jones in a housedress and not even consider them in a sexual way. He didn't care about those things. One summer in the early '90s, a harpist had broken his heart on a bench in Tompkins Square Park, and after that he was through with love, and more or less through with sex, too. He had a life and wasn't going to waste it chasing strange tang around California.

On this glorious day, Slim was feeling light and lucky. He hadn't paid for this weekend, just like he never paid for anything. Assistants got charged a $35 registration fee, but Bolster had ponied for that. In fact, he was feeling so good that he stopped in front of the Reiki Hut and lit a fat bowl of something that smelled like the citrus section at the farmer's market and tasted like a spice carousel.

Bury me baked, he thought, as he blew out a cloud of smoke that enveloped his face.

Of course, getting stoned in the gloaming has its detriments, particularly if you're in unfamiliar surroundings. Slim had no idea where his bunkhouse was. He stood for a minute, looking at his hands, and then realized he had no idea where *anything* was. Well, he was on a path, and in one direction was the main lodge. He'd just come from that area. Instead, he decided to follow the path onward. That didn't always lead to the best outcome, but it did always lead to a different one, and Slim was all about different outcomes.

This path led into the woods.

Slim walked along, maybe for ten minutes, and the path seemed to close behind him, leaving the Hart Center™ behind. The trees weren't thickly foliated through here—it had actually been kind of a dry season, and the fire risk was high—but they were plentiful, and plenty tall. The sun hadn't quite set yet so the light was still flickerish. A thin breeze whistled lightly; the air was warm and desiccated, vaguely entropic. Slim had not chosen the correct path, but this didn't bother him. When you didn't really care what came next, no decision could be truly wrong.

He stopped for another puff and then pivoted to walk back.

There was a man behind him, his face obscured by what looked like a cobra hood.

"Who are you?" Slim said.

"You're late for the ceremony," the man said. "You were supposed to get here *before* six."

"What ceremony?"

"You don't have to be cryptic. It's OK. We're all here for the same reason."

"We are?"

"Shh," the man said. "Give me your hand."

Slim did. The man put two little white pills in his palm.

"Take these now. If you do, you'll still get the full effect."

"Cool," Slim said, and he popped them in his mouth.

He wasn't one to turn away pills from a stranger. One time in New Orleans he'd bought half a bottle of some stuff from some kid in a bar. "I made them myself," the kid said. "They have *vitamins*." Slim spent the subsequent two days sweating and grinding his teeth in a hotel room. Pills always brought something to the party.

The man waved Slim along.

"Now go," he said. "They're waiting."

"Aren't you coming?" Slim said.

"No, I'm the gatekeeper," the man said. "They need me in case someone tries to run away."

"Why would someone do that?" Slim asked.

The man looked at him sternly.

"Just go," he said.

Slim walked down the path for a couple of minutes. His hands were feeling tingly, like he'd been napping on them funny. He came to a rise and looked down. Instinctively, he dropped behind a tree. Which was probably good, because he saw something very weird.

A half-dozen people, all wearing cobra hoods like the man from the woods, sat around a roaring bonfire. Some of them were men, some women; all were perfectly formed. Their legs were crossed into lotus position, and they had their hands folded across their chests in *anjali mudra* as they hummed softly. Slim felt his legs grow rubbery. He looked at his hand. It appeared to be getting smaller and then larger and was maybe threatening to change shape on him.

After a time, one of the cobra-head people stood and raised his arms to the sky. He said, in a voice as deep as Topol's:

"I bow to the two lotus feet of the Gurus, which awaken insight into the happiness of pure Being. We will experience the complete absorption into joy, the jungle physician, eliminating the delusion caused by the poison of Samsara, otherwise known as conditioned existence."

Yoga is so weird, Slim thought.

The cobra-man continued:

"I prostrate before the sage Patañjali who has thousands of radiant, white heads, for he is the divine serpent Ananta. He has assumed the form of a man holding a conch shell, a wheel, and a sword."

Weird, Slim said to himself.

All the cobra hoods chanted together:

"Om, Shanti Shanti Shanti."

Then the Sanskrit began.

"Vande Gurunam," chanted the leader.

"Vande Gurunam," responded the others.

"Caranaravinde."

"Caranaravinde."

And so on it went, sonorous, two-toned, and very serious, until he reached the last bit:

"Sahasra sirasam svetam Pranamami patañjalim."

"OMMMMMMMMMMM," he went, and everyone joined him, including Slim, who was feeling oddly light and spirited, and besides, he knew that word.

A silence fell over the woods.

After a minute, the man spoke:

"Patañjali," he said, "healer of worlds, dissembler of delusion, I invoke thee."

He pulled a little canvas pouch out of his jeans pocket. Slim didn't understand why a guy wearing a cobra-priest hood also had on jeans. But this was California, where even rituals tended toward laid-back style. He opened the pouch and waved his hand toward the fire. White powder came out, and when it hit the flames, it evoked a dramatic *whoosh*.

A plume of smoke headed up out of the fire and began to swirl above it. From his hiding place, Slim watched the smoke mutate and begin to shape itself into the form of a man. He held a conch shell, a wheel, and a sword, and stood there serenely.

"*Vande Gurunam*," the hooded people chanted. "*Vande Gurunam. Vande Gurunam!*"

The cloud man's head vanished.

Whoa, thought Slim.

In its place emerged a ten-foot-tall hissing cobra's hood. And then another, and another. The cobra eyes glowed red and angry as the figure shook and writhed, and his worshippers opened their arms to the skies in ecstasy. Head after head sprouted, some of them tiny and some of them reaching toward the sky, all of them spouting angry venom. Slim saw it all. He couldn't believe it.

"WHAT IS HAPPENING?" he shouted.

The cobra-hooded people turned their heads and saw Slim. Their leader pointed. The snake thing in the sky rotated as well, looked at Slim, and hissed horribly.

Slim shrieked, stood, and ran from whence he'd come, past the guy in the clearing. He looked behind him, and the snake demon was hovering over the trees, watching him.

"No!" he shouted. "No, no, no!"

I have to warn Bolster, he thought.

Slim ran, but there was less light now, and the woods seemed a lot less friendly. The snake god loomed above him, laughing. In the sky, the cobra heads hissed, but he saw them on the ground, too. Tree branches were sprouting hoods. On the ground, sticks turned into tiny cobras. In the distance, he heard the blowing of a conch shell. Then the demon grew larger still, filling the world with his infinitude. Slim could see nothing else, and he could hear nothing other than a sonorous *OMMMMMMMM*, the universal sound of pure awareness, breaking apart the air, encasing multitudes.

He sweated and panted. If he could have looked in a mirror, he would have seen that his pupils were the size of arcade tokens. He'd only felt this way once before in his life, during a Widespread Panic show in Tahoe in 1998. That night had ended with him passing out pantless and facedown in a dirty trailer full of fema beads. There was actually only one prominent similarity between that night and this one, but Slim wasn't in a condition to understand that right now. Instead, he just found himself hoping that this situation would turn out better for him. But it wouldn't.

Slim came to a fork in the woods. To the right, fewer than three hundred yards away, sat the safe haven of the Hart Center™. If he'd turned that way, he would probably have prevented a lot of trouble that came later. But he took the road less traveled by, snagged on a root, and sprawled down. His right shoulder hit first. Slim knew how to roll. He dropped into a tumble like his *sifu* had taught him. But when he straightened out, he found himself at an eighty-degree angle, sliding down, very fast. Rocks and brambles tore at his Bruce Lee T-shirt. Slim flipped once, and then again, and then he instinctively did another tuck as he hit the ground sideways, a movement that probably spared him a broken leg. But it didn't spare him from hitting his head on a rock.

Slim lay in a ravine, which seemed to be spinning like a carnival centrifuge ride after the bottom dropped out. *This is how it's going to end*, he thought. Above him, the infinite-headed snake god hovered, watching incredulously, arms crossed, his massiveness consuming the sky from Santa Barbara to Palmdale.

The snake-thing threw back its heads—all thousand-plus of them—and laughed.

"Patañjali . . ." Slim moaned.

And then the night swallowed him.

CHAPTER EIGHT

Bolster spent dinner eating alone in a corner of the dining room, like a friendless transfer student on the first day of school. His usual companion Slim was missing. Bolster wondered what had happened to him, but with more curiosity than worry. Slim would often disappear for days, weeks, or months, sometimes returning with a freshly stamped passport. He couldn't take care of himself (in the sense that he didn't have money, or skills that involved anything other than martial arts and playing obscure musical instruments), but the world, in general, seemed to watch over Slim's well-being. Bolster guessed Slim was off partying somewhere.

Suzie Hahn came bounding up to Bolster, a puppy off-leash, looking bright as a dime. It was a little after seven o'clock.

"How's it going?" she said.

"Fine," Bolster said. "How's it going with you?"

"Great!"

"Don't you ever have any problems, Suzie?"

"Nope!" Suzie said. "The world is amazing!"

"If you say so."

"I used to have problems, of course, but then I started doing yoga."

"The usual story."

"It is!" she said. "So, listen, Bolster, I have an extra VIP lounge pass if you want to come back there with me when you're done eating."

"VIP lounge?"

"It's just a place where special guests can chill during the Gathering."

"I know *what* a VIP lounge is," Bolster said. "I'm just kind of surprised there's one here."

"Why?"

"You understand the problem. The students have to stay outside while the teachers get a special hang."

"Not *all* the teachers," Suzie said. "Just the VIP ones. And their special guests. Like me!"

"You're making my point for me, Suzie. Yoga is supposed to be about erasing differences, not creating them."

"Put yourself in Tom's place," Suzie said. "If there wasn't a VIP lounge, he wouldn't be able to go anywhere around here without being totally mobbed by people. He needs a place where he can just sit and think quietly."

"That's why there are hotel rooms."

Suzie's face constricted. She actually looked a little stern. This made Bolster uneasy. He'd never seen her turn her facial volume down anywhere past cheery. Her voice lowered to a whisper.

"Dammit, Bolster," she said. "I had to persuade a lot of people to get you on the roster this weekend. No one had any idea who you were, and they still don't, but I talked you up so much that they let you come. I realize you don't care that much about being here, but this is part of my work, and it's important to me. Now you have an opportunity to meet Tom Hart. I know he's not the pope or anything, but he's about as famous as American yoga teachers get. So why don't you stop overanalyzing everything and just come with me without complaining?"

Bolster had been righteously spanked.

"All right, all right," he said.

"Don't blow this," said Suzie.

"Yes, ma'am."

The VIP lounge was a four-room, 1,100-square-foot job at the far western edge of the property, attached by an almost-always-locked door to Tom Hart's private suite—the true inner sanctum of the inner sanctum. Unless someone told you otherwise, there was no real way to figure out where or what it was, since every building on the property, including the laundry shed, looked exactly the same from the outside: all faux-rusted metal, cool white concrete, aloe vera plantings, and smooth pebbles imported from the "remotest beaches of Thailand," or so the supplier said.

Bolster and Suzie approached the front door. She took a plastic key card out of her pocket and slid it over a panel. A green light went on. She opened the door.

In the entryway, they removed their shoes. Bolster saw luxury in action. There was a wet bar, staffed by a black-tie bartender who Bolster hadn't seen anywhere else during the weekend. The jet-black Silestone counter held a tray of smoked meat and fish, the Gathering's first non-vegetarian options. The room's floor was blond wood, impeccably maintained. A flat-screen TV, forty-eight inches at least, had been mounted on a wall, above a fully operational wood fireplace. A fire burned in the hearth and also on the TV, an effect that Bolster hoped was meant to be ironic. There were comfortable chairs and little glass-topped tables on which rested clay bowls full of roasted nuts. And more than a few half-drunk cocktails.

The rear glass wall revealed an unobstructed view of mountains, just now vanishing into night. A purplish-blue corona vaguely outlined them as the day said good-bye to the Hart Center™, which had treated it with such kindness. On the terrace sat wicker chairs with high-thread-count white cushions, a hot tub built for at least eight, and another fire, this one in a pit, though equally roaring. It was all very billionaire-ski-lodge. Clearly, for Tom Hart, yoga did more than just pay the mortgage.

In the center of the room, Hart lounged on a divan in the manner of a Roman noble, or at least an actor playing a Roman noble. Though the black pants and white linen shirt he wore made him look like a stage musician, or a professional flamenco dancer. His skin shone like the hood of a freshly waxed car, and his hair looked as though it had been recently washed. On one side of him sat Kimberly Wharton, busily poking an iPad with alternating index fingers.

There were two other people in the room, besides the bartender, who, by professional obligation, didn't really exist: a trim, serene guy with receded curly gray hair and glasses, who had to be somewhere near seventy years old; and a serious-looking late-thirties type, vegan-thin with a rough beard and a T-shirt depicting a young T. Krishnamacharya sitting in lotus position.

"I think that tomorrow, I want to talk about the swirls," Hart was saying. "Really in-depth. People need to understand how they underlie the poses, and we can have some real philosophical depth to the discussion. Are you getting this, Kimber?"

"I'm getting it," Kimberly Wharton said.

"The swirls" were, in fact, something that Hart had completely made up out of a misreading of someone else's misreading of a misinterpretation of an ancient text that may have never existed, Bolster knew. But people bought into it anyway. Once Tom got talking, it was easy to get lost in the folds.

"People have the wrong idea of what they're about," Hart said. "They get them confused with *chakras*, or spirals, but they come from a different source, right, Andy?"

"Yeah," said the bearded guy. "A lot of that spiral stuff comes from the *Kurunta*, but I have access to different seminal texts that reject that in favor of a more organic theory of energy distribution throughout the body. You could talk about that, too."

"This is why I surround myself with yoga scholars," Hart said.

"The medieval Tantrics believed . . ."

Hart interrupted him.

"We can hash that out later," he said. "Sound good to you, doc?"

"Whatever keeps your blood pressure down, Tom, I'm for it," the older guy in the room said.

"Well, it does do that," Tom Hart said. He looked toward Bolster and Suzie.

"But I'd better stop showing my cards," he said, winking at Suzie Hahn. "The press is here."

"Your secret yoga formula is safe with me, Tom," Suzie said.

Tom Hart laughed, a bit too loudly.

"You crack me up, Hahn," he said.

"I brought a guest," she said. "This is . . ."

"I know who it is," said Hart. "I recognize him from the flier. Matt Bolster, Yoga Detective."

"Yep," Bolster said.

"Man," Hart said, extending a hand. "That is *so* cool."

Bolster shook it. Hart's grip exuded warmth and perfect alignment. Clearly, it was full of swirls.

"Glad to have you here, man," Hart said. "Sorry I didn't sit in on your class yesterday. I had my Air Module."

"I've been hearing that a lot," Bolster said.

"So what do you think of our little Gathering, yoga detective?" Hart asked.

"Honestly?"

"Why not?"

"I think it's a fucking cult."

"HAH!" Hart said, a little too loudly. "Maybe it is, a little."

Bolster suspected Hart had heard that before, and he'd decided that the best way to disarm your critics is to agree with them. Especially when almost no one else cared about the critique.

"It's always a danger," Hart said, "when you get popular. People become attached to you, and they expect so much. I just want them to feel good and be happy."

Kimberly Wharton was still attacking her iPad with her index fingers.

"This is all off the record, Kimber," Hart said.

"I know," she said. "I'm just coordinating your flight to Chicago for Monday."

"Make sure I get an aisle," Hart said, and then turned back to his company. "Matt Bolster. Siddown. Have a drink."

Bolster sat in one of the comfy chairs.

"What're you having?"

"Red wine is fine," Bolster said.

"Oh come on, Bolster, order a man's drink."

"Red wine is good for you," said the doc.

"Bolster," Hart said, "this is my personal physician, Dr. Mitchell Cohen. He saved my life, more or less, almost thirty years ago."

"And now look at me," Dr. Cohen said.

"Hey, at least you're still working, old man," Hart said. "So, come on, Bolster, what are you drinking?"

"Scotch, neat," Bolster said. "But only one."

Everything in moderation.

"Blue Label OK?" Hart said.

"Only the best," Bolster said.

Hart nodded toward the bartender, who poured and brought the drink over silently, and one for Hart as well. Suzie Hahn had red wine. So did Dr. Cohen. They all sipped comfortably, as fires both real and virtual burned inside the room and out. The silence broke when the bearded scholarly guy said, somewhat awkwardly,

"I'm Andy Barlow."

"Did you write that book about the yogin warrior caste in medieval India?" Bolster said.

Barlow's eyes brightened.

"Yes!" he said. "It was my Ph.D. thesis."

"I loved it," Bolster said. "Really interesting stuff. Yoga is never what you think it is. How did you go about researching that?"

"Well, there's this library in Lucknow," Barlow began.

Bolster could see that Barlow was excited, which he could understand. Scholarship was yoga's least-traveled path, so it was rare that anyone showed even a passing interest in that kind of work, and even rarer that someone was actually familiar with it. But Bolster was, and he knew that Barlow was on the path to becoming one of the world's leading yoga scholars. Not that there was a ton of competition for such an honor. Still, it could be considered an accomplishment.

Tom Hart, who hadn't read a book since he'd thrown away his Bible in 1986, certainly didn't care. He kept Barlow on retainer for purposes of intellectual legitimacy, but he was always so busy talking that he didn't pay attention to anything Barlow was saying. This arrangement wasn't quite to Andy's taste, but a good-paying gig was rare in yoga scholarship. And Hart rarely bothered him, only trotting him out for expedience. Most of the time, he was independent. The only downside was that Hart sometimes mocked him in public, like a jock knocking off Poindexter's glasses.

"I don't think anyone's interested in that right now, Andy," Hart said.

"Actually, I am," Bolster said.

"You guys can talk on your own time," Hart interrupted. "We're here to talk about me."

He didn't say this with any kind of a wink. It was as though he were a seven-year-old only child, holding court at the dinner table. Everyone tried to keep their poker faces, but you could tell they were uncomfortable. When you ordered up the great man, he came with a side of boyish petulance.

"I'll catch up with you later," Bolster said to Barlow, who looked at him gratefully.

"So how much do you really know about Hart Yoga, Bolster?" the boss said.

"Only what I read on *The Huffington Post*," Bolster said. "Which is kind of a lot, actually."

"Yeah, I buy editorial space there," Hart said. "I gave Arianna a private Water Module."

I bet you did, Bolster thought.

"So you probably know that I got started in yoga because of Dr. Cohen here."

"That part I heard."

"And then I went to India and traveled around for a few years, studying at ashrams and picking up wisdom."

"Which ashrams?" Bolster asked.

"It doesn't matter," Hart said. "They were totally authentic. But my one complaint, and I know this makes me sound like a selfish, spoiled, lazy, urban Western yogi . . ."

That's a lot of adjectives, Bolster thought, *all of them accurate.*

". . . was that their yoga was *boring*. Overly serious. I mean, I agreed with everything they told me, and I admired their sincerity, but I just didn't think it was going to translate to American audiences. We like a little flash, you know."

"As opposed to Indian culture, which is *so* dry and boring," Bolster said.

Suzie gave Bolster a disapproving look, as if to say, *don't challenge the boss like that*. But Hart didn't seem to care much. He dismissed it flatly, as though there was simply no way he could be authentically challenged.

"I see where you're going with that, Bolster, and I appreciate it, but there's a big difference between Indian popular culture and yoga culture. To people in India, yogis are skinny old bearded guys who live in huts by the river and cover themselves in ash and only eat one meal a day and survive by begging. Or it's just like, you know, health care."

"It *is* health care," Dr. Cohen said.

"Yes," said Hart. "But it's also about feeling good and having fun, and there's nothing wrong with that, right?"

He glanced at Mitchell Cohen menacingly, as though to say, *You will be a yes-man now.* Bolster was starting to wonder how much control this guy actually had over his followers. Emperors often behaved this way just before their fall.

"Absolutely," the doctor said.

"I mean, all those Indian ascetics, the ones telling you that you need to meditate four hours a day, they're not happy, right? The Buddha tried that and he almost died. He didn't start to get better until that little girl gave him some rice under the tree. Then he got enlightened and started walking around, but he was *fat.* The Buddha didn't exercise at all!"

Bolster looked over at Barlow to see his reaction to this idiotic bastardization of humankind's noblest spiritual parable, but Barlow sat stoically, as his training and discipline required. Hart gulped down his Scotch and signaled for another. The great guru was getting his drunk on.

And that wasn't all. He pulled a little portable vaporizer out of his pocket and took a big pull, letting out a puff that smelled like sweet plums. Hart offered Bolster a hit, and Bolster gladly obliged. Gore Vidal once said that no one should ever turn down an opportunity to have sex or to appear on television. To that, Bolster wanted to add: *Never say no to getting high with a famous person.* You never know what the fuck is going to happen, though usually it just means the famous person talks a lot about himself.

"Of course, I'm not the Buddha," Tom Hart continued. "The people who practice with me are my friends, not my followers. It's been that way ever since I came back from India in 1997 and opened that little yoga studio in Pomona, just next door to Dr. Cohen's office. Isn't that right, Mitchell?"

"Absolutely," said Dr. Cohen. "I funneled all of the patients your way."

"What is it they say?" Hart went on. "When the student is ready, the teacher appears?"

"I guess they say that," Bolster said.

"Well, that seems about right to me. I just happened to have a message that they wanted to hear. And a training they wanted to pay for. HAH!"

Go on, Bolster thought. He wasn't sure exactly why Hart was talking to him. Sometimes, people just need fresh audiences for their bullshit, and Bolster knew how to present a neutral stance. Or maybe the fact that he'd called Hart Yoga a cult meant that Hart now really wanted to impress him.

"Life doesn't have to be about struggle," Tom Hart said. "It should be easy. It should be fun. It should be relaxing. All you have to do is open your heart."

That pretty much killed the conversation. It wasn't the kind of statement that really brought about a reply. Everyone there was complicit in a lie, and everyone knew it, but no one wanted to say or do anything about it, because the lie was paying a lot of bills for a lot of people. Bolster felt vaguely complicit himself. Two hundred bucks and unlimited spa treatments seemed to be about his price, at least for a weekend.

Tom Hart clapped his hands together.

"All right," he said. "Who wants to party?"

CHAPTER NINE

Saturday night was when the Gathering took flight. The DJ had things going pretty good in the main lodge by the time Bolster got there. A massive dub beat permeated the room with a tabla underscore, a louder, faster version of the *vinyasa* flow soundtrack that booms out of trendy coastal studios during prime yoga hours. Large ceiling fans blew overhead—unnecessary temperature-wise, since it was 62 degrees outside, but necessary to create a flowing effect for the red and white silk streamers. Bolster guessed that some unlucky staff members—probably supervised by Kimberly Wharton, who seemed to do everything here—had spent the afternoon tying them to the rafters. Multicolored gel lights whipped around the room as well, both from the ceiling and the floor, adding to the hippie-disco ambience.

There were about a hundred and fifty Hart Yoga devotees in that room, 80 percent of them women. And, this being Saturday night, many of them had shed their yoga-pants and sports-bra skin in favor of flowing skirts or comfortable pants that puffed at the waist, and bright-colored blouses. Light-brown henna tattoos virally spread up their arms and necks. Many had pashmina scarves that they were moving across their shoulders and hips like soft, spiritually oriented dental floss, dancing rhythmically and mostly alone, getting deep into their yoga groove, as the brochure copy advised them to.

Bolster had attended far too many of these sorts of things in the last few years. He kept saying he wouldn't go, but a temptation—usually female—always arose at the last minute. He often couldn't resist the urge to *do something*, that universal tug. It's hard to turn down an invitation to a party, even when that party is a yoga rave.

Usually, Bolster went to these things, paid his money, had an organic energy drink if there was a free bar, and stayed a half hour—give or take twenty minutes spent talking to Suzie Hahn, who always went to everything. But there's a big difference between showing up at a party anonymously and showing up in the entourage of the party's raison d'être.

Tom Hart entered the room. A bolt of lightning would have gotten people's attention more slowly. He was like a human glow stick, and his followers like bugs drawn to the flame. Andy Barlow and Bolster looked at each other and grinned. You couldn't deny the cheesy heat that surrounded the guy.

"Easy, folks, easy," Tom said. "I'm just here to dance!"

DJ Shiva Rama Lama (birth name: Richard Smith) was really pounding out the beats now. A circle developed. Tom Hart stepped into the center of the Saturday Night Yoga Fever. His followers whooped like they'd never seen such a thing.

This middle-aged man began to gyrate and shimmy like someone twenty-five years younger, forcing the crowd's attention upon his strength and grace. He presented a perfect picture of balance, attention, and joy, a stance long cultivated to garner maximum enthusiasm from his audiences. His face lit by the gentlest of smiles, Hart suddenly threw himself into a backward handspring, like a preteen gymnast. Maybe three other men his age on Earth, all of them employed by circuses, could make their spines do such a thing. He had an extraordinary gift for gyration. Hart sprung back up, whirled, and lowered himself, not as gently as he could have, into a full split.

If Bolster had tried that, he would have torn his groin muscles away from the bone for the rest of his life.

Then Tom Hart was back dancing again, waving his arms, encouraging the circle to close and to dance around him. Bolster didn't join. He stood against a wall, arms crossed, next to Barlow, who handed him a pill.

"What is this?" Bolster said.

"It's synthetic," Barlow said. "Engineered for your enjoyment."

"I don't think so."

"It'll help you get through. I can vouch for the chemist. He was my roommate at Santa Cruz."

"Do you pop these often?" Bolster said.

"Only when I have to."

Bolster popped it.

"Tastes like a Smartie," he said.

"That's part of the engineering," said Barlow. "Just kind of a funny touch. You definitely only want one, though."

Bolster looked around the room. *What happened to Slim?* he wondered. He was thinking about him, because Bolster knew Slim never met a strange pill he didn't like. His buddy had been missing for several hours now. If nothing else, Slim usually showed up for the party. Maybe there was some other, better party somewhere else. Or maybe Slim had hitchhiked to Santa Barbara for no reason. Both outcomes were possible.

But Bolster's attention was soon drawn elsewhere. Tom Hart still stood at the center of the circle, which had now constricted. The dancing began to coordinate. Hart threw up his arms, and so did a hundred other people. When he flowed around, moving his torso in a circle, they followed. He did a little three-step tap dance, and so did they, an act so campy and inappropriate that Bolster found himself almost hissing with embarrassment. And yet, creeping around the edges of sensation, he felt a little tingle in his limbs and a warmth in his heart. He felt it coming on.

Bolster was gonna tweak.

He wasn't sure exactly when Tom Hart had gotten hold of a headset mic—maybe he always had one on, ready to be activated—but Bolster definitely heard Hart's voice amplified now over the lodge's sound system.

"Feel the music deep in your cells, the essence of your being," he said. "Inhale it. Exhale it. The divine calls from within you, wanting to dance her way out. Give in now. It's Saturday night. Flow. DANCE!"

Bolster wasn't sure there was some sort of feminine spirit inside him just waiting to flow, but he did feel himself beginning to sway to the sound, which was picking up irresistible speed. His mind was dissolving, his spirit loosening. He *felt so good*. Next to him, Andy Barlow had already let loose and was whipping his arms around like it was the Summer Of Love. All around the room, people were grinding, alone and in pairs, lost in the ecstasy of the weekend. With the exception of Suzie Hahn, who stood off in a corner, smiling, recording the whole thing with her tablet.

"Our yoga has four modules," Hart blathered on. "There is water, the most common. And air, which we're all floating on this weekend. But there's one other, the rarest, and most important one of all. It burns inside our bellies, craving activation. It wants to come out. It must come out."

The music hit a peak of frenzy, and the crowd floated. It felt, to Bolster, like someone had torn out his spine. He had no bones, and he moved accordingly.

"Ladies and gentlemen," Tom Hart said, throwing up his arms. "LET THERE BE FIRE!"

There was a pause in the music, and then Chelsea Shell appeared from behind a scrim, wearing yoga clothes that she simply could not have afforded to buy herself. Maybe she'd scored a sponsorship, Bolster thought, or maybe Tom Hart had bestowed upon her a wardrobe, or, who knew? Chelsea worked the yoga grift better than anyone—the long con, the short con, and everything in between. She could have had a hundred scams going simultaneously, and most of it wasn't even malicious or intentional. It was simply in her nature to use and manipulate people. But because of the yoga, she also made them feel good, both physically and mentally. This made Chelsea the most confounding person that Bolster had ever known. She certainly had *him* running laps. Was it possible to want to fuck someone because you found them deeply annoying? Apparently so.

Then Bolster remembered that he was tripping. Sometimes even the lightest drugs take you to the darkest place. *I need to just let it flow*, he thought, and then his head became immediately lighter. He was starting to get the hang of Hart Yoga™. *We are all one, we all are elements,* he thought. Also, he realized he had a huge boner, like artificially large, as though someone had inflated him with a pump. These were some drugs.

Chelsea wore a two-piece number, black tights and a black top, also tight. Both had flame designs running up each side, muscle-car decals for the thighs. A bright-red headband finished the job. Chelsea's eyes were very reflective in general, so on this night, they glowed. The whole effect made her look like 1980 Olivia Newton-John, but in hell. To Chelsea's credit, she was able to pull it off. She was remarkable at walking the tightrope between sincerity and kitsch.

Tom Hart beamed at the scene. This moment meant so much to him. The best possible outcome he'd ever imagined was happening right here, right now. He'd always been a child of the spirit, but now he had real apostles, and they were very well dressed. People who he genuinely (if not deeply) loved were loyally following him into the heart of a divine reality that he'd created himself.

He'd *built this*—not just the LEED-certified facility in the woods, but everything, down to the intellectual property. He'd spent decades creating a fresh, modern spin on ancient techniques, with only a slight upcharge for late registration. All his modules were trademarked and copyrighted, as much a part of the fabric of American ingenuity as mass-produced cars and social networking. He was more than a yoga teacher; he was a cultural *entrepreneur*, a visionary, a seeker, a thought leader for the new millennium, and tonight, he had to admit to himself, a party demigod.

The Gathering showed, beyond doubt, that hundreds of people had given Tom their souls, the part of them that mattered most. Some of them had given him much more. And he was grateful. So he was celebrating his glorious spiral-shaped victory with them, thanks to a soundtrack from DJ Shiva Rama Lama.

Nothing would ever bring him low.

Chelsea had hoops around both of her arms, and they were on fire. She wagged her hips, kicked her legs up, and then launched herself into a cartwheel with the hoops still whirling around. The crowd reacted in a frenzy that would have embarrassed a Vegas audience. But she could really dance with the flame hoops, whirling, flipping, up and down.

Chelsea continued her dance of danger, adding a hoop down the middle, which an assistant lit on fire. She shimmied to the beat of conga drums, fast, West African dance style, all hips and whipping the head around. Then it slowed, and she began to slink, a seductive, Lycra-clad Theda Bara of the yoga plains. In the middle of the room, Bolster could see Hanuman and the Hanumaniacs doing their handstand routine, but everyone moved around them to get a better look at Chelsea, who was offering a fresher show. Handstand exhibitions were for lunchtime. The sun had fallen, and the masses demanded release.

Suddenly, Chelsea turned, posed sharply, and whipped up the hoops, one by one. She caught them, and when they hit her hand, by some sort of *Mindfreak*-style physical manipulation, they extinguished. The last one went up, and she caught it, flipped it offstage, and then threw herself into a wheel pose so deep and fully expressed that it looked like she was going to roll *herself* offstage as well. Instead, she sprung up, the DJ fired up the tunes, the lights went crazy, and confetti blew everywhere. Chelsea plunged into the crowd, dancing in a frenzy.

The great Vedic philosophers, their names lost to the infernal mists of time, teach that the point of yoga practice is *citta vritti nirodahah*, the cessation of the fluctuations of the mind. In that stillness, they say, people find the true nature of reality, which is nonjudgmental, nonchanging, and eternal. Life should be lived, of course, fully and with enthusiasm—but only a calm mind, without attachments, makes that truly possible. People should take their *vritti*, their distractions, the little bugs that make them unhappy, and wipe them away by concentrating and honing their perfect minds.

That is yoga's goal: to get clear.

But for those looking to teach people such a lesson, plying them with synthetic drugs and throwing a rave in the woods probably isn't the best vehicle. It's hard to have a clear mind when you're part of a hot scrum of athletic bodies grinding under a multicolored strobe light show while the hottest possible trance rhythm plays around you. That is a veritable *plague* of *vritti*. Your *vrittis* are *vritting vrit*. They are multiplying. Good feelings like this cannot, by nature, last very long. They create attachments, because you always want to feel that good, and misplaced desire is the essence of human suffering.

Bolster was grinding his pelvis against the wall. Barlow pulled him off.

"Save it for someone who cares," Barlow said.

"What?" Bolster said.

He was feeling a little disoriented.

"Dude, you're dry-humping wood."

"Oh, that's bad," Bolster said, disengaging himself.

"Once you've been to a few of these things," Barlow continued, "you learn how to pace yourself."

Bolster hoped so, because right now he felt ready to float away completely. He looked out on the floor. Tom Hart had waded into the middle of the floor, where he was wiggling rhythmically, his arms in the air, surrounded by a dozen girls.

"What about him?" Bolster said.

"You don't need to pace yourself when you're the boss," Barlow said. "Besides, look at him. He knows exactly how to play."

Bolster saw. The girls were keeping a few inches of distance from their great leader. You could sense the desire coming off their fingertips, like lightning.

Just like that, Chelsea slithered up to Bolster.

"Hello, boys," she said.

"Hello," said Barlow, but she wasn't really there to talk to him.

"Did you enjoy the show, Matt?" she said.

"You were good," Bolster said.

"Stop being so stoic, Bolster," she said. "It's unbecoming."

"Sorry," he said. "These drugs are strong."

"Aren't they, though?" she said. "They'll be even stronger at the after-party."

"This isn't the after-party?" Bolster said.

"This isn't even the *pre*-party," Chelsea said.

"Oh, man."

"You'd better be around tonight," she said.

And then she wiggled out the door.

"Dude, are you fucking her?" Barlow said.

"On and off," Bolster said.

"That's a lot of diva," said Barlow. "You have my condolences. Seriously, though, I'm a little jealous."

"Don't be," Bolster said. "She fills me with grief."

But Bolster's grief was just beginning.

CHAPTER TEN

Chelsea Shell moved at a steady pace away from the main lodge, gratefully peeling away her false eyelashes. The chemicals coming off these things were going to give her retinal cancer someday, she just knew it. And the crotch in this hemp costume was rubbing her raw. But the night's show had enhanced her legend, and that was important. *People are such idiots*, she thought, *so easily entranced.*

She resented everything and everyone, and she was especially tired of giving performances for Tom Hart. Admittedly, he'd pulled her out of a tight spot after that mess with Ajoy, and he'd set her up better than ever. She'd had some fun, for a while, but then it got less fun. When she started with Hart, he'd had an ego, but his yoga was light and playful. There'd been a change in the last six months. The air around him had gone stale and weird. Everything became much more serious and intense, his desires more fervent. He'd gone from light tickling to heavy petting. She'd never given Tom an inch of sexual quarter beyond a shoulder rub, but suddenly he was drooling around after her, and after every other woman in his purview. Chelsea couldn't quite figure out why. Sometimes the shadow just descends. But because of that, she had to stay at the top, because that was the only way she'd have any power. Tom was picking the low-lying fruit. Those girls had no choice other than to let him suck their juice. But Chelsea was still allowed to have a lock on her door.

Soon, she'd get out. There was some money in her checking account again, and she had a lot of valuable new contacts that could set her up with teaching gigs. Maybe, she thought, she could settle into something more legitimate. Not a lease—those tied you down for at least a year—but maybe a sublet, something temporary (and nice) from a rich idiot who was going to Brooklyn for a year to explore his or her creative side. Chelsea knew people like that. It was possible. Sleeping in the same bed for more than five nights in a row would come as almost unimaginable relief from the usual hustle. She wouldn't be Tom Hart's dancing peacock anymore.

In the midst of this grim reverie, a man stepped into Chelsea's path.

"Who leaves their own pre-party?" he said. "Certainly not the star."

"What do you want, Hanuman?" Chelsea said.

"The question is," Hanuman said, "what do *you* want?"

"Actually, that's not the question," she said, "although it is, technically, *a* question."

"Some of us have been with Tom for a long time," he said.

"So?"

"So we don't appreciate someone cutting in line. Someone who might not have earned that place."

"For God's sake, dude, I'm not trying to replace you! Do you think I care about any of this bullshit? I just want to teach yoga and pay my bills."

"You're doing a lot more than paying your bills."

"Only because I don't have any."

"Just stay away from the Hanumaniacs," he said.

"That will be the easiest task of my life," she said.

A pause.

"Can I keep walking now?" asked Chelsea.

Hanuman stepped out of the way and extended an arm. He walked away, his synthetic dreads flapping in the wind. *What a weasel*, Chelsea thought.

This was not why she'd gotten into yoga. Like a lot of people, Chelsea had come from athletics, thirty-mile runs, surfing, skiing, the occasional distance swim. One weekend afternoon in January, she was snowboarding in Tahoe and went over a mogul. When she landed, her knees twisted until they were almost parallel to the ground. She heard a horrifying popping noise, and a grinding, and she screamed. The pain shot all the way up her body, through her throat. She leaned over on her side, vomited, and then passed out, cheek up. She was twenty years old, a sophomore in college.

Two years and three knee surgeries later, Chelsea's best exercise was coming from jogging in place in a therapy pool. She could barely ride her bike to the farmer's market. Her psych-major homework hardly held her interest, and her work-study job at the student-union cash register made her soul shrivel. Chelsea's edges were dulling, her personality receding. And then along came yoga.

Later, yoga created more problems for Chelsea than she was able to solve herself, but the first two years had been a delicious platonic romance of healing. At first, she limped through a few beginner's classes at a neighborhood studio whose owner was kind and patient and provided her with all the props she needed. Within a few weeks, thanks to a little simple home practice with some rubber tubing and some helpful advice to activate the quads while bending forward, Chelsea was making it through basic sequences relatively unassisted, though she was sweating way more than usual. That was normal, her teachers told her. *We always sweat a lot at the beginning. Our bodies are purging themselves of physical and mental impurities.*

At core, Chelsea was an athlete, with an athlete's obsession for training. Orchids like that tend to bloom quickly when grown under the right *asana* conditions. Soon enough, she'd started working out every day, and hard, putting the power back in power yoga. Some people spend a lifetime working through the Ashtanga primary series. She roared through it in six weeks and said, "Let's do some headstands." And while yoga isn't really meant to be a competitive sport, at least not outside of yoga competitions, she was clearly at the top of her three-hundred-hour Yoga Jock™ teacher training. Chelsea received her certification with honors. The studio had hired her to teach before she'd even graduated.

Then, of course, she'd moved to L.A., and everything turned to shit, like things usually do there. But she was still cranking out the poses. She'd be looking good long after most of these trendy idiots had moved on to their next pseudo-spiritual hobby.

She entered the communal bathroom at the women's dorm, which, for some reason, didn't have en suite accommodations like the men's did. Maybe Tom Hart had drilled some peepholes in the showers. It was in the realm. Regardless, Chelsea couldn't wait to change into something a little less Cirque du Soleil.

Chelsea washed her face, looked up, and heard sobbing from the direction of the toilets.

Great, she thought. *Now I have to be sisterly.*

She opened the door to the stall. Kimberly Wharton sat fully clothed on the toilet, sobbing.

"What are you doing?" Chelsea said.

"I thought everyone was at the party," Kimberly snuffled.

"Apparently not."

"I'm sorry. I just had to get away."

Kimberly blew her nose on some toilet paper, which made Chelsea wince.

"What is wrong with you?" Chelsea said.

"I hate these nights," Kimberly said. "They're getting worse."

"How?"

"It's Tom. At the last teacher's training, he took me into his bedroom and made me tie a yoga strap around his neck. Then he had me stick a cucumber up his ass."

"Are you serious?"

"He said it would be good for my spiritual development."

"And you did it?"

"It's my job."

"It is never *anyone's* job to do that."

"He dipped his fingers in Tiger Balm and put them in my vagina," Kimberly said.

"*What?*"

"He said I needed to feel the fire."

"That is rape, dude."

"Tom means well," she said. "He's just having a hard time adjusting to his new powers."

"He doesn't have any powers!" Chelsea said. "He's just a man, and he's kind of fat. You are a strong, beautiful, intelligent woman, and you don't need to put up with his crap."

"*You* do."

"That guy doesn't touch me unless we're being photographed together," Chelsea said. "If he ever tried, I'd rip him apart."

Kimberly sighed.

"But I love him," she said.

Chelsea offered Kimberly her arm.

"Let me make you some tea," said Chelsea.

"I have to get back to Tom."

Chelsea assured her it would be a short cup.

She had found an exit strategy.

CHAPTER ELEVEN

About an hour or so later, the dance party having scattered in favor of slightly more personal gatherings, Matt Bolster was staggering around the grounds of the Hart Center™, looking at his hands. They seemed so big, and then so small. *I've never really looked at my hands before*, he thought. But of course he had. He was on drugs.

Barlow was just ahead of Bolster. He sat down on a bench. Bolster sat down next to him. Barlow turned his head upward.

"The universe is full of infinite stars," he said. "You don't really understand that until you look at them."

Bolster sighed.

"Women," he said.

"That's what you're thinking about?" said Barlow.

"That's what I'm always thinking about."

"In yoga, we call that an attachment."

"I know. I see them naked in my mind, all the time. It's a serious weakness."

"Well," said Barlow, clearly not wanting to have this conversation. "It's something to work on."

"What about you?" Bolster said.

"What about me what?"

"And women. Or men. I don't care either way."

Barlow sighed, as though he were tired of explaining.

"I practice *bramacharya*," he said.

"OK," said Bolster, skeptically.

"It's the ancient Vedic art of sexual self-restraint."

"I know what *bramacharya* is, man. But no one actually practices it."

"I do."

"So you're *celibate*?"

"No," said Barlow. "*Bramacharya* isn't celibacy. I haven't renounced my desires. They're still present. I merely *control* them."

"All the time?"

"Every day and night."

"Even when you're by yourself?"

"Especially then."

"You're a man," said Bolster. "Once in a while you've got to beat one out."

"The fluids stay inside," Barlow said. "It keeps you vital."

"That's just sad."

Barlow stood up.

"You know, just once, I would like to have a conversation that wasn't about drugs or fucking," he said.

"Sorry," said Bolster. "Most people like talking about that stuff."

"See, this is the problem," said Barlow. "We all go around saying and thinking it's all good, it's all fine, we're all in the flow, when, in fact, all we're doing is looking for distractions from the *actual* flow."

"Sounds pretty human to me," Bolster said.

"We're supposed to be more than human," said Barlow. "Better than human. We're supposed to *overcome* things."

Then the night was silent.

"I think I just need to go back to my room and read," Barlow said.

"Understood," said Bolster. "See you in the morning."

"Later, man," Barlow said.

Barlow turned to walk away, his posture a little less perfect than usual.

"Hey," Bolster called out to him.

Barlow turned around, looking a little hopeful.

"Where's the after-party?"

"At the VIP lounge, where it always is," Barlow said.

"OK," said Bolster.

"The party never stops."

And he walked ascetically into the black.

With Barlow retired to his monkish chamber, Slim mysteriously MIA, and Suzie Hahn simply not a late-night option worth considering, Bolster found himself in an unfamiliar place. He was perilously sidekickless. Bolster spent most of his life wandering the world alone in a daze. Now that he was even more dazed than usual, he wanted company.

He looked up, finally taking Barlow's suggestion. The universe was a luminous smear of wonder, vast enough to almost appear sinister. Against such a backdrop of eternal flame, what was one pathetic, lonely human ego? Nothing more than the mangy growl of a starving alley dog. The self was a thin bulwark against the immensity of all creation. *Best to shed that layer as soon as possible*, Bolster thought. *Enjoy yourself, enjoy yourself. It's later than you think.*

Bolster's head felt light, and his heart was beating way faster than healthy. It felt like he'd taken ecstasy laced with an adrenaline substitute, which was probably something close to the truth. Time to press on, to be subsumed into the master's den.

The bartender let Bolster into the VIP suite, which was loaded with half-full martini and wine glasses, but empty of people. Everyone was outside, sitting around the enormous fire. Tom Hart was there, holding hands with beautiful Hart Yoginis on either side of him. The rest of the circle was composed of ten women and two men, only one of whom, mercifully, was Hanuman. Bolster noted, with some disappointment, that Chelsea Shell wasn't among them.

"Look, it's Matt Bolster, Yoga Detective!" Tom Hart said.

"I'm not really a . . ." Bolster said.

"Join us!" Hart said. "We were just getting ready to invoke the spirit of Shakti, the embodiment of divine desire."

Hart's definition of Shakti, while technically true, was also a little thin. Bolster didn't much care to invoke cosmic forces he didn't particularly understand. And he didn't trust Hart much to be able to control his *siddhis*, the extraordinary powers that fully developed yoga practitioners sometimes can cultivate.

"I don't know," Bolster said.

"That was an order," Hart said. "Not an invitation. If you come to the after-party, you play by the after-party rules."

Well, there you had it. Bolster sat down, grabbed a hand on either side of him, and closed his eyes. Hart began to chant:

"Ommmmmmmmmm!"

Everyone *ommmmmmmmmed* right back at him.

"*Ong namo guru dev namo*," he chanted.

"*Ong namo guru dev namo!*"

He chanted back. So did Bolster. The drugs were still in effect. They came and went. His mind was full of stars. So was his self. All the beautiful yoga voices chanted together, lost on a universal wave of harmony, for seemingly infinite minutes, until all was lost but the sound and the air.

The chanting stopped. Bolster opened his eyes. Tom Hart had his tongue halfway down the throat of the woman next to him. That was one way to awaken Shakti. The woman on Hart's other side had a hand on his inner thigh and was licking the neck of the guy next to her. Bolster realized there was a hand on his thigh as well, and a tongue in his ear. He looked across from him. Three women sat in a nearly closed circle, playing with one another's hair, pygmy chimps in $400 sarongs.

The party seemed to be drifting toward the hot tub. Sarongs came off, some of them revealing bathing suits underneath. Bolster considered skimming the froth himself, but then he saw Hanuman dipping into the waters. He decided not to take that bath. If Bolster was going to be at this party, he was going to do it right, and that did *not* encompass getting cockblocked by the monkey prince, not to mention by Tom Hart, the King Lingus. Instead, he drifted inside.

There, two versions of Jacqueline Bisset circa 1974 waved together in front of the divan, their hand and body movements coordinated, their eyes locked as though they were trading some sort of eternal secret. Next to them, Kimberly Wharton sat in a chair, thwacking away on her tablet, as always. A barely sipped martini sat on the table beside her.

"Aren't you going to join the fun?" Bolster said.

"Hah," she said. "I'm working. I'm always working."

Bolster looked at Kimberly. Unlike most of the women here, who had gorgeous faces but storky limbs and hungry-looking torsos, Tom Hart's assistant had curves and texture and also seemed to be capable of thought—if not necessarily independent thought. The other women were straightaways, but Kimberly was the whole racetrack.

"I wish you would," he said.

"I can't, Bolster," she said.

Bolster tried giving her the pouty eye.

"You're cute, but I really, really can't. Tom wouldn't like it."

Bolster looked outside. Tom Hart was in the hot tub, one woman on each knee.

"He looks pretty busy right now," Bolster said.

"I'm still here when they all leave," she said, sadly.

"Oh."

"He always says dessert is the best part of the meal."

Sometimes Bolster learned things that he didn't really want to. Whether he paid them or not, Hart did whatever he wanted with people. He was a big old baby who wanted to play with all the toys.

Bolster sat down, feeling heavy. The two Dusty Springfields on the dance floor were way too busy to notice him. Only *he* could come to a hot-tub orgy and not have a good time.

"It's OK, Bolster," Kimberly Wharton said. "Just open your heart."

The door to the suite flung open. There stood Chelsea Shell in a black wifebeater, her hair tied into a stern ponytail, looking very Starbuck. The door banged against the wall and made the groovy dancing ladies look up, surprised. Chelsea had a flair.

She stomped over to the bar.

"Give me a shot," she said.

"Of what?" asked the bartender.

"It doesn't matter."

The bartender poured something dark and thick. Chelsea belted it. She slammed the glass on the bar. Then she saw Bolster.

"Watch this," she said, and winked.

Chelsea walked over to the sliding glass doors and slid them open in a rush. Bolster bolted up, following her. If Chelsea told him to watch something, he usually complied.

Tom Hart had his head arched over the lip of the hot tub. He was getting licked and stroked in various places. The noise of Chelsea opening the door made him look up, though.

"Hey, Chelsea," he said. "Where are your hoops?"

"I shoved them up your ass," Chelsea said.

"Hey, wait," Hart said, standing up. "You can't talk to me like that."

Bolster wasn't particularly pleased to see that Hart was naked.

"You don't have any power over me," Chelsea said. "I know about things that you did. Things you don't want people to know about. You know?"

"No," Hart said. "I really don't."

"Let me give you a sample," she said.

Chelsea walked over to Hart, put a hand on one close-cropped temple, and bent his head down toward her mouth. He looked on impassively. She whispered in his ear. For a second, Hart looked shaken. Then he just looked angry. Chelsea released her grip.

"That's just the first," she said.

"You know, Chelsea," said Hart, "if you're jealous, I could always include you. God knows I've paid you enough to take the privilege."

She slapped him across the face, hard. He didn't flinch. Hanuman scrambled up from his seat in the tub, looking ready to pound her. Bolster tensed, ready to defend his dysfunctional lady. But Hart calmed everybody with a hand gesture.

"It's all good," he said. "Everyone stay calm. It's just a difference of style. Also, Chelsea seems to forget that I have excellent balance."

Chelsea slapped the other cheek then, a little harder, combining it with a little push. This time, Hart stumbled, half out of the hot tub, and landed one foot on the deck, catching himself on the rail before he stumbled completely over.

Everything seemed to freeze for a second as Tom Hart faced the Ojai Valley, hands holding the blond wood tightly. His middle-aged yoga ass shone like the moon.

"Get out," he said.

This time, Hanuman, also naked, charged Chelsea for real. Chelsea steeled for contact, but Hanuman would have worked her good. He was much bigger and stronger and seemed to have no internal check. Bolster stepped in. Not all his training was in yoga. His riot-squad training may have been twenty years in the past, but the principles stayed the same.

He charged Hanuman, landing a hard one on the jaw, sending the dreadlocks reeling. Walking forward fast, Bolster followed this with a quick punch to the gut. Hanuman bent over. Bolster walloped him under the chin. Hanuman spit a little blood, dropped to his knees, and then pitched forward.

Suddenly, the deck was a scene of screechy panic, as everyone scrambled for towels and robes, trying to get inside and away from Bolster as quickly as possible. But Bolster wasn't about to go on a rampage. He'd only been defending his lady. Even if she wasn't actually his lady.

"Out," Tom Hart said, hand extending toward the door. "Now."

Chelsea Shell pointed at him.

"Everyone's gonna find out," she said.

Meanwhile, Hanuman was staggering to his feet. He was actually pretty tough, Bolster had to admit. But not tough enough to want more.

"Just leave, Chelsea," he said. "And take your boyfriend."

"He's not my boyfriend," she said. "He's my muscle."

She turned out of the room. Bolster followed her.

Once they were outside, walking away from the complex, she said:

"That went well."

"It wasn't what I expected," Bolster said.

Back in the VIP lounge, Tom Hart was still facing the great beyond in his birthday suit. Kimberly Wharton came up behind him and draped a robe over his shoulders. He slid his arms in and cinched the belt. The music had stopped, and so had the conversation. Even the hot tub jets were off. All that remained was the faint crinkle of a big gas fire.

Turning around, he said, "All right, folks. There's obviously been a disruption. Time to leave the party."

Everyone was halfway out the door already, looking for an excuse. The room was clear within three minutes. Only Kimberly, Tom, and Hanuman remained. Hanuman's chin and lower lip were looking pretty raw where Bolster had clocked him.

"You go, too, Jones," Hart said. "Sleep it off."

"Can I at least get some ice?" asked Hanuman Jones.

"Have the bartender get you some," Hart said, "and take him with you."

Hanuman, as befitted his namesake, did what his lord commanded. Soon he was gone, and so was the bartender. Kimberly walked around the suite, picking up glasses. Hart brushed up behind her. She could feel him under the robe.

"I'm glad you stayed," he said.

"Just thought I'd tidy a bit," she said.

He brushed past, toward his bedroom door, the sanctum sanctorum.

"Don't worry about it," he said. "That's why we have housekeeping."

"I just thought that maybe, tonight . . ."

"Oh, no," he said. "Tonight especially. This is the weekend of the Gathering. I have plans for you."

"Tom, please," Kimberly said.

He looked at her sternly, standing full in the doorway. He extended his right arm about halfway and wagged his right index finger, giving a look somewhere between adorable and stern. Kimberly found him neither. Just inevitable. She put down the glasses.

Hart stood aside. She brushed past him and sat down on the edge of the bed. As the guru turned to face her, he removed his robe. It dropped to the floor like a drape coming off a statue. His foot kicked the door shut.

It was late.

CHAPTER TWELVE

Bolster woke up next to Chelsea Shell. They were on the bottom bunk in his dorm room, both of them wearing their clothes from the night before. By the time they'd gotten back, it had been long after midnight. Bolster's fist had been sore, and Chelsea was in no mood for anything. And so, for the first time in their lives, they'd slept together—actually slept.

Chelsea was awake, staring at him.

"What?" he said. His mouth felt gummy and acidic.

"You look horrible," she said.

"That's not surprising," he said.

Bolster had been here before, but not for a while. It felt like the fluid had drained from his spine. His brain was eggy, his joints jagged around the edges. This wasn't a physical problem that *pranayama* was going to solve.

"Excuse me," he said.

He rolled out of bed upward, flung open the door, and staggered down the hall to the communal bathrooms, which were mercifully empty. But he didn't make it all the way. A foul broth of vodka mixers and vegan sushi erupted from his stomach. This actually happened more often during Bolster's yoga decade than before. He took much better care of his body now, so when he treated it badly, the body rebelled. Even though it spent 95 percent of its time in Los Angeles, it wasn't used to toxicity.

Bolster looked at himself in the mirror. By any standards, this was the old version of himself. Sometimes when he stared, the light fell a certain way, and it was like a portal into the past, one where he was twenty-five pounds lighter, both in body and soul. But more often, it was a gaze into the future: heavy, tired eyes, ear hair, and skin the color of old wallpaper glue. This was a future day, and Bolster didn't like it. Right there, he vowed to lay off everything for weeks, to detoxify his body, mind, and spirit.

I've done it before, he thought.

When he got back to the room, he loaded a bowl and sparked up. Chelsea was up, too, her hair in a ponytail, not looking too much the worse for last night. He offered her a hit. She demurred.

"I don't get high before breakfast," she said. "Or ever, really."

"Me neither," said Bolster. "I just did this for the nausea."

"Right."

She patted him on the head.

"Shower up," she said. "You smell like a sheep. I'll see you at breakfast. I have things to do."

"Like what?" Bolster said. "It's Sunday morning."

"I have my own agenda," Chelsea said.

That's for sure, Bolster thought.

At breakfast, on the patio, Bolster sat alone. No one came anywhere near him. Suzie Hahn, if he knew her, had eaten at six thirty and already taken two classes by now, and Slim was still suspiciously absent. Otherwise, Bolster had only made enemies at the Gathering. Hanuman and his Hanumaniacs were a few tables away from him. Bolster felt himself on the opposite end of a light glower, but nothing else. Hanuman may have gotten seconds from the buffet, but he didn't want them from Bolster.

That had been a dark night, for sure, but from the happy chirping around the breakfast area, it was clear to Bolster that almost no one at the Gathering was aware of what had gone down in the VIP suite the night before. These were happily paying customers, living their dream in proximity to their yoga idol. They'd been posting pictures of themselves—smiling, glowing, hugging—to their Facebook pages all weekend. As far as anyone outside knew, they were all standing serenely like cranes in a perfectly manicured garden, their gazes fixed unjudgmentally on some unmovable, eternal point.

Slim burst onto the patio. His hair was matted with dirt and twigs and leaves, his face and arms covered with scrapes, his T-shirt a mess of blood and moss. He looked worse than usual.

"Patañjali!" Slim shouted. "He's alive!"

"What?" Bolster said.

"I saw him. A snake demon. He was sixty feet tall, and he wanted to rip out my heart."

Someone on the patio said, "I want what *that* guy's been smoking." People laughed. But Bolster was concerned. He'd known Slim a lot of years. This guy could handle his drugs. If he'd seen something, then he'd seen something.

"I need water," Slim said.

Slim moved toward the buffet table, wild-eyed. He picked up a pitcher of ice water, put the spout to his tongue, and downed three-quarters of it while everyone watched. Then he went back over to Bolster.

"Better," he said.

"All right," said Bolster. "What happened to you?"

"Well, I was out walking in the woods after my volleyball game yesterday, and . . ."

Bolster heard a scream. The sound filled the air from the valleys to the walls of the canyons, a near-echo of pure terror. There was another one. He pinpointed it, down the hill and to the right. The VIP suite.

He was vaulting over the rail and running down the path before the sound stopped. A huge gaggle of worried-looking yogis dashed just behind him, in a pack, like some sort of perverse viral-video fantasy sequence. Bolster arrived at the suite, breathing hard.

A woman from housekeeping sat, sobbing, on the step.

"It's horrible," she said.

The door was open. Bolster walked in. The room glowed with warm, soothing light, the night's detritus scrubbed away via the magic of underpaid labor. The door to Tom Hart's inner sanctum was also open. Bolster got in there quickly.

Hart sat in hero's pose on the bed, his back leaning against the headboard, his butt resting between his heels. His hands were tucked at his chest into *anjali mudra*, the sign of prayer. But his chest had been ripped open, as though with a hammer and chisel, and then with a crowbar. Flies had already begun to nestle at the edges of the gaping hole. The guru's heart was missing. It had been shoved, juice and muscle still fresh, into his mouth, which was as wide open as his eyes.

Bolster thought: Twenty-four hours a day everywhere in this world, thousands of people are practicing yoga, grinding and stretching and resting their tired, sad bodies and minds, and someone is trying to teach them. But they're never sure who they're looking at, out there on the horizontal teacher's mat. Millions of people are flipping their dogs, discretely and discreetly, dropping back into full camels, listening to the sound of their breath as they open up into warrior two. They're finding a greater peace than they've ever known through the magic of postural adjustment, but also snapping ligaments, tearing hamstrings, knocking their sacra out of alignment, and slowly going crazy. Yoga will save some of them, but not most. They'll quit, unsatisfied. But even if they stick to a plan, even if they master poses and people, yoga will still be the relentless engine of their ultimate destruction.

That had certainly happened here.

Tom Hart would flow no more.

Other people arrived in the room. Screams of horror began afresh. The sheets and walls were splattered with their guru's bloody, stinking guts.

At least I won't have to teach my eleven o'clock, Bolster thought.

He had real work to do now.

CHAPTER THIRTEEN

The moment he saw Tom Hart's eviscerated body, Matt Bolster went into cop mode. Hart had been ripped open, his chest exposed as if he were a rubber Halloween lawn zombie, his heart stuffed in his mouth in an act too taboo and gluttonous even for *Bizarre Foods*. It made Bolster gasp, and he'd encountered a lot of gore in his life. These cosseted yoga Barbies and Kens also weren't reacting well. As soon as the first couple of Gathering attendees followed Bolster into the room, the screaming began.

"Back away!" Bolster said. "Do not touch the body, do not touch anything in the room!"

The trickle of humans would soon turn into a deluge, Bolster saw. The couple of women who'd made it to the door frame were howling and clawing at the air. Bolster bumped them away from the door.

"Out!" he said.

"He was our light!" one of the Gathering moaned.

"This is a crime scene," Bolster said. "Every minute every one of us is in here, it becomes a little more compromised. Do you want the FBI to find your DNA anywhere near that body?"

That got their attention. Slowly, the room began to clear as Bolster shooed people away like pigeons. He closed the door. Housekeeping could let the cops in with a master key. For now, the scene needed to be secure. Outside, he saw people trying to climb over the back gate.

"And stay off the patio, too," he said.

Ordinarily, he would have posted Slim there as a guard, but Slim was back at the lodge, covered in dirt and blood, murmuring about having been attacked by an ancient Indian snake god. Bolster had to deal with that situation, too, but right now this was more pressing. The crowd of twenty or so who'd begun to gather was acting restless. Bolster knew that this group wouldn't respond to excessively authoritarian speech, so he moved into Kind Yoga Teacher mode. Or at least tried to.

"Hey, guys, I think it would be coolest if you all headed back to the lodge," he said. "Please, please, please. Obviously this is very traumatic for all of us, but we can't disturb the crime scene. Also, I need someone to call the police."

Kimberly Wharton stepped out of the scrum.

"I already did," she said, "the second I heard the screaming."

"You're awfully calm," Bolster said.

"Panicking never helped anyone," Kimberly said. "I can be sad later, in private, when I'm away from these bozos."

"Sad about what?" Bolster asked.

Then he heard someone running around the compound, screaming, "Tom Hart is dead!" That alleviated his suspicion. Somewhat.

"Everyone back to the lodge," Kimberly said, and now they listened. As much as anyone at the Gathering, she spoke with Hart's voice. Which was somewhat ironic, Bolster thought, since Hart would never speak again.

"What happened?" she said.

He told her, in detail.

"Oh my God," she said, a little too quickly and obviously.

Shoving Hart's heart in his mouth had been a nice baroque touch. TMZ was going to love that.

Kimberly joined the yogis and yoginis on their sad brunch-time exodus, leaving only Bolster standing in front of Tom Hart's VIP suite. The crime-scene tape would be along soon enough. For now, he was a one-man guard.

He pulled a one-hitter out of his pocket, lit up, and dragged. That would clear his head. Or calm him down. Or maybe this wasn't such a great time to be getting high. Maybe he should stop trying to avoid challenging situations in a constant search for ephemeral pleasure. Maybe it didn't matter. And maybe no one else cared or was paying attention. Regardless, in the present moment, the deed was done. It was hardly the worst thing that had happened at the Hart Center in recent hours.

Suzie Hahn was walking down the path toward him, tapping at her iPhone. Bolster was sure she was getting a post ready for Tumblr. But no one would allow her to post pictures of Hart's body. This was no time for murder-scene selfies.

"Is it bad, Matt?" she said.

"Brutal. Beyond your imagining," Bolster said.

"Wow," said Suzie. "Who do you think did it?"

"I don't know," said Bolster. "Everyone who slept here last night is a suspect. Including me. Including you."

"Oooh, a real mystery," Suzie said. "How exciting!"

"This isn't *Scooby-Doo*, Hahn," Bolster said. "A man is dead."

She snapped a photo.

"And Matt Bolster is on the case," she said.

That was going on Instagram.

"I need you to stand here and not let anybody past you," Bolster said, "until the cops get here."

Bolster knew that Suzie, size-wise, probably wasn't the best person to play murder-scene bouncer, but she was a neutral third party, and she was a decent worker. He could trust her. That meant something in a deputy.

She gave him a little salute.

"Can I go online while I do it?" she asked.

"Can I stop you?"

"No."

Bolster didn't mind. Suzie would guard the perimeter well. She was a force of pure will. This gave Bolster a few minutes to stealthily case the grounds, not that much stealth was required since no one else was paying attention at the moment.

It was hard for Bolster to tell if there had been any security breaches, or anyone running from the scene. First of all, the Hart Center™ was 60 percent undeveloped, so cursory glances along the hillsides didn't reveal anything. Also, there had been some crazy partying the night before, so the whole joint was a bit disheveled. When a crime scene spans multiple acres and empties out into a forest, there are infinite avenues for escape, Bolster knew. He'd tried to track criminals in Griffith Park, and this was a lot less familiar.

He decided to go see if Barlow knew anything. It wasn't as though Bolster suspected him—though, to be honest, he didn't know him very well—but Barlow had seemed pretty alienated the night before and could maybe at least provide some context clues.

Bolster knocked on Barlow's door. There was no answer, but the door was unlocked, so Bolster opened it. Barlow was sitting on a cushion in the middle of the room, meditating, his eyes turned down softly, *vipassana*-style. It looked like he'd been at it for a while. The air felt mildly electric, which Bolster thought was mildly weird.

"Barlow," Bolster said.

Barlow held up a finger, in an impatient and vaguely threatening way.

Om mani padme om, he chanted, *om mani padme om. Om mani padme om.*

He opened his eyes and looked at Bolster, calmly.

"What?" he said.

"Tom Hart is dead."

"Holy shit!" Barlow said, in a voice that indicated—or at least imitated—genuine surprise. "How?"

Bolster told him.

"Jesus fucking Christ!" Barlow said.

An appropriate reaction.

"Did you see him at all last night?" Bolster said.

"Why?" said Barlow. "Am I a suspect?"

"Right now everyone is a suspect," Bolster said. "Including me."

"I didn't see him after we left the party. I went to bed early. I didn't sleep much because I was hallucinating my balls off."

"That was strong stuff," Bolster said.

"Yeah, I got up and walked around the property at around four thirty, but it was really quiet. Just a couple of women doing *pranayama* by the pool."

"Did you go anywhere near Hart's suite?"

"Define near," Barlow said.

"Close to."

"I might have gone over there to see if the party was still happening, but I didn't hear anything, so I went back to my room and crashed."

"It broke up early," Bolster said, "when I punched Hanuman in the face."

"That guy's a tool," Barlow said.

"He is. So you were near the suite before dawn, and there was no one else around."

"Yes."

"Huh. OK."

The room was quiet. There was still residue from Barlow's meditation vibe. This guy would need to answer some more questions later. Those were a lot of unaccounted-for hours.

"I guess I need to start looking for paid work," Barlow said.

The yoga scholar walks a lonely road, Bolster thought.

Bolster went next door, to the women's dorm. Chelsea's door was wide open, the room empty, her stuff gone. She'd even taken the sheets and towels, which hadn't been hers. But that was never really an impediment for Chelsea, who was no stranger to purloined thread count. She bailed whenever she wanted, with whatever she wanted, and didn't care who she left behind. This time, though, Bolster had to find her.

He was wearing the same shirt as the night before and wanted to change. Back in his room, there was a piece of paper on the bed. A red lip imprint had been pressed onto it, above the typed words *Namaste, Bolster. Kiss.*

That woman's gonna drag me under, Bolster thought. *But at least she doesn't use emoticons.*

Was Chelsea capable of killing Tom Hart? Certainly. Did she tend to leave situations at the wrong time for obscure reasons, thereby throwing undue suspicion upon herself? Without question. Had she and Bolster been working each other over all weekend? Unfortunately. His prints would be all over her, inside and out. Hers could be all over everything, too, including Tom Hart's cheek.

Dammit.

By the time Bolster went outside, the cops had begun to swarm around the Hart Center, really throwing the Gathering into a tizzy. The tape went up around Hart's suite. The parking lot entrance gained a guard. No one was getting in or out for a while. Meanwhile, a half-dozen yokel cops and a couple of state troopers were looking around but appeared to be unsure of what they were looking for.

And then Bolster remembered Slim. He went back to the deck. His buddy was still sitting where he'd left him, covered in dirt and blood and scratches. Dr. Cohen, ever kindly and caring, had brought Slim a cup of herbal tea. Slim sipped on it, looking scared and numb. He still had the shakes.

"It was so big, Matt," Slim said. "As big as the sky. With infinite heads. *Patañjali*. He is lord of the snakes."

"Snap out of it," Bolster said.

"It was real!" Slim moaned.

"What kind of drugs did you take yesterday, Slim?"

"I didn't take any drugs!"

"Really."

"Wait, does weed count as a drug?"

"Yes."

"So that, and nothing else."

"All right."

"This guy wearing a cobra hood gave me a pill when I was lost in the woods after volleyball."

"You're kind of burying the lead here, man."

"What do you mean?"

"When did you start seeing the snake god?" Bolster asked.

"About fifteen minutes after . . ."

Slim paused.

"Oh," he said. "Maybe I *was* on drugs."

"You think?" Bolster said. "That still doesn't explain why you look like *this*, though."

"Because I thought he was chasing me, and then I tripped and fell into a ravine."

"Did anyone see you go in or out of that ravine?"

"No. I mean, maybe the cobra guys, but they were looking up at the sky mostly. Also, their faces were covered, so I have no idea who they actually were."

Why do I ever leave the house? Bolster thought.

"OK," he said.

"You don't believe me?"

Slim didn't exactly fit a conventional profile on a normal day. But now he was sitting around a murder scene, looking like he'd accidentally walked into a cockfight. Plus, he had a misdemeanor rap sheet, mostly drugs. They were all in for a long day. But Slim's would probably be longer.

"I believe you," Bolster said.

CHAPTER FOURTEEN

Detective Vijay Malik of the Ojai Police Department sat on his living room sofa, enjoying Sunday morning alone. Normally this would have been family time, but his wife had taken the girls to Brownies. Vijay liked being involved with the kids. He had no problem sitting through ballet recitals or soccer games. But he drew the line at scouting. He just didn't understand what the girls were doing at those meetings.

Which was fine, because now Vijay had a chance to really enjoy a plate of eggs. He was joined—on the TV, at least—by CNN's Fareed Zakaria, a personal hero of Vijay's. That guy had it all: brains, dry wit, and a hot rich blonde American woman at his side. He was someone to emulate. Even though Vijay could have done without some of the boring interviews with Paul Krugman and Henry Kissinger, and actually didn't under- stand about half of what Fareed was saying (particularly the stuff about the Eurozone crisis), the show was still one of the highlights of his week. It was like having a sensible friend over for brunch, but without the extra food costs. Lesser men might have watched football with their guy time, or smoked weed or had a beer. But Vijay didn't like sports much, and he was a decent cop, so he didn't do drugs. Beer was for after work, but he definitely hadn't worked today. Vijay was perfectly satisfied with Fareed Zakaria and a breakfast scramble. He settled back into the couch with a happy sigh.

His Android rang. He looked at the screen. It was a city number with three zeroes at the end. The office. Dispatch didn't usually call on Sunday. So he decided to answer.

"Malik," he said.

It was his chief.

"I hope you're not busy," his chief said.

"What do you think?" said Vijay.

"Guessing not."

"Right."

"We have a situation up at the Hart Center."

"What's the Hart Center?"

"It's that big luxury yoga compound up Route 150. The one with all the Cabrios in the parking lot."

"Oh, right. So what kind of situation?"

"It's a murder situation."

"Really?"

"We're going to have to investigate."

Vijay gulped.

"When you say murder, what kind do you mean?" he asked.

"The kind where someone ends up dead at a yoga center."

"OK."

"It's in our jurisdiction. You need to represent us."

"Brian," Vijay said, because the entire force was on a first-name basis, "don't you think *you* should represent us?"

"Yes, but not until after lunch," the chief said, not explaining why, though he was probably golfing.

I guess I need to investigate a murder, then, Vijay thought.

He put on some clean pants, an off-brand polo, and a decent pair of shoes, and combed a little water into his hair, swished some mouthwash, and headed for the door in fewer than five minutes. On his way out, he texted his wife:

Had to run out. Murder investigation.

MURDER???? she wrote back.

Yes, he replied.

Aren't you fancy? she said.

Very fancy.

OK. B careful.

Vijay had assisted a couple of homicide investigations back when he was a trainee in Cabrillo, but not since. Mostly he investigated small-time theft: unlocked mountain bikes getting lifted at the farmer's market, rakes missing from garden sheds. Ojai crime was enough to keep him busy, but not enough to keep him up late with worry. He always had his paperwork done by five.

The town had about one assault—usually minor—per week, and one domestic-violence rap every four or five months. The population—farmers, hippies, and, on the weekend, wine-besotted Hollywood executives in their mountain-fetishist second homes—didn't exactly exude menace. At community meetings, the chief was always griping about Ojai's "gang problem," but "gang" was just a synonym for "teenagers with spray paint." They didn't even have a significant college in town, thus reducing the chance of public drunkenness by about 90 percent.

About three years ago, the cops had found a guy in an orange grove with his head bashed to hell. That might have been something. But the guy had just tripped and hit a rock. There hadn't been an actual murder in Ojai for almost twenty years.

But it looked like they had one now.

Vijay drove his government-issue car (a Camry hybrid, boring but more than good enough) up Route 150 to the Hart Center, wondering what in the world a murder at a yoga center would look like. As far as he was concerned, yoga was something his nan used to do in the mornings after feeding the birds. Like a lot of thoroughly assimilated Indians, he thought Americans were pretty ridiculous walking around with their colorful mats and wearing their $125 workout pants. Hearing Anglos say "namaste" to each other was almost offensive to him. How would they like it if he went into a church and shouted "Howdy, Jesus!"? They would not.

But it's not as though he cared much. Yoga was just part of the firmament in this part of the world, like sour fruity frozen yogurt, free-range meat at the farmer's market, and brush fires. The fact that it originated, thousands of years ago, in the place where his grandparents were born (as opposed to Gardena, where *he* was born) held little interest. Lemon pickles also came from India. He didn't like those either.

Vijay pulled into the Hart Center parking lot, waving at the police guard, who he knew, at the entrance. It was quiet, calm, piney on the grounds. Vijay really needed to get outside more often. But TV trumped nature most of the time. *This will be the year I go hiking more than once*, he said to himself as he parked at the end of a row of squad cars. There were all of Ojai's patrol vehicles, plus a couple from the county. The state police wouldn't be far behind, either. Maybe the feds, too. Or maybe Vijay would solve this one all by himself.

He had a brief flash of himself being interviewed by Fareed Zakaria. "My next guest," Fareed would say, "is the hard-working California police officer and devoted father of two who solved a yoga murder despite tremendous budget constraints." Then, after the interview, he and Fareed would go out for croissants and talk about the pressures of being working dads. They would be friends forever.

This delicious reverie came to an end when Vijay walked into the lobby of the Hart Center, which was full of worried people who'd paid good money to draw close to enlightenment and instead found themselves detained on suspicion of homicide. Several yogis and yoginis, their natural beauty disturbed by worry lines and hangover, were frantically confronting the cops, who looked puzzled by these strange urban (or wealthy exurban) creatures. Some of the people wanted information. Some of them wanted consoling. Most of them just wanted to go home. But that wasn't going to happen right now.

"You have to let me out!" one woman pleaded. "I promised the weekend nanny I'd be home by six, and she absolutely has to leave. She's going to France with her other family on Monday! I've got no one to cover!"

"If you'll just be patient," the officer said.

"We're like *refugees*!" the woman said.

Vijay approached a cop cowering in the corner and sucking on an energy drink.

"Hey, Malik," the cop said.

"Tell me," Vijay said.

"They found the guy who runs this place dead this morning."

"OK."

"Someone had torn out his heart and shoved it in his mouth."

"*What?*"

"People are totally frantic. I guess he was their guru or something."

Vijay heard someone shout:

"We are running out of coconut water!"

This evinced a fresh round of ululation and weeping. Two women ran up to Vijay.

"Are we going to starve to death?" one asked. "*Are* we?"

"You can't keep me here!" shouted the other. "My husband is the executive vice president in charge of animated feature film development at Paramount!"

"Please just give us a little time, and then we can let you go," Vijay said.

"He used to be at Dreamworks," said the woman who was, for some reason, worried about her husband's career status. It turned out to be warranted when, two years later, he was working out of a two-room "independent production office" in Van Nuys, and she was doing free yoga on Sunday mornings in Griffith Park instead of attending $3,000 luxury retreat weekends. It was a cruel and dirty business.

"Where's the body?" Vijay asked the cop.

The cop shrugged and pointed noncommittally.

"Some building behind there," he said. "But good luck getting through this bunch."

The guru-less yogis were braying like goats and tapping their smartphones relentlessly. Up and down the West Coast, attorneys were coming out of their Sunday brunch stupors to some really juicy gossip. The knives of a hundred lawsuits began to sharpen.

"Today was the day Tom was going to give me my mantra!" someone screamed.

"This is a problem," Vijay said.

A guy in his midforties approached Vijay. He was about six-two, with slightly receding sandy-blond hair close to shoulder length, and three days of graying stubble. He wore light brown pants a little baggily around the hips, and a T-shirt depicting The Flash battling Captain Cold. The guy didn't seem stressed out at all.

"Maybe I can help," he said.

"How?" said Vijay.

"They need to be told what to do," the guy said.

He turned to the crowd and threw up his hands.

"Everyone have a seat," he said.

To Vijay's surprise, everyone did—except for the cops. Yoga students were well trained to follow orders.

"I'm Matt Bolster," he said to the crowd. "I was supposed to teach today at 10:00 a.m. Obviously, that's not going to happen. If you live in the greater L.A. area, you can check out my regular Tuesday evening flow class at Prana Mala on Abbot Kinney."

He continued: "But right now I need you to stay very calm. These guys haven't come here to make your lives hard. They're here to do a job, a very tough and stressful one. So I'm asking you, as a fellow yogi—and a former cop—to extend some empathetic thoughts to them. Even while you're grieving."

He seemed to have their attention.

"Place your hands on your knees, palms up," he said. "Close your eyes. Focus on your breath. Let it move in and out of your lungs. Count slowly, gently, down from ten on the exhale. Hold at the bottom. Inhale for ten, and hold at the top. Let the rhythm of your breathing caress you. Listen to the sounds in the room, and beyond, and remember that you're part of something greater than yourself. All is calm. All is perfect."

To Vijay's amazement, the room suddenly seemed to be enveloped in a peaceful haze. Matt Bolster looked at Vijay and said:

"No one expects the Relaxation Response."

And then he winked.

For someone who was trying to help Vijay, this guy sure seemed like a lot of trouble.

CHAPTER FIFTEEN

Bolster sat in a conference room at the Hart Center with Vijay Malik and a couple of state troopers, who appeared to have some authority over the half-dozen other state troopers who were now swarming the grounds looking for nothing in particular. One of the troopers, with a name badge that read JOHNSON, said:

"Who the fuck is this guy?"

"This is Bolster," Vijay said.

"I was supposed to teach at the Gathering this week," Bolster said.

"What is the Gathering, and what were you teaching, and why are you in here?"

This guy didn't know anything, which gave Bolster an advantage.

"Did you invite him, Malik?" Johnson asked.

"He kind of invited himself," Vijay said.

"The Gathering is the fancy name for this weekend retreat," Bolster said. "I came here to teach yoga. My friend Vijay asked me to sit in because I used to be an LAPD homicide detective."

"Wait, you're a yoga teacher, but you used to be murder police?"

"Yes."

"Huh."

Vijay said, "I thought that Detective Bolster . . . Can I call you that?"

"Not officially," Bolster said. "I'm privately employed now. You can call me Señor Bolster."

"OK, I thought that Señor Bolster here might have some insight."

"I was kidding about the Señor," Bolster said.

"He seemed to really calm down the crowd earlier," Vijay said.

Johnson sat with his arms crossed. He was a hard-ass, but probably not a moron.

"OK, Señor Bolster," he said. "Enlighten us."

"I know a lot," Bolster said.

"Great," said Johnson.

"I'm not sure if Tom Hart, the victim, had a lot of enemies. But I do know that he'd built a pretty substantial yoga empire here. And when there are yoga empires, there are money problems, and rivalries, and a lot of sexual jealousy."

"Are there a lot of yoga empires?" Johnson asked.

"More than you might think," Bolster said. "And this one has gotten pretty large. Or at least it had. I don't think it's going anywhere now."

"So what was this empire all about?"

"Controlling people, like all of them are," Bolster said. "Hart's specialty was 'heart-opening poses,' and rapid-breathing exercises. Pretty physical stuff, for a mostly young clientele. There was also a kind of pyramid training scheme where the more you paid, the higher a module you'd get to take with Hart. The wealthier you were, the more access you got to the boss."

"So kind of like Scientology," Vijay said.

"A little," said Bolster, "but not as organized. From my brief exposure, Tom Hart just seemed like a party guy who liked to smoke pot and flirt with women. The yoga was just an excuse."

"Wait, I'm confused," Johnson said. "You're involved with the organization how?"

"I'm not," Bolster said. "I'm just a guest here this weekend. They invited me because I got a little famous from solving another yoga murder."

Johnson looked incredulous.

"Another yoga murder."

"Yes, in L.A."

"And you solved it."

"More or less."

Bolster couldn't help it. He puffed with pride a little.

"This is a real thing," Johnson said, sipping on a portable cup of highly leaded coffee. "Yoga murders."

If you knew anything about yoga at all, he thought—but didn't say—*you'd know that murders aren't that surprising. In fact, they're almost inevitable.*

"Yes, like I said. So I came up to the Gathering."

"And you didn't know anyone."

"Except for the people in my car."

"Bolster," Vijay said, trying to redirect, "maybe you could tell us what you *do* know."

"All right," said Bolster. "The night of the murder Tom Hart had a little pre-party in his VIP suite."

"A pre-party?" Johnson said. "Pre to what?"

"A real party."

The cops were rolling their eyes, but also looking a little intrigued. Everyone liked to get invited to a party, even a weird yoga one.

"OK. So who was at this pre-party?"

"Not too many people. Me, my friend Suzie Hahn the yoga blogger, a yoga scholar named Andrew Barlow, and Dr. Mitchell Cohen, Tom Hart's personal physician. Tom's assistant Kimberly. A couple other people, I think. Oh, and a bartender. That was the first time I actually met Tom Hart in person."

"And what were your impressions?"

"Hart seemed kind of insecure."

"Insecure about what?"

"Everything."

"So what happened at this pre-party?"

"We drank, talked, smoked some weed."

"Weed as in marijuana?"

"Yes."

"That's illegal."

"Are you investigating a murder or trying to make a dime-bag bust?" Bolster said. "This is California. I have a prescription."

Bolster could break out the tough-guy if he needed to. Any cop who still cared about pot these days was just looking for a cheap collar. The courts and jails were full. Time to let the stoners run free.

"All right, so what happened after the pre-party?" Vijay said.

"There was a rave."

"A rave?"

"With a DJ."

Vijay slumped in his chair a little, as though he was beginning to realize what this case would entail.

"At a yoga conference?" he said.

Bolster shrugged.

"It happens all the time," he said. "There was dancing, and I took a pill."

"A pill? Like drugs?"

"A mild hallucinogen, I think," Bolster said. "Though it mostly just made my legs feel heavy."

"You were tripping last night?"

"A little," Bolster said.

Vijay put his head in his hands.

"Jesus Christ," he said.

"I've had just about enough of this guy's bullshit," said the state trooper who wasn't Johnson.

"Hang on, hang on," Bolster said. "I'm trained to observe situations even when I'm on drugs."

Johnson leaned in.

"Really?" he said. "So what did you observe? While on drugs."

"I went to the party with Hart."

"Did he give you the drugs?"

"No," Bolster said. "The scholar did. I don't know where *he* got them, though. A lot of people seemed happy, like they were doing them."

"What happened at the party?"

"Hart danced for a little while. He was the center of attention. Women were swarming all over him. I got pretty horny. Not because of the dancing. Probably because of the drugs. Then I left."

Bolster was losing his audience. Nobody wanted to hear about how horny he'd been.

"Then there was an after-party," he said.

That got their interest back.

"And you attended," Johnson said.

"I did," said Bolster. "The hot tub was going. People were making out."

"How many people?"

"Twenty, maybe twenty-five. About twice as many women as men. They were starting to get naked."

Now he *really* had their attention.

"And they were making out?" Vijay said, his voice cracking a little. "Like it was an orgy?"

"Getting there."

"With Hart?"

"He was definitely in on it," Bolster said.

"What about you?"

"I considered," Bolster said. "How could I not? But I didn't really get a chance."

"Why not?"

"Because Chelsea Shell came in."

The troopers leaned in. This was all bullshit to their minds. But it was a pretty good story.

"Who's that?"

"It's complicated."

"Tell us anyway."

"Well, she's a yoga teacher who's pretty high up in the Hart organization. He wanted to sleep with her, but she wouldn't let him."

"Why not?"

"She let him a couple of times but then it stopped."

"OK."

"In any case, she walked in and slapped Hart, twice."

"Slapped him, like hit him?"

"Yeah, I'm not sure why," Bolster said. "She whispered something to him first. Then Hanuman got up out of the hot tub and wanted to hit her."

Johnson held up a hand.

"Wait," he said. "Who is Hanuman?"

"This guy. The number-two yoga teacher in the organization. I think he felt threatened by Chelsea, or maybe he was trying to defend Tom. I don't know. But he lunged at her."

"And then what happened?"

"I hit him."

"*You* hit him?"

"Yeah, three times. He ended up on the deck."

"Why?"

"Because Chelsea and I have a past."

"How much of a past?"

"A substantial past. It's a long story."

"We have a little time."

So Bolster gave them a brief outline of his history with Chelsea, during which the three cops sat there like ladies who lunch, absorbing the juiciest gossip. The non-Johnson trooper scribbled furious notes. It would have taken them weeks to get this much background, if ever. Bolster clearly had his uses.

"And what happened after you hit Ham?" Johnson asked.

"Hanuman," Bolster said.

"Whatever."

"I left. With Chelsea. We went back to my room."

"Did you sleep with her?"

"I don't remember."

"How could you not remember?"

"It was late. I fell asleep right away."

"Where is she now?"

"I don't know," Bolster said. "We woke up together, and then I went to breakfast. I went back to look for her about thirty minutes after they found Hart's body and she was gone. She got out before you guys got here."

"But she can't be a suspect, right?" Vijay said. "She was with you all night."

"I don't know," Bolster said. "Like I said, I was asleep."

Bolster didn't *think* Chelsea had killed Hart. She didn't tend to do anything that was against her best interest. But why had she slapped Hart? What did she know? The cops wanted to find the killer. He wanted to find Chelsea. He was hoping they weren't the same person.

"Do you have any idea where she might be headed?"

"Could be anywhere. She doesn't have a fixed address."

They went around like this for a few more minutes.

"Thanks for your help, Mr. Bolster," said the trooper.

"Sure," Bolster said. "I can keep helping if you want."

"Anything you can do."

"For a fee."

"You want us to fucking *pay* you?" said non-Johnson. "Because you did drugs and went to an orgy?"

"Services rendered," said Bolster. "I'm a professional."

"I could arrest your ass right now."

"Calm down, Mark," Johnson said. "We appreciate your offer, Bolster, but we're going to take it from here."

"Suit yourself," Bolster said.

He got up to leave. The conference door opened.

"Sergeant Johnson," a trooper said, "we've got a guy on the deck who's causing problems. He's covered in blood and dirt, and he's ranting about a snake god."

"A snake god?" Johnson said.

"He means Patañjali, the original author of the *Yoga Sutras*," Bolster said.

The troopers looked at him.

"Oh, right, you don't need me anymore," Bolster said.

The troopers left. Bolster and Vijay Malik sat the conference table, looking at each other.

"That guy who was ranting was my friend Slim," Bolster said. "I drove him up here. He's covered in blood and dirt because some guy wearing a cobra hood slipped him a pill, and then he hallucinated and got scared and fell into a ravine."

"I do not understand this situation," Vijay said.

"Me either," Bolster said.

They went outside. The troopers had Slim handcuffed and were walking him to a car. Clearly, despite all the wonderful information they had in hand, they'd taken the easy path.

"What's going on?" Bolster said.

"This guy is covered in blood and can't offer a plausible explanation of where he was last night," Johnson said.

"It's his *own* blood, not Tom Hart's!" Bolster said.

"How do you know that?'

Bolster didn't.

"After all I just told you, you're going to arrest a guy just because he looks weird? Come on! You know this goes deeper."

Slim saw Bolster.

"Help me, Matt!" he said.

Bolster followed the deputies to the parking lot, where they loaded Slim into the back of a car. Just before they closed the door, Slim said:

"Don't let them take my didge."

"I'll get you out of this, buddy," Bolster said.

The troopers drove off, apparently proud of their shoddy work. But they had what they cared about: a guy they could trumpet to the media. Shortly after, CNN announced: "California state police have taken a man into custody who they suspect in the grisly murder of Tom Hart, the world-renowned yoga guru. Charles Slimberg, age thirty-eight, is reportedly a drifter with a checkered rock 'n' roll past . . ."

Bolster was stunned. He hadn't known that Slim's real name was Charles Slimberg. But he knew now, and he also knew that Slim had cruel parents.

Over the next week, YouTube videos of Slim playing the didge with Nine Inch Nails and Widespread Panic would go viral. *The Smoking Gun* would obtain copies of his marijuana possession arrest reports, and Defamer would post clips of the one-man show in which Slim read aloud the poetry of Charles Bukowski while sitting naked in a cemetery. They didn't bother to ask why Slim, a man with no record of anything but the most innocent consensual crimes, would commit a hideously violent murder against a man he'd never met.

Well, Bolster would ask. And so would Vijay Malik.

Back at the Hart Center, Vijay gave a sigh.

"They may not need you," he said. "But I do."

"I'll consider it," Bolster said, "for my friend."

Vijay pulled out his wallet, opened it, and peeled off five twenties. Bolster took the money.

"That'll about cover my gas here and back," said Bolster.

"We'll find more," Vijay said.

CHAPTER SIXTEEN

Two weeks passed. The Hart Center emptied out, becoming a living evidence drawer, as abandoned and ghostly as some old Western movie town in the hills around Palmdale. Slim was arraigned and stayed in jail. To Bolster's great surprise—and also Slim's—they'd found a substantial amount of Hart's dried blood on Slim's body. The DNA tests matched it perfectly. The people and Nancy Grace cried: Guilty!

The judge set a million-dollar bond, which no one who Slim knew could pay. Everyone else went home, even Bolster, who returned to L.A. to look for a decent lawyer, preferably someone who specialized in springing railroaded hippies. That was a specialized skill set for sure, but probably not too hard to find in California.

Bolster felt guilty about leaving Slim behind, but he had to teach yoga. Since his status in the world had improved, he'd taken on a ten-class-a-week load. Sitting shiva at the Ventura County courthouse wasn't going to help anyone.

Like O.J., Bolster vowed to find the real killer. He was operating at a 99.99 percent level of certainty in his friend's innocence. Slim was a freak, but he was a sweet freak, and no killer. The stupidity and laziness of the arresting officers really nagged at Bolster. This wasn't *Easy Rider*; it was the era of Burning Man and techno-punk and Dog the Bounty Hunter. Weirdoes ruled the Earth. Admittedly, the circumstances had been strange, but that's why you hired a yoga detective. Bolster had read most of the Upanishads and had worked the LAPD's murder squad. That was a specialized combination. He knew his shit.

But instead, Bolster was subbing the 10:30 a.m. "Sweat and Surrender Lotus Flow" at Santosha Shala, a white-walled, wispy-curtained second-story joint above a yogurt shop and cell-phone store in Westwood. If Bolster had been in charge—which he never seemed to be, no matter the situation—he would have just called the class "yoga," since it was all the same, but these joints had to justify their $21 individual class prices. Even the ten-class passes ran $180, hardly a bargain. So they gave the classes fancy names and promised eighty-minute escapes. There was no grounding in tradition, no imploring to practice long and slow and hard over a period of many years. Just "sweat" and "surrender," and you'd be fine. Which was true, to some extent. Yoga teachers got into trouble whenever they started to promise their students anything other than some safe exercise and a little peace of mind. Look at Tom Hart. He'd sweated and surrendered plenty in his life, and now he was just a slab of meat in a mountain coroner's basement.

This place made Bolster uncomfortable. Most yoga studios did. These owners clearly made a nifty profit off their spiritually starved clientele. The custom-cut mat cubbies, stacked six high and six across and topped with rubber plants, probably cost more than all the furniture in his apartment. But he'd walk out with a pocket full of twenties, and no one would get hurt.

Usually, Bolster kept his practices grounded, but he wasn't in the mood today. He had the students, mostly actresses and USC trust-fund girls, focus on backbends. When he taught at the Santa Monica Senior Center, it was a victory if one of his students could touch their toes. These girls could handle five straight wheels with pauses to rest on the tops of their heads, and not even sweat.

Look at them, he thought, as they dropped back into camel, their hyper-elasticized quads barely even straining, their lumbar regions as loose as vending-machine change. *So young and supple and innocent.* Lesser men than Bolster would take advantage. Many of them did. And so did a lot of women.

"You guys are doing great!" he said. "Try not to let your necks hang."

The room smelled like non-animal-tested perfume, with a slightly rancid patchouli undertone. Most of the sweat was coming from the three guys in the room who were lucky enough to have a free hour at ten thirty on a Wednesday morning. They were working hard, but also clearly having fun. Bolster envied them. If he'd discovered yoga in college, his life would have been a lot calmer. Maybe he wouldn't have spent most of his twenties and thirties getting shot at in the hills around Lincoln Heights.

Around the forty-five-minute mark, it seemed like the class would never end. But less than half an hour later, it was basically over, and the twenty-five inhabitants were drifting gratefully into *savasana*, half-asleep, half-awake, half-enlightened.

Bolster roused them, had them sit for a minute, watching their breath, and then led them in a long, sonorous *om*.

There was some post-class flirting, which Bolster kindly deflected. As often happened, a couple of students asked him if they should take teacher training.

"If you want to further your education, great," Bolster said. "But the world already has enough yoga teachers."

They giggled, but Bolster wanted to say, *I fucking mean it*. Yoga makes you want to share, but there are already way too many teachers out there on the market. Every succeeding generation got a little younger and knew a little less. Like a game of telephone, the teachings had been diminished until they were little more than nonsense words tied up with a fancy cloth strap.

Bolster rolled up his mat, already dreaming about the twenty-four-ounce mango Robeks he was going to slurp down as soon as possible. He looked up. There stood his old partner, Esmail Martinez, leaning against the door frame, shoes still on against all yogic etiquette. Martinez didn't remove his shoes, he said, unless he was going to bed or taking a shower, and sometimes not even then.

"I like the sleeveless look," Martinez said.

"My pits get sweaty," said Bolster.

"You look gay."

"Don't be a bigot," Bolster said. "Gay or straight, we are all one under the watchful eye of *Brahman*."

"Whatever, *culo*," Martinez said. "Why'd you call me, Bolster?"

"How'd you like to help me solve a murder?" Bolster said.

"You need *my* help?"

"I need someone to drive me around so I can get stoned."

"You are a true professional."

"Before you say no," Bolster said, "let me buy you breakfast. I'm sure you need it."

"If you're offering to buy," Martinez said, "you must be serious."

Martinez took full advantage of Bolster's offer, ordering two heaping plates of *chilaquiles*, with extra sour cream and avocado. He believed strongly in eating his way out of a hangover, though the Bloody Mary he had alongside his gut bomb probably didn't help much. Bolster ate light, just a bowl of house-cut granola with soy, and a fruit smoothie with a little spirulina boost.

Bolster looked at Martinez. He was wearing cowboy boots and a golf shirt that couldn't contain the belly spilling over his jeans. That was in sharp contrast to Bolster's hemp pants and light blue sleeveless top with the *om* symbol on it. But they both were going to try to solve a murder.

First, though, Martinez talked of women, a topic about which he was stunningly unfamiliar.

"Here's the thing I don't understand about women," he was saying. "Why do they always say they want to do one thing when they actually want to do another thing?"

"I don't know," Bolster said.

"I'm like, 'Hey, it's cool if you don't want to watch *Gladiator*. I totally understand that it's not for everyone. We could watch something like, like one of the Bourne movies. But then don't fall asleep or say you have to leave early because you have to work in the morning."

"Right," Bolster said.

Bolster felt sorry for women who encountered Martinez, because he was actually a *good* option: employed, a homeowner, a decent driver, not a pervert or an obsessive or a control nut. His idiosyncrasies added up to a personality rather than a psychosis. He was a grouch and a cynic, but Bolster knew there was love somewhere in Martinez's heart. Bolster wanted to tell Martinez, and all men, that if you actually *liked* women and were willing to see them, without fear, as people just like you, then you'd never be unsatisfied in their company. Then again, what did Bolster know? He had a lot of female friends, and he certainly enjoyed them, but most nights he slept with a cat. A fat, angry male cat. Which hated him.

"Can we talk about this case now?" Bolster said.

"Sure," Martinez mumbled through a mouthful of scrambled eggs and tortilla strips, which he'd smothered with enough *sriracha* to strip the paint off a Hyundai.

"They've got Slim locked up in Ventura."

Martinez knew Slim. Two less compatible people didn't exist on the planet. His sympathies were muted.

"Could be worse," Martinez said. "Could be Riverside."

"That's true," Bolster said, "but he's still facing life."

"Not good," Martinez said.

"So here's what we know," Bolster said. "Slim showed up in the morning on the day the body was discovered, after being missing for twenty-four hours. He was covered in Tom Hart's blood and dirt and said he'd passed out in a ditch after some guy wearing a cobra hood gave him some sort of pill that made him hallucinate a giant Indian snake demigod."

"The usual," said Martinez.

"Right," said Bolster.

"What is it with you yoga people?"

"It's a mystical art," Bolster said, nonchalantly. "Obviously, all that makes Slim a suspect of sorts since he couldn't account for what happened to him the night the murder happened and no one saw him. The thing is, he'd never met the victim and had absolutely no motive to kill him."

"What about—and I don't believe I'm saying this—some sort of mind control?" Martinez said.

"I suppose," said Bolster, "but that doesn't account for the fact that Slim remembers falling into a canyon, and that no one saw him do it. It seems to me like it was just kind of an accident, and he stumbled onto something weird in the woods."

"Knowing him, that's plausible," said Martinez. "So who else have we got?"

"Could be anyone," Bolster said. "There were three-hundred-plus people in the compound when it happened."

"Not helpful, Bolster."

"I do have some finalists."

"That's good."

Bolster pulled a pad of paper out of his bag and started to idly doodle, sketching out blocks, drawing lines between them. It wasn't a schematic of the case, in any way. But sometimes making random shapes helped him draw connections.

"Well, first there's this doctor," Bolster said.

"OK, said Martinez, eggs dribbling down his chin.

"An old Jewish guy, got a practice out in Pomona."

"And we all know how much old Jews like to kill."

Bolster ignored that calumny and continued:

"All weekend, he stood around Tom Hart, whispering in his ear. There was something very Dr. Feelgood about the whole thing that made me skeptical."

"Sounds like he's worth visiting."

"I've put a lot of miles on Whitey lately."

Martinez huffed.

"I can drive, Bolster."

"That's what I wanted to hear," Bolster said, smiling.

"So who else?"

"Hart had this assistant—really good-looking, full hips, beautiful curly tawny hair. She was really sharp and together."

Bolster's voice must have sounded a little excited, because Martinez said,

"Is she a suspect or do you want to fuck her?"

"Maybe a little of both," Bolster said. "There was this vulnerability to her that I found a little unnerving."

"I find all women unnerving."

"That's your problem right there. In any case, she had a lot of access to Hart. She lives up in the East Bay, where Hart lived, so there's another six and a half hours on the car if I want to go check her out."

Martinez was so tired of hearing about Whitey.

"Jesus, Bolster, just buy a new car already."

"Yoga teachers drive old cars," said Bolster. "That's what we do."

"Yeah, yeah," Martinez said. "So Pomona Jew doctor and sexy capable assistant lady in NorCal. What else?"

"Up in Berkeley there's this yoga scholar named Barlow," Bolster said. "Hart kept him on retainer, but it seems to me that Barlow felt kind of unappreciated. I liked him, but he was a little too intense. Sometimes you can be too into yoga, you know?"

"I don't."

Bolster waved this off.

"He had a distant look that I didn't totally understand. I'd like to check him out again, too."

"OK."

"And then there's Chelsea Shell."

Martinez moaned. He remembered Chelsea Shell from the Ajoy situation.

"*She's* involved again?" Martinez said. "That broad really gets around."

"This is 2013. You don't call women *broads*."

"Yeah, but she does. Did you fuck her?"

"Only twice."

"Dammit, Bolster."

"I can't help it, man," Bolster said. "She and I have *energy*. Every time I see her I'm just flooded with desire."

"That's why God gave you saliva and a right hand."

"Nice."

"So what was she *doing* there?"

"As far as I can tell," Bolster said, "after Ajoy she drifted up north and into Hart Yoga."

"Needed someone to follow?"

"You'd think, but Chelsea doesn't follow anyone. She needed someone to grift. Something went down with her and Hart because at the orgy the night before . . ."

Martinez put his elbows on the table, his eyes glistening with excitement.

"The *orgy*?" he said.

Bolster saw how excited Martinez was getting, so he leaned back, feeling cocky. He liked Martinez to think his life was full of glamor and adventure.

"It was probably going to become an orgy," Bolster said, "but Chelsea busted in and slapped Hart across the face. She knew something about him."

"Did she tell you?"

"She doesn't tell me anything except for 'Bolster, I like your butt.'"

"That's something," said Martinez.

"Doesn't help in this case."

"So where is she?"

"I don't know. She split before the cops arrived."

"No information?"

"She left me a note."

"What'd it say?"

"Nothing."

"So she could be anywhere?"

"I'm guessing California. Probably near the coast. Or maybe Squaw. Or Mammoth. It'll be somewhere nice, though."

Martinez was basically licking his plate.

"That's not helpful," he said. "We have no resources, and I'm doing this on my day off."

"Maybe you could get Ojai to give me a little money? They're barely paying for snacks."

Martinez laughed, ruefully.

"Let me see if I can get my PayPal to work," he said. "Meanwhile, you've got me for a few hours. Let's do something. Got any local leads?"

Bolster had done some checking. All the official Hart Yoga™ studios within a thirty-mile radius had closed—some temporarily, some permanently. Their websites were tastefully illustrated with candles, and their Facebook feeds were rife with lamentation and unhelpful inspirational quotes. Without the teacher, there was no practice. But there was one unaffiliated joint off Sunset, near the entrance to the Ravine, that didn't appear to have ceased operations at all. In fact, they'd added classes. That was where Hanuman made his nest. Bolster wanted to see if the monkey man had any tricks left.

"How about we cruise up to Echo Park?" Bolster said.

"I've been trying to get away from that neighborhood my entire life," said Martinez. "Guess I picked the wrong job."

The bill arrived. Bolster had agreed semi-willingly to pay. Martinez *was* doing him a favor, after all. He examined it.

"Sixty bucks before tip," he said. "Screw this town."

CHAPTER SEVENTEEN

The floor-to-ceiling mirror ran the length of the back wall of the studio. There were mirrors along the side wall, too. The wall facing the street was all windows, leaving just a small corner for a bathroom, a stairway entrance, a donation table, and a gilded shrine to the monkey god that served Rama so well. Once upon a time, in myth, it took giant steps across the world to defeat the armies of evil.

Mostly, though, it was a mirror room, which gave Hanuman Jones a lot of opportunity to look at his own body while he practiced. Yoga was about self-reflection, but for Hanuman it was also about *actual* reflection, his physique thrown back at him for constant contemplation. Today, as always, he liked the view. Hanuman pitied the mindless gym rats with their outdoor lifting and their CrossFit deltoid obsessions. *His* body—sleek, drawn-out, almost starving—was unlike other bodies, with muscles as raw as jerky and joints as sharp as flinted arrows. He didn't need a six-pack; he had a one-with-the-universe pack, plus breath control.

The transformation had happened steadily for Hanuman, under Tom Hart's semi-watchful eye. Hanuman had been just another frat-boy loser, with his backwards baseball caps and his rubber chin and his wagging tongue. His birth name had been *Chad*, for God's sake. Chad Jones from Anaheim. And Chad had twisted and squeezed and lifted and bent and struggled and sweated and grown his hair into *magnificent* dreadlocks, shedding the pounds and the bro-dentity until he was reborn into something strong, elastic, early-rising, incredible—a living avatar of Hanuman, the Hindu god of help and friendship, his head topped by a shining crown of glory.

Now Tom was gone, which was good for Hanuman, an obstacle removed. The old man's power had been waning, too caught up in ego and world-traveling and feeding the empire. He'd lost sight of transcendence. Hanuman's followers, the Hanumaniacs, were the true yogis. They didn't number many, but their power couldn't be denied. Tom's followers had drifted upward, airy and stupid. The Hanumaniacs, on the other hand, were rooted in the earth, hard and firm. They were bound by tradition and, occasionally, straps. The great Patañjali wrapped them in all his eight limbs, and they emerged transformed. The pills helped, too. There were so many pills, and they tasted so real.

Today, they were working on one-armed handstands. This was an advanced class, so they numbered only eight, including Hanuman. Not all of them were getting up on the palm. It required tremendous strength and balance, and it came at the end of a three-hour workout, so the floors were pretty slick. Some of them were trying it against the mirrors, leaving little smudges with their feet and backs. They looked like dancing penitent tattooed skeletons. They were the base of the mountain.

"Feel the strength in your *mula*," Hanuman said.

The *mula*, the root chakra, was the key to it all, the true source of human power. Hanuman knew that it grounded you and lifted you up. All breath traveled to and from there. He could feel energy in every inhale and appreciated the gift of every exhale. You could bounce a dime off Hanuman's perineal floor.

As he balanced there, with effort that was no effort at all—skirting around his edge like a skater around the rim of an empty swimming pool, inhaling for a count of twenty, exhaling for the same amount, slowly, carefully—Hanuman thought about filling the gap left by Tom's death. Someone had to do it. Most of the Hart Yoga™-certified sub-masters were busy rending their garments and wallowing in the wake of the tragedy. But Hanuman wasn't one for sentiment. He'd mourn in a unique way, by establishing his own empire in the ruins of Hart's. He'd been planning to do it anyway. Tom's murder had just been the parting of the sea that led to Hanuman's ultimate liberation.

Hanuman had many plans for the future. He couldn't throw a "Hanuman Festival" because some trendy usurpers in Boulder had already claimed that name. But that was OK, because festivals were for the weak and unambitious. *Everyone wants to be part of a crowd,* he told his Hanumaniacs, *but they don't understand that they already have a crowd inside of them. That's where the light gets in.* He didn't actually understand what that meant, but he knew it was true anyway. You just had to do the work, and the followers would come. Soon enough people would be sending him plane tickets and $5,000 honoraria checks to teach on the big festival stages. It would be the Age of Hanuman.

He had other ideas. Already, without telling his followers, he'd trademarked a brand name: Monkey Man Yoga™. It was mostly yoga for bros, otherwise known as "broga," but he also owned Monkey Woman Yoga™, because a lot of women did yoga, and he felt like he had something to offer them, including a Monkey Woman clothing line. There would, of course, be a chain of Monkey Man studios, patented Monkey Man sequences that Hanuman designed himself, and a Monkey Man YouTube channel that would totally redefine online yoga and would establish Hanuman as the hot new yoga star to watch, though he wouldn't ever appear on morning shows, because he had a three-hour self-practice in the morning and it was important to remain pure to his lineage. Overall, it would be so awesome and rad. He'd spread the love, and then America would no longer be depressed and angry and fat, because of him, Hanuman. No thanks would be necessary. It was all about yoga. Yoga was everything.

Hanuman descended from his perch. He walked around the room, encouraging, touching lightly, giving adjustments. The Hanumaniacs didn't need his help, though. They just practiced on, their eyes glassily satisfied. Eventually, they all came down. After an extended child's pose, they folded back into *savasna*.

The room stank like hell. Hanuman had to get out. He knew he was supposed to sit there and hold the space for them, but they were going to be there for a while after this practice. He went outside with his fanny pack, which contained two joints, a lighter, and a grinder.

The air was coolish. It smelled like Echo Park: dog shit, *pupusas*, motor oil, with an overlay of gentrification.

Hanuman lit a spliff. It was his vice. It was everyone's vice. Including Matt Bolster's. And that's who Hanuman saw coming up the stairs, followed by a huffing, big-bellied Mexican guy wearing cowboy boots. Not who Hanuman wanted to spend his afternoon with.

But the Monkey Man always needs to be ready, he thought. He took a puff.

When Bolster asked Martinez to go to Echo Park with him, he hadn't realized the Dodgers were playing, one of those weird Wednesday matinees against the Marlins, an off-brand game that counted in the standings but nowhere else. The team marketed these as family days, which is why Bolster never went. His Dodger fandom could be traced back to Steve Garvey's rookie year, 1974, and he'd hated family days even then. It was all about hot dogs and beach balls and nothing else, arriving in the third, leaving in the seventh. Bolster rejected that shit. He went for the *game* and nothing else, the raw experience of watching, which is why he bought tickets on Mondays and Tuesdays when the crowds were smaller.

"I've got this guy online who sells admission in bulk," he was telling Martinez as they crawled along Sunset, past the dollar stores and the stupid hipster foraging restaurants and the Casbah with its pricey tea service. "I buy the two cheapest loge tickets I can find, out in left field. And then I just move over to the third-base line, like seven rows down. No one's ever there, because those are corporate seats, but not the good field-level ones. You get an eighty-dollar value for like twenty bucks.

Usually there aren't a lot of kids, either, because it's too expensive."

"Whatever," said Martinez. "I'm an Angels fan."

"The Angels are not a real baseball team," Bolster said.

"I got a 2002 World Series Championship T-shirt that says otherwise."

"Balls."

"Give it up for the OC!"

Bolster moaned. It had been a long time since Kirk Gibson had run around the bases pumping his fists. This is one of the reasons why Bolster did yoga. The Dodgers hadn't given him a transcendent moment in a long time.

They pulled into the parking lot of a two-story strip mall that had been thrown up in a hurry in the 1960s, next door to an oil-change joint. Now it housed the usual mix: a Salvadoran restaurant, a CPA office that never seemed to be open, a tarot-card reader, a Comedy Defensive Driving school, and, occupying the entire eastern wing of the second floor, a Hart Yoga™ studio, though that moniker didn't really apply anymore. This was an outlier. Hanuman yogaed here.

"I need you to be alert," Bolster said. "I already had it out with this guy once this month."

Martinez patted his belt, in which he'd lodged his department-issue piece.

"Cocked and locked," he said.

"Don't say that again," said Bolster. "Just give me backup."

Martinez waited at the bottom while Bolster headed up the steps, which were coated in pebbles. The average toddler could have fallen into the gaps between the stairs. At the top, Hanuman was leaning against the railing, gaunt and sweaty and smoking a fatty. He blew out a cloud.

"Back for more, Bolster?" he said.

"I'm the one who decked you," Bolster said.

"I know," said Hanuman. "I'm a peaceful guy."

"Sure," Bolster said. "I want to talk to you about Hart's murder."

"Worst thing that ever happened," said Hanuman. "No doubt."

"Is that so?"

"Wish you hadn't brought your crazy friend Slim along to the Gathering, but at least they caught him."

If Hanuman had been wearing a shirt, Bolster would have ripped the collar. Instead, he flung himself onto the landing and grabbed Hanuman's dreads, hard.

"Watch the hair!" Hanuman said.

"I've got questions for you, monkey man," Bolster said, not knowing that was actually the name of Hanuman's trademarked brand of yoga products, "and you're going to answer them."

"I'm not telling you shit unless you let go of my dreads," Hanuman grunted.

Bolster relinquished.

"I get it, man, you are relentless in your pursuit of justice," said Hanuman.

"Do not fuck with me," said Bolster.

"Come inside and we'll talk."

Bolster signaled Martinez, who came up the stairs the rest of the way.

"Stand guard," he said.

"OK, chief," said Martinez, immediately looking at his phone.

Inside, the shades had been drawn. The Hanumaniacs were lying on their mats. They looked dormant. Hanuman emitted a long, slow *ommmmmmmmm*. One by one, the maniacs began to rise.

"*What are you doing?*" Bolster whispered.

"I thought you might want to talk to all of us," Hanuman said. "At once."

The Hanumaniacs stood there, slackly.

"This is Matt Bolster," Hanuman said. "He wants to ask us all some questions about what went on at the Gathering."

"Yeah," Bolster said. "So . . ."

"And what would Patañjali say about that?" Hanuman asked.

Patañjali? Bolster thought. Slim had been muttering about Patañjali when he'd emerged from the woods.

Fuck.

Hanuman gave a little whistle. His maniacs started to shuffle forward, menacingly. There were eight of them, including Hanuman. Too many, especially since they had the expanse of the room behind them, and Bolster had nothing but a doorway and a cleaning-supplies cubby. They would be on Bolster in a second, and then Bolster would be meat.

He picked up a gilded statue of the monkey god and chucked it at the maniacs. They skittered a little, like roaches, enough to buy him a couple of seconds of time to bolt out the door.

Martinez was outside, texting. Bolster dashed past him.

"RUN!" Bolster said.

"Why?" said Martinez.

The door flung open, and a half-dozen loincloth-wearing yoga-men charged out, their quads pumping with purpose.

"Oh," Martinez said, "that's why."

He ran behind Bolster, several steps slower and way more out of shape. They got halfway through the parking lot, a full complement of dreadlocked handstand freaks following hot. A couple of them were whipping yoga straps around their heads, the buckles reaching a point of deadly acceleration. Bolster hit the sidewalk along Sunset. Martinez stood his ground and showed his badge.

"Detective Esmail Martinez, LAPD!" he shouted. "Hold up!"

Martinez pulled out his gun, looking nervous. The Hanumaniacs kept coming. One of them whipped his strap toward Martinez, like a bolo. It snapped around Martinez's knees, bringing him down. Bolster couldn't stop it. Martinez fell. His gun fired. The shot missed Hanuman—and the freaks, and everything else except the gas tank of Martinez's Dodge Charger.

It exploded.

CHAPTER EIGHTEEN

The explosion blew Bolster onto his ass, sending him skittering onto the sidewalk on Sunset. He lodged against the substantial side bumper of an old Toyota Avalon, a car designed for safety and comfort, though not exactly under these circumstances. A white-hot piece of Martinez's muffler zinged over his head, smacking the hood and skidding onto the street behind the car. Bolster's ears were ringing, but he was OK.

He looked over at Martinez, who was upright and leaning against the iron parking-lot fence. He was a little bloody from a cut on his cheek but otherwise intact.

"What was that?" Bolster shouted at him.

"I don't know," Martinez said.

Martinez stared at his gun as though he weren't exactly sure what he was supposed to do with it. But the gun's work was already accomplished.

Across the parking lot, his car was on fire.

"That's a real durable ride you've got," said Bolster.

"Better than yours," said Martinez, still trying to shake away the fuzz.

The explosion had unhinged Martinez's rear side door and hurled it through the window of the *pupuseria*. Damage to humans was as yet unclear, but judging from the caterwauling that had sprung up, there was some. The air smelled like gasoline and fried dough; the lot was crackling with fire and metal.

The Hanumaniacs, in their loincloths, had taken the brunt of the cartillery. They were sprawled around the lot in various stages of injury. Those who could stand clutched their arms or their heads, staggering, not really interested in Bolster anymore. Hanuman, their leader, seemed relatively unharmed. He kept coming toward Bolster.

"That's why they call him the Leader of the Pack," Martinez said, moving toward Hanuman, but Bolster waved him away as if to say, *I'll take this one.* Bolster straightened, feeling steady enough, and squared off, hands lightly and calmly clenched just above his waist.

Bolster had been too far out of the blast radius to be knocked back hard, so Hanuman had no advantage. Hanuman saw this. He'd met Bolster's fists before and knew he couldn't win a one-on-one. He got within a few feet of Bolster, crouched and feinted like a tailback, and bolted eastward, toward Elysian Park Boulevard.

The sirens had already begun to scream. With ambulances came chasers and all sorts of attendant problems and delays. Bolster quickly looked at Martinez, who nodded, indicating that he was relatively stable.

"I'll clean this up," said Martinez.

"Use a mop," said Bolster.

Martinez would see that the scene got coordinated, and that the news crews got placated. This was his mess, and he'd fix it like a grown-up professional, even if that meant lying to the cameras.

But Bolster had an ancillary mission. He took off after Hanuman.

The explosion had slapped a layer of chaos onto an already crowded day. Even a weekday matinee Dodgers game drew thirty thousand people to the Ravine. The town just had a bottomless supply of fans, the stadium was essentially in the middle of the city, and you could usually get tickets for pretty cheap. Dozens, hundreds, of fans, all of them wearing snap-new Dodgers hats and jerseys, ranging from the sincerely rabid (Kemp, Kershaw, Puig) to the nostalgic (Koufax, Robinson) to the ironic (Gagné, DeShields), streamed down the Sunset sidewalks enthusiastically, but as far as Bolster was concerned—and he was a fan, mind you—today they were just a nuisance wall of human traffic.

The frantically running dreadlocked man, wearing little more than a thong, barely registered with the crowd working its way down Sunset and turning to make the long uphill march toward Dodger Stadium. Such is life in L.A. They'd have given Hanuman a hassle only if he'd been wearing a Padres or Giants jersey. Hanuman threaded the needle, with good yogic reflexes. But Bolster followed a few paces behind, just as fit as Hanuman and not as nervous. Hanuman looked back, and Bolster gave him a friendly wave. He had no intention of losing the chase to the Monkey Man™.

They hit the hill of Elysian Park, and the sidewalk cleared a little bit, the crowds slowed by the incline. There were a couple of lanes of open pavement. Hanuman swerved onto one of these. Bolster followed, gaining an inch with every step. Unlike Hanuman, he hadn't been on the mat for three hours, so he had more in the tank.

Just before the parking-attendant booths, at the middle of the incline up Elysian Park, Hanuman cut into the street, where he was almost run over by a black Silverado full of *cholos*. The truck swerved and honked. A guy in the back threw a half-drunk tallboy at Hanuman's head.

"Hippie faggot!" he shouted, which was incorrect, because Hanuman wasn't gay, though he did sometimes refer to himself as "pansexual."

Bolster stood on the periphery and smiled. He and Hanuman were facing each other, a ten-thick row of streaming fans between them. Bolster crooked his index finger, to summon Hanuman toward him. He could see that the Monkey Man was nervous. Hanuman was looking out of place among the baseball dudes, but Bolster *was* a dude, which is what made him so effective.

Hanuman shot forward. Bolster moved in parallel but ran into a phalanx of fat-asses taking their time up the sidewalk. This gave Hanuman just a beat, of which he took full advantage, cutting through the crowd and into the brush along the hillside. Bolster marked the spot with his eyes and followed.

He immediately lost his footing and started to skid. The ground was all rocks and dirt and weeds and glass and condom wrappers, graded at sixty degrees, with no branches to hold. Bolster turned sideways so he could at least slip against the grain. It was amazing how quickly L.A.'s piss-soaked concrete could turn into dead chaparral once you went off the prescribed path.

He reached the bottom of the ditch quickly. Hanuman was curled up against an abandoned shopping cart, clutching his knee. He wouldn't be folding that joint behind his head any time soon. Served him right for running around the Eastside barefoot.

Bolster landed unscathed. Hanuman raised his hands in surrender, a gesture Bolster ignored.

"What's your plan, Bolster?" Hanuman said. "You going to hit me with your big swinging dick?"

"I've got better things to do with that," Bolster said.

Hanuman had no shirt to grab, so Bolster crouched down, took Hanuman's sweaty, dirty shoulders, and smacked him hard across the face.

"That's what you get for running from me," Bolster said.

He smacked him again.

"That's what you get for turning your goons on me."

Then he popped Hanuman on the bridge of the nose.

"And that's because I don't like your face."

Hanuman was looking woozy.

"I thought you were a man of peace," he said.

"Like Arjuna, I go to war when I need to," Bolster said.

He figured Hanuman, of all people, would get the *Bhagavad Gita* reference.

"Just leave me alone," Hanuman moaned.

"Not likely," Bolster said. "I want to know why you killed Tom Hart."

"I didn't kill him."

Bolster sighed. Why was this never easy?

"Yeah, well, you had plenty of reason to."

"He was going to burn himself out eventually. I was just waiting. The yoga world needed something more pure. My practice was perfect."

"And look at you now."

"I'll recover."

"My best friend is in jail. Is *he* going to recover?"

"Beats me."

"He said he saw some cobra-hooded guys in the woods. Maybe you know something about them."

"Maybe I don't."

Bolster grabbed Hanuman by the hair.

"Maybe you *do*," he said.

"OW!" Hanuman said. "Watch the dreads. I cultivated them."

"Cultivate *this*," Bolster said.

He tugged again. Hanuman shrieked.

"OK, OK," he said.

"*What* was going on in the woods?"

"There was a core group of us," Hanuman said.

"Who?"

"The guys you saw today. Maybe a couple of other people. We'd been trying out some rituals. We wanted to see if we could invoke the *siddhis*. Those are higher powers that they say you can achieve through—"

"I *know* what *siddhis* are," Bolster said. "They're serious business. Don't mess with what you can't understand."

The *siddhis*, "extraordinary powers" as outlined in the *Yoga Sutras*, couldn't just be a playful hobby for a gaggle of fly-by-night *asana* addicts. They required a lot more seriousness and a lot more intelligence. Hanuman attempting them was like a toddler trying to operate a ray gun. Bolster feared them, but not from this guy.

"Whatever, it was all pretty low-key," said Hanuman. "Just some chanting and some sitting and a few poses. I thought the cobra costumes would be kind of fun while we were in a circle."

"*So* much fun," Bolster said ruefully. "Did you happen to invoke anything while you were at it?"

"We did the chant for Patañjali."

"Funny, Slim came out of the woods talking crazy about Patañjali. But it was like he'd actually *seen* him. How would that be possible?"

"I don't know."

Bolster tugged on Hanuman's hair again.

"There were drugs!" Hanuman said. "All right? But I'm not sure how your buddy could have gotten hold of them."

"He said there was some guy on the path handing them out."

"Oh, right," Hanuman said. "The sentry. I guess he thought your friend was one of us. He kind of looks like us, right? But I had no idea he was there, much less taking the pills."

"What kind of pills?"

"This new synthetic stuff."

"What's it do?"

"Engineered for hallucinations."

"A giant avatar of an Indian snake deity is a very specific hallucination," Bolster said.

"Cohen is good, and that's what I ordered," said Hanuman. "It usually lasts for about an hour, maybe a little less, though there's a lingering feeling—that could last for days—that makes you imagine that what you saw was real. That's something we've had to fight through in our crew. There were some pretty rough rehearsals. One guy freaked out and jumped out an open window. So it was probably tough for your friend to deal, considering he didn't know what he'd taken."

"I always tell him not to accept pills from strangers, but he never listens," Bolster said.

"Are you his mother?"

"Kind of," Bolster said. "Were there other side effects?"

"I don't know."

"Blackouts, murderous rages, that sort of thing?"

"Not sure," Hanuman said.

Hanuman was actually being pretty helpful, Bolster realized, though the next question challenged that perception.

"Where did you get the pills?" he said.

Hanuman sat silently. Bolster looked up. A guy in a Dodgers hat was peeking through some bushes. Bolster shooed him away. The guy, who'd just seen what looked like some vagrants fighting over a shopping cart, complied. This was none of his business. But it reminded Bolster of the perils of conducting a public interrogation of an essentially naked man.

"Where did you get them, Hanuman?" Bolster repeated.

Hanuman was silent. Bolster took hold of one of his dreads and set it, toward the root, atop a rusty hinge sitting on top of the shopping cart. He began to saw.

"You're going to tell me," Bolster said.

"Not my hair . . ." Hanuman moaned.

"You do yoga," said Bolster. "You should know that your hair is impermanent."

"Stop!"

Bolster kept sawing.

"I'll do this to all your fucking dreads," he said, "unless you tell me what I need to know."

"Fine!" Hanuman said. "The pills came from Dr. Cohen."

"You mean that old guy from Hart's suite?" Bolster said.

"Yeah, he's been cooking them up for us. He made all of Hart's drugs, except the weed. Which is from the Earth."

"Why?"

"Ask him. He's still got that alternative-healing center out in Pomona. The guy is really good at cooking. He can make anything."

"All right," Bolster said. "I will. You got anything else for me? Any idea what happened to Hart?"

"No, man," said Hanuman. "After you kicked the shit out of me that night, I hung around for a little while, but then Hart said he didn't need me anymore, so I went back to my room and crashed hard."

"When was that?"

"Around midnight."

"Was anyone else there?"

"Just Kimber Wharton."

"Hart worked her too hard."

"She did a lot of stuff for him off-hours, if you know what I'm saying."

Bolster was disappointed to hear that.

"I think I do," he said, "unfortunately."

He finished sawing off the dread. It came off easily in his hand, spongy and sweaty, an elongated wet strand of steel wool.

"Goddammit, Bolster!" Hanuman said.

"It's cool, man," said Bolster. "You can pin it on your ass and wear it like a tail."

He was done with Hanuman, who, much to Bolster's disappointment, didn't appear to be guilty. Bolster headed back toward the incline. Hanuman cleared his throat. Bolster turned around.

"Maybe a little help?" Hanuman said.

Hanuman's knee was very swollen. It looked like a ripe eggplant. Bolster felt terrible. This guy may have been his adversary, but he was still, in the end, just a suffering human. At their core, all beings just want to be happy.

Bolster went over to Hanuman and grabbed hold of his arm. Hanuman moaned a little, but he was sturdy; his good leg was *very* good. Bolster gagged a little. The Monkey Man smelled like the chimp house at the L.A. Zoo.

Bolster looked around. There appeared to be some concrete steps maybe five hundred feet down the wash, which would mean that he'd emerge into the Dodger Stadium parking lot half-hugging a hippie. But he'd done worse.

It took them a few minutes to get down there, and a few more for Bolster to drag Hanuman up the steps, but they surfaced soon enough, and they could hear Nancy Bea playing "It's a Beautiful Day for a Ballgame" on the Hammond. The air smelled like beer and peanuts and maybe a win for the Blue.

"Thanks, man," Hanuman said. He extended his hand. Bolster shook it. He would never call Hanuman his friend, but yoga could be a brutal and dangerous game. It was always better to have an ally than an enemy.

Bolster got out his phone to call Martinez, to see how things were going back on Sunset, and whether he could spare an ambulance. A guy approached him.

"Anyone need tickets?" the guy said. "I got two in the loge down the left-field line. Twenty dollars each."

That was a good deal. Bolster could sneak around to better seats, like he usually did.

"Your friend's gonna have to wear some pants, though," said the scalper.

"He doesn't like baseball," Bolster said.

"I do, actually," said Hanuman.

Bolster briefly thought about taking the ticket and going to the park, after Hanuman got taken away. He could have used the break. But that would have been a bad idea. Not only did he have work to do, but AT&T provided pathetic coverage inside the park. He'd be totally shut off from reality, and from Slim, in case he called. Every minute that Bolster wasn't investigating, Slim was getting closer to life in prison. Bolster declined because he needed to find a killer.

There'd always be another home stand.

CHAPTER NINETEEN

After returning to the scene of the explosion (no major injuries, one very angry Salvadoran restaurant owner), Bolster made a call.

"Hey, Matt!" said Lora Powell.

"Hey," Bolster said. "My ride blew up."

"Oh no! Whitey blew up?"

"Not Whitey."

"That's good. I love Whitey."

"It was this cop car I was riding around in."

"That's a drag."

"Pretty much."

"You need a lift?"

"If you can."

"Of course! I have to lead a sit at the Self-Realization Fellowship right now, but I can get you around three thirty."

A "sit" was hipster Buddhist slang for *vipassana* meditation. Lora was always sitting but never seemed to have any back pain. That was part of her magic.

"That's fine," Bolster said. "I'll walk over to Intelligentsia."

"Big spender!"

"The coffee's good," Bolster said.

"I usually get my coffee at the gas station," Lora said.

"I'll be the guy not pretending to work on his screenplay," said Bolster.

Bolster had a half-hour walk. His hams were starting to feel the strain, but he was alive and breathing in the present moment, so that was good. His phone rang, which distracted him.

"Namaste," he said.

"It's Vijay Malik," said the voice on the other end.

"Who?"

"From the Ojai Police."

"Oh, hey. You got any money for me yet?"

"I scrounged up two hundred bucks."

"That'll almost pay my utilities."

"Working on it, Bolster."

"OK, I have faith. How's Slim doing?"

"He's made a lot of friends in the jail. It doesn't really seem to bother him."

"That's normal for him," Bolster said. "But he doesn't do too well without sunlight for extended periods. He's like a plant."

"I've been watering him."

"Funny. So what's up?"

"Well, we finally tracked down Kimberly Wharton in San Francisco. She told us where we could find a list of numbers and addresses for conference attendees."

"Can you e-mail them to me?"

"We only have hard copies."

"Scan them and e-mail them to me."

"We don't have the resources. We could make you a copy and send it COD."

"I've really got to get a better client," Bolster said.

"We don't tend to do a lot of serious investigations."

"Obviously."

"But we *do* have a pathologist's report."

"Anything good?"

"Depends on your definition. Tom Hart's heart was cut out of his chest, but it was a remarkably clean removal, almost perfectly circular, like someone popped it out like a cork."

"Weird."

"We haven't seen any other examples of this sort of thing, obviously. But it strikes me that the whole thing would have been a little bit gorier than it actually was. I mean, there was a mess, but it wasn't an *unbelievable* mess."

"Any theories?"

"None. They found no drugs in Hart's system, other than marijuana and a little alcohol, so it doesn't seem like he'd been sedated."

"You mean he was *awake*?" Bolster said.

"Yeah, I mean, it doesn't much seem like something a person could sleep through."

"Huh."

"You should probably come up here and take a look at the paperwork."

"Is tomorrow OK?" Bolster asked. "I'm about two hours and twenty miles away from my ride."

"I'll be at my desk at eight thirty," Vijay said.

Bolster realized he was standing in the middle of the sidewalk doing crescent pose. This was Silverlake, so no one gave him a second look. A guy stretching his hip flexors didn't count as a sin.

"Too early for me," said Bolster. "See you after lunch tomorrow."

Bolster got to the coffee place and waited in line for twenty minutes to get his cappuccino, which the barista decorated with a little *om* symbol in milk foam, a nice touch. The outdoor patio was full of guys who looked like the banjo player in the Geico commercials, all talking excitedly about their very original creative ideas, as well as quite a few attractive women who were with their dogs and therefore off-limits for conversation, and more than one ripped-jeans set of parents dragging their Dylans and Bowies in for a hot chocolate, post–violin lesson at the music conservatory.

They were all avatars of smug, trendy victory, representing the establishment consensus triumph of the techno-artistic yuppie, playing their little instruments of self-advancement while Rome burned. Bolster sniffed at the pretense of it all but didn't have a real basis to judge. He was a yoga detective. It didn't get much more precious than that.

The coffee sharpened his brain and gave him a chance to think clearly about his case. He really wasn't any closer to figuring this out than when he'd started. Hanuman looked like a dead end; he could have been lying, but he really didn't seem smart enough to lie, at least not to the extent necessary. The big question, to Bolster, was how Hart had ended up getting, well, de-hearted.

If there were no signs of a sedative, it had to have been some sort of unknown drug. Hanuman had said that Dr. Cohen was cooking. It was possible that a toxicology report, especially one up in the hills, wasn't going to be reading any sort of synthetic hallucinogen. Police science couldn't keep up with the fancy designer stuff.

So maybe Cohen had slipped Hart some drugs somehow. But then why would he kill him? He also probably had some surgical skills. But why? There was no good reason.

Bolster went onto his mobile browser. He got the number of Cohen's clinic.

"Alternative Medicine Institute," said a chipper voice on the other end.

"How late are you open?" Bolster said. Because he couldn't resist, he added, "I need to realign my chakras."

"We're open until six, but you need an appointment," said the voice on the line.

Not for what I need to do, Bolster thought. His evening was starting to come into focus.

A few minutes later, Lora pulled up in her Honda Civic, which was even older and shittier than Bolster's car, if that was even possible. The backseat was full of blankets and papers and what appeared to be an entire thrift-store dresser's worth of costume jewelry. Bolster knew lots of people who had crap in their car, but Lora always had *different* crap, every time he saw her.

"You are some sort of automotive hoarder," he said to her.

"It's a free ride, pal," Lora said. "I cleaned it out for you."

This was clean?

"Man, the 10 is going to be a nightmare," she said.

"Let's take the 2 up to the 110 over to the 60," Bolster said.

"That's not going to get you home."

"I need to go see a doctor in Pomona. It's important."

"Bolster, can't you just buy your weed in Venice?"

"Not that kind of doctor," he said. "It's for my investigation."

"What's in it for me?" Lora said.

"Ten free *asana* classes?"

"I'm a lucky woman, then."

Bolster couldn't tell if she was being sarcastic or not. Either way, Lora started driving toward Pomona. Yoga tells you to express gratitude, something which most people acted on superficially. Gratitude wasn't always easy for Bolster. He didn't pass it out like Halloween candy. But he *was* always grateful for his friends.

As soon as she'd left the Hart Center, Chelsea Shell went upstate. Maybe south would have been a better option, far south, but she didn't know anyone in Mexico, and she didn't have any money to get there. She also didn't really know anyone in San Diego. Encinitas was just too obvious. East wouldn't cut it unless she was going to hide out in Tahoe, but that's just not where she went. More than twenty minutes west would have put her sunning on the rocks, with the seals.

So it was north, where she had bestie safe houses in places from Santa Cruz to Healdsburg, people who were always glad to see her in exchange for some free *vinyasa* flow on the deck and, if the situation called for it (which it often did), a well-timed three-way.

Now she'd been hiding for weeks, though admittedly her version of hiding involved walks in the woods and sitting in hot tubs and drinking a lot of wine until her host got sick of her. High-end freeloading was all Chelsea knew; she'd been doing it so long that she didn't really even understand any other mode of living. She drifted from situation to situation, accumulating fabulous experiences that didn't belong to her, mindful of the present moment but completely blind to the big picture. This time, though, her life-float was sprinkled with paranoia, like a little sifted powdered sugar atop dessert, and with good reason. A guy was dead.

She *had* to stay in hiding. Not that she'd killed Tom Hart. *I didn't*, she kept telling herself. But she was part of something, maybe not willingly, and certainly not out of deliberate intent. The water causes the flood. But the person who opens the dam valve is culpable, too.

But at some point, you can mooch too much white wine and caprese. Chelsea could sense that it was almost time to move along. There she was, at a three-thousand-square-foot cabin overlooking the rocks at Big Sur, just up the road from Esalen. Her current marks, a couple of rich, young, retired tech executives who she'd met in a teacher training three years previous, seemed to be reaching their limit. Jarrod and Lisa were clearly getting tired of her. She could tell, because while she was sitting on the couch in her sports bra and panties watching *Rehab Addict*, Jarrod just walked by her without even giving her a sniff, whereas ten days earlier he'd straddled her crotch and licked her neck like a slobbering bull terrier. The things she did to get by.

In the kitchen, Lisa was chopping herbs. Chelsea tried to offer a peace frond.

"I thought maybe we could all go for a hike tomorrow," Chelsea said. "Take a picnic."

Lisa kept chopping.

"Maybe rekindle . . ."

Lisa stopped chopping.

"Listen, Chelsea, we had a little fun, but Jarrod and I need our life back. We're developing apps."

"I totally get it. Work is work," said Chelsea. "I can get out of the way during the day."

"It's more of a full-time commitment, not a daytime one."

"Of course."

"So we're going to need you to leave. Preferably tomorrow."

"Listen, if this is about me buying Spotify Premium on your account, I'm totally good for the ten bucks," Chelsea said.

"No, it's about the fact that you're staying in my house for free and fucking my husband."

"I'm fucking *you*, too."

"You licked my tit. One time. When we were drunk."

"I would have done more."

"That's not the point."

"But what about the yoga?" Chelsea said.

"You don't do *yoga*," Lisa said. "Yoga is something comprehensive that's supposed to bring inner calm. You're just a goddamn pose-witch."

That's hardly fair, Chelsea thought. *I'm trying to survive here.* Besides, who was Lisa to judge what yoga was or wasn't? Lisa had made her money. She had her half-Taiwanese husband and her trial subscription to Google Glass and her solar-powered home. Chelsea had nothing in this world but a bag of exercise pants, trampoline-taut abs, and a trail of dead gurus.

Some of us still have to hustle, bitch, she thought.

"Fine," she said. "I'll leave tonight. But I need to borrow your phone."

She'd had to ditch hers in a hurry, smashing it to bits at a Santa Barbara gas station, just minutes after disconnecting her account. There would be no electronic trail of her movements. Chelsea Shell had no geolocation.

"Please don't call another country," Lisa said.

"There goes my plan to get back at you by running up your phone bill," Chelsea said.

MRRRRRROWWWWWWW!

Chelsea took Lisa's phone. Out of her purse, she pulled a business card. On it was a number she'd really hoped she wouldn't have to call. The other person answered on the second ring.

"It's Shell," Chelsea said. "I know I wasn't supposed to get in touch . . . Don't worry, Bolster has no idea where I am."

Pause.

"I need a place to crash," Chelsea said.

CHAPTER TWENTY

The drive to Pomona took awhile. Lora's Civic topped off at 65 mph before it started to shudder. Every tortilla truck from Lompoc to San Ysidro seemed to be clogging the right lanes on the 210. Also, Lora didn't have a CD player. When her car had been manufactured, Bluetooth was just something you got from eating a sno-cone. So Bolster had to listen to the same *All Things Considered* segments several times. When had radio reporting gotten so casual-sounding?

"It's all naive mumbling!" Bolster complained, during the second airing of a report on retrovirus tracking in West Central Africa. "I want radio news to sound like it's coming from a British expert. This guy is like a junior camp counselor saying, 'Hey, you guys, check out my awesome lanyard.'"

"Oh, Bolster, don't be such a grump," Lora said. "Smoke some more weed."

He complied.

"So imagine, people, that you're living in Egypt, 2013," Bolster said, continuing regardless. "For NPR News, I'm like whatever."

"You're silly," said Lora.

They pulled up in front of Dr. Cohen's office at quarter to six. Bolster was coated in sweat and highway soot. He needed some integrative healing.

"Do you want me to come in with you?" Lora said.

"You're welcome to," Bolster said. "But you have to be quiet."

"I'm always quiet."

"That's true."

The office grounds had been well maintained, but the building still looked antiquated and splintery, giving off a 1982 wheat-germ vibe, all wood beams and yellowed, outdated type-faces. The outdoor wind chimes carried Bolster back into the past, to a time when *asana* was still a secret, ascetic thing. How he longed to be a part of that era of yoga, when it was practiced quietly by obsessives in dark and dusty rooms. Instead, he found himself living day-to-day in a glossy, overcommercialized exercise nightmare.

But you can't choose your time. You can't even choose to be happy. You just have to practice every day and hope you die in peace.

They walked into the reception area, all leafy wallpaper and dated linoleum countertops. There was a stack of *Inside Sports* magazines on a side table, a magazine so dated that you couldn't even really find it in thrift shops anymore. That's when Bolster knew this was a front. Dr. Cohen hadn't done any real doctoring in a long time.

The receptionist, who didn't look all that healthy herself, was chomping on gum and looking at Facebook.

"Can I help you?" she said.

"We're here to see Dr. Cohen."

"He's with a patient."

"Is he, now?"

"Yes, and then he's leaving for the day."

"I've got to talk to him."

"You need to make an appointment."

"Tell you what," Bolster said. "I'll make an appointment with my friends at the DEA. Then you'll be out of a job, and probably in jail."

She looked at him to see if he was serious. Then she looked at Lora, who was sitting in a waiting room chair, palms in her lap, eyes closed, meditating. These were not the usual clients. She picked up the phone.

"Dr. Cohen," she said. "You have a visitor."

"Matt Bolster," Bolster said.

"A Mr. Bolster."

"Tell him I'm here about Tom Hart."

"He wants to talk to you about Tom Hart."

Bolster waited a second while the receptionist listened.

"I'll buzz you back," she said.

Bolster looked at Lora.

"You coming?"

She opened her eyes.

"If you like," she said.

"Might keep me from hitting an old man."

"Only if you introduce me as your associate."

"I can do that."

"Then lead the way, yoga detective."

The door buzzed.

Bolster and Lora walked through.

Dr. Cohen was sitting in his office, which looked about as cluttered as Bolster expected, papers, manuals with red leather spines, and posters depicting the healing properties of various herbs. If you lived in Pomona and needed an update on acupressure points, this was the room. Or at least it used to be. The cleaning crew hadn't been allowed back here for a long time. Instinctively, Bolster sneezed into his arm.

"Bless you," Dr. Cohen said.

The doctor stood, looking pretty trim for a man in his seventies, a testimony to yogic longevity. His curly gray hair slinked halfway down his neck. He had a pair of bifocals propped on his forehead.

"Nice to see you again," he said, extending his hand.

"Likewise," Bolster said. "This is my associate, Lora Powell."

Lora put her hands at her chest in *anjali mudra* and bowed. Dr. Cohen bowed back.

"Such a shame about your friend killing Tom," Dr. Cohen said. "Are you—"

"My friend didn't kill Hart," Bolster said, cutting to the point. "I'm wondering if maybe you did."

Dr. Cohen clicked his tongue on the roof of his mouth.

"Of course I didn't," he said. "Tom was one of my best friends. I *introduced* him to yoga. Why would I kill him?"

"Maybe because the yoga you taught him got out of control? Because he was corrupt? Because he'd perverted the teachings?"

"There's some truth to that," said the doctor, "but do you really think that would drive me to murder?"

"It's happened before in this world," said Bolster.

"Tom got a little caught up in trends sometimes, but he had good intentions."

"Some people might doubt that," Bolster said.

"Now now," said the doctor.

"I also have some questions for you about drugs."

For the first time, Cohen's demeanor seemed to hitch. He looked worried.

"What about drugs?" he asked.

"Certain ones. Where they come from."

"Of course," Dr. Cohen said. "But I'm being rude. Can I offer you some water?"

"Sure, thanks," Bolster said.

The doctor opened up a minifridge and took out two bottles, unmarked, and handed one to Bolster, who surprised himself by chugging it all down in one gulp. He was thirsty from the long drive out. It tasted good and cold. Lora took hers as well. She was better than Bolster at controlling her appetites, so she just took a few sips.

"You ask about drugs," the doctor said, "but it's all just part of the progression of yoga in this country, Bolster. When I started practicing in the seventies, you really had to look hard to find a *hatha* yoga teacher. *Lilias, Yoga and You* was on PBS once a week, and that was about it. I found an old pamphlet in a used bookstore, and I used it for almost a year. Then I just kept going. Even still, when Tom came to me the first time after he'd been ill, yoga was still pretty rare. So when he went to India and fell into that ashram circuit, everything felt fresh to him, not like received wisdom."

"Sure," Bolster said, "but what about—"

"Hold on," said Dr. Cohen, "you must let an old doctor have his ruminations."

Bolster wanted to protest. He had questions to ask. But his legs and tongue were feeling surprisingly heavy. He looked behind him. Lora's eyes were closed, as though she were meditating deeply.

Trouble.

"Then Tom came home after a couple of years, and I could see the excitement. Yoga had always been something calming and healing for me, but in his hands, it was more like a revolution, a burning flame. Rather than resist, I decided to flow with it. That's what yoga teaches you to do, right?"

Bolster wasn't talking much.

"He said to me, 'Doc, I learned so much there. We should develop our own sequence. We could make millions if we trademark it.' I tried to tell him that there weren't poses to trademark, that the sequences were already set, but he was young and hungry and excited. I didn't really like what he was doing; it was all energy expansion, no grounding. But that's clearly what people wanted. In five years, he built an empire like nothing I've ever seen, and it just kept getting bigger.

"Meanwhile, I was dealing with a lot more competition here. When I started, no one was doing holistic health. But then regular doctors started prescribing herbs and yoga. You even had health insurance—at least in California—covering it. Suddenly everyone and his uncle was doing *reiki* energy work. Business started to dry up. Tom asked me if I wanted to work for him instead. That was the best offer I'd had in decades. But I kept the office. Why not? I bought the building in the seventies and paid it off years ago."

"Drugs," Bolster gurgled, remembering the reason he'd come in here in the first place, and realizing that he'd been slipped some in the water. He hadn't felt like this since a backpacking trip he'd taken to Guatemala in his early twenties. Someone had brewed him a potion made from flowers and he'd woken up two days later in the basement of his youth hostel. This was at least twice as strong.

Bolster looked behind him. Lora's head was dropped to her chin. At least she hadn't finished her entire bottle. The dose would have probably killed her.

"I thought you might be interested in *that* aspect of my career," Dr. Cohen said.

To Bolster, Cohen's voice was sounding deep and slow, echoing in the cloud chamber that Bolster's brain had become. But yes, he was interested.

"After a while, there wasn't much use for my services inside the Hart Yoga world," the doctor said. "Everyone was so young and healthy; they didn't need diet and nutrition advice from an old hippie fart like me. *I* was the one whose health was slipping. When I'd first gotten into medicine back in the—God, I guess it was the sixties—it was because I was a chemistry dork. To me, the human body was just a big science experiment. I wanted to make it better. And then yoga *did* make it better. Almost ideal. But the yoga people wanted more, always more. Tom wanted to push himself harder and further, better.

"A few years ago, he asked me for some experimental herb mixtures. I pulled together some recipes and tried them out on him and a few others, with not a lot of results. I started to get worried that he'd consider me obsolete. That was around the time that synthetics really started to take off. So I cleared out a couple of my old treatment rooms. They weren't getting used anyway. I pulled some formulas out of online forums, and I cooked. I cut and synthesized and mixed stuff.

"Hart and his followers, particularly this one guy called Hanuman, were taking just about anything I gave them, and paying good money for it. It was all dudes; the yoginis, with a few exceptions, tend not to go in for anything stronger than wine or weed.

"Eventually, they started asking for specific hallucinations. That was harder to come up with, but I had a couple of these guys—Hanumaniacs, they call themselves—up to my cabin in Idyllwild for a weekend, so I could try out some visions on them. They wanted to see Patañjali. He's the snake god who . . ."

"I know," Bolster blurted through his haze.

"It took a little while, and I think I might have burned a cerebrum or two finding the recipe, but I made something good. Hanuman certainly seemed happy. And I was happy, because I had customers again. It wasn't what I'd intended, but it was work."

This guy was a pusher trying to pass himself off as a humanitarian. Bolster hated hypocrites. If he could have stood up, he would have punched the old guy in the face.

"Then someone came to me looking for something else," Cohen said.

"What?" Bolster said.

"A paralytic. A really strong one that would stop the heart. Not entirely, of course, but something that would slow it down to the point where it seemed like it wasn't beating. Something to give the illusion of death. That was a trick that Krishnamacharya used to do for visiting camera crews. Really high-end yoga stuff. They wouldn't say why. I think they just wanted to experiment on themselves."

"Who was it?" Bolster said, feeling more than a little paralyzed himself.

Dr. Cohen wagged his finger.

"Ah, ah, Mr. Bolster. You ask too many questions. I didn't kill Tom Hart. And I don't know who did. But I do know that if you're asking questions about drugs, then my business is in danger. That, I can't have."

"Who was it?" Bolster grunted. "Who wanted the drug."

Dr. Cohen reached into his desk drawer. He took out a syringe and gave it a few taps.

"I'm going to invoke doctor-patient confidentiality on this one," he said. "Enjoy your trip. If you survive, maybe I'll tell you."

He pulled up Bolster's right sleeve, raised the needle above the deltoid, and plunged it in.

"But you probably won't," he said.

CHAPTER TWENTY-ONE

Once upon a time, deep beneath the eternal ocean (which had not yet become gentrified), Lord Vishnu sat in a meditative state. He'd chosen Adisesa, the sacred serpent, as his couch. Adisesa was a bit scaly and wiggly, but way more comfortable than the futon Vishnu had recently discarded. Next to Vishnu lounged Lakshmi, his consort and *Top Chef* host, looking graceful and blissfully stoned, and nearby sat Garuda, the giant transporting eagle, who was a real sweetheart once you got to know him.

It was a fun night in the Vishnu household. The recent season of *Mad Men* had just ended, so, as alternate entertainment, the royal family celebrated the sacred dance of Lord Shiva, who was really getting his freak on. Vishnu enjoyed the dance so much that a beautiful lotus emerged from his navel, an image that has no erotic implications whatsoever.

However, the show wasn't quite as much fun for Adisesa, the snake-couch. Vishnu became so absorbed in Shiva's dance that he began to vibrate, which made him heavier and heavier, increasing Adisesa's burden, until Adisesa was close to collapsing, gasping for breath, and hoping the dance would end soon. Finally, it did. Vishnu returned to his usual form, which was comprised of pure light and thereby greatly cut down on the electric bills.

Adisesa found himself amazed by Vishnu's transformation. He asked how it had occurred. Vishnu said to his couch that the majesty and beauty of Shiva's dancing had created a similar vibration in his own body. It had been an act of divine mimicry.

"That's incredible," Adisesa said. "I want to learn how to do it, too."

"Of course, my snake-couch," said Vishnu.

He called Shiva back into the room. Shiva was shirtless and had a magical towel draped around his neck.

"What's up, boss?" Shiva said.

"Adisesa wants to learn how to dance."

Shiva thought about this for a second.

"I will teach him," Shiva said, "and he will develop perfection in time."

Awesome, thought the snake-couch.

"But first, he must write a series of inscrutable commentaries on yogic grammar."

"Are you kidding me?" Adisesa said. "That sounds *boring*."

Adisesa's intransigence angered Vishnu, who realized his couch had become cosseted and spoiled.

Meanwhile, on Earth, humanity was fucked. The world had become plagued with disease, overcrowding, delusion, and pop-up video ads. It seemed that the end of the world was approaching. A few brave souls approached the only yoga teachers who hadn't yet sold out to clothing corporations and prayed to them for deliverance from suffering. In return, the teachers prostrated themselves before Vishnu, and you know how painful that can be.

"Great Lord Vishnu," they wailed, placing their hands together at their hearts in *anjali mudra*, "please send us help."

Vishnu removed his Bluetooth headset and heard their plea.

I've got a snake-couch I want to get rid of cheap, he said to himself. Without a second thought, he sent Adisesa to the earthly realm as his envoy of hope. As part of the greatest practical joke of all time, humanity would be saved by God's used furniture.

One of the wise people praying to Vishnu was a woman named Gonika. She was a vegetarian (though not a vegan because she raised her own chickens) and had recently completed her five-hundred-hour RYT training at the Sacred Flower Yoga School in Chapel Hill, North Carolina. She'd also studied with many prominent yoga teachers around the world, including Maty Erzraty and Chuck Miller, during a weekend retreat in Maui. She truly believed in yoga's power to transform and heal.

But she was also, sadly, single and found herself wishing for a son to whom she could impart her wisdom. She felt it would be easier to raise a son, because the cultural environment had grown very hostile to women. Her wishes were answered, to a point.

After praying to Vishnu, Gonika opened her eyes and unfolded her palms. She saw a tiny snake wriggling there.

"EEK!" she said.

She threw the tiny snake down on the ground, where it quickly grew into a full-sized human.

"Mama," it said.

This wasn't the fate that either of them wanted, but now that it had happened, they decided to make the best of it. Gonika called her new child Patañjali: the "anjali" part from the sacred hand position, and "pat" after her grandfather, Patrick. The tilde that bonded the two syllables together was a mere linguistic affectation.

Patañjali assumed a form that was half-human, half-serpent, and all sexy. Most of the time, he had a normal human head but could manifest his snaky form if threatened, or to show off at parties. He had four arms and carried a conch, a disc, and a sword. Patañjali was a mighty warrior, as well as a scholar who wrote the *Yoga Sutras*, the most important boring book of all time. He was to spend eternity wandering the cosmos, looking for someone who could understand what the hell he was talking about in Section Three.

Matt Bolster was one of the few people who'd ever tried.

Bolster found himself walking in an unforgiving forest with no entrances or exits. Above him, the canopy was dark and impenetrable. The earth below was spongy, and crawling with terrible bugs. To his right stood trees, ancient and cruel. To his left, also trees. It was a forest, after all. The wind blew light and cold, and the birds sounded mean. This was no place to spend a Friday night.

These drugs are strong, Bolster thought.

The mind is a trap, the seat of *avidya*, a potent word that means, in ancient Sanskrit, the misunderstanding of the true nature of reality. Dr. Cohen was well studied. He knew this. And he knew that many people die, either actually or metaphorically, inside their prisons of self-consciousness, kept from happiness by their narrow, petty minds. Whatever chemical he'd cooked up mimicked this process, enhanced it, made it nightmarish.

So even though Bolster knew he was under the influence of Dr. Cohen's synthetic hallucinogens, they had entered his bloodstream all at once, probably in a higher dose than what Slim had taken. The forest was his mind, but he couldn't get out of it. *That's the worst place a yogi can find himself,* Bolster thought.

Actually, there was someplace worse.

Bolster approached a clearing in the woods. It looked like all the trees had been removed in a perfect circle, like cut biscuit dough. The ground had been scorched, even though the sky above was as gray as a frat boy's bed sheets. There were logs around the perimeter, as though this had once been some sort of low-rent Ultimate Fighting pit. In the center, there was a pile of ash and wood chips. A fire had burned here, though how recently Bolster couldn't tell.

On a log sat a man. He had four arms. Three of them were holding, respectively, a conch shell, a silver disc, and a sword. The fourth hand was drawn into a complicated *mudra*.

Bolster knew who it was immediately.

"Patañjali," he whispered to himself.

Unbidden, Bolster walked toward the man, who raised his head and said, calmly:

"Yoga citta vrtti nirodha."

Bolster knew this phrase, the second of Patañjali's many *sutras*, which translated, very literally, as "thought fluctuation cessation." This sounded like something from *Star Trek*. But it meant something more like, "a mind free from all disturbances is Yoga."

"My mind *is* free," Bolster said. He couldn't tell if he was speaking Sanskrit or not. Usually, he didn't spend his time talking to epic mythical yoga demons underneath a gray-purple hallucinated sky.

Patañjali rose up. His eyes glowed red.

"*Yoga citta vrtti nirodha!*" he said.

"Listen," Bolster said, "it's really interesting to meet you. Much respect, jungle physician and all, but I've got a friend in jail, and I just need to get out of here."

Patañjali stood. He seemed to be ringed with flame. His sword hand raised high, as he bellowed:

"*YOGA!*"

Then he raised the disc.

"*CITTA!*"

Then up went the *mudra* hand.

"*VRTTI!*"

Finally, he blew the conch shell, which gave off a horrific bellow, seeming to echo off faraway mountains, into the realm of the infinite.

"*NIRODHA!*"

For a second, the air was still. Then Patañjali's head disappeared into his neck.

Uh-oh, Bolster thought.

A small cobra's head emerged in its place. Well, that wasn't so bad. But then it started to grow—a foot tall, two feet, six, and then up and up, toward the top of the tree line. Bolster felt his eyes began to bulge. His mouth widened. His heart felt like a turbine. The drugs were really kicking in now, to the point where Bolster was almost unaware of their existence. He was too focused on the fact that the snake head, which just kept rising, now also appeared to be hissing blood and fire. And then another snake head emerged and grew just as tall. And another. They just kept coming, at a speed Bolster couldn't track.

Patañjali, the sage with so many cobra heads, had revealed his true form.

Bolster tried to breathe and gather his mind. Maybe he could run. But the circle no longer appeared to have any way in or out. The trees seemed glued together, and drugs no longer seemed fun.

At some indeterminate point—Bolster couldn't tell if the process had taken hours or five seconds, even though at some distant point deep in his sizzling cerebrum, he must have known that it wasn't, in fact, taking place at all—the heads stopped sprouting. In some versions of the Patañjali myth, the sage has an infinite number of heads, and in some he just has a thousand. Bolster was relieved to discover that his imagination ran toward the latter.

Of course, it didn't really matter *how* many heads Patañjali had when he started swinging his sword.

Patañjali whirled the blade around his head. The sword made a whooshing noise, almost like it was a whip. It was shiny silver with a gold handle, encrusted with diamonds. This was ridiculous.

Bolster didn't have anything to fight with. He broke a stick off a tree, which would have been great if he'd been a kid defending himself against a school bully. But he was fighting an immortal Indian snake god, and, in addition, he was doing so in a hallucination, so he really didn't have a chance. Dr. Cohen hadn't stuck Bolster with this dose so he'd have the illusion of winning.

The sword came down toward Bolster in a straight chop. Bolster dodged neatly. It cut one of the logs in half, like the log was a brick of soft cream cheese. Patañjali lifted the sword again, whooshed it again, and swung in a circular motion again. Bolster jumped like he was skipping rope, and it missed, again. He could feel air on the back of his legs. He had to get out of there.

Bolster started running. The grove of trees was a perfect circle, and it was sealed. There was no path in or out. It was, in fact, Bolster's mind, and he was trapped inside it. He knew the feeling of being trapped.

Once when Bolster was a cop, he'd chased a couple of junior Avenues gang members, who'd knocked over a liquor store as part of some kind of initiation, into a concrete wash alongside the 110, near the Forty-Third Street exit. That wasn't a good neighborhood. It was crawling with reinforcements for the guys he was chasing.

Bolster was plainclothes then. He looked like just any other guy. Though he was in really good shape, he wasn't much of a match for the Avenues, who'd been beating the shit out of tougher guys than him since before he was born. There were five of them, maybe six. Bolster ran under a bridge. The walls of the wash sloped upward so steeply that he didn't have the opportunity to scramble up. He would have slid back, and he would have been dead. Instead, the guys he was chasing doubled back, and then they were chasing him along with the reinforcements.

Finally, Bolster ran into a drain pipe, which smelled like human piss and rat turds and garbage, and there was probably a dog carcass in there too, but Bolster couldn't tell because it was dark. The back of the pipe was covered with thorny brush.

It looked like the cover of a junior book of dark fairy tales. Bolster had been trapped.

But there were differences between that situation and this one. Then, Bolster had a gun, which he knew how to use. He'd squatted behind a concrete barrier and let off a couple of shots. It was probable that the Avenues had guns too, at least a couple of them, but they didn't fire back so he wondered how prepared they really were. Also, he had a radio. Within two minutes, there was a chopper overhead, sweeping the wash with spotlights. The Avenues scattered quickly.

Situations like that were a big reason why Bolster had taken up yoga in the beginning. Who needed that shit? It was stressful. But in a lot of ways, it was better than dodging imaginary swords while under the influence of strange synthetic drugs. Or was it? Bolster wondered what would happen if he just let the sword slice through him. But not enough to actually let it happen.

So instead he ran around in a circle for a while, dodging big clumsy sword blows, and then once in a while, one of the cobra heads that covered the gray-purple sky like a hideous canopy would come swooping down, hissing and spitting some foul-smelling liquid on the ground, just to remind Bolster who was boss, as though Bolster didn't know.

"Cut it out, man!" Bolster said. "I do yoga!"

"*CITTA VRTTI NIRODHAA!*" Patañjali bellowed.

Cessation of thought fluctuations.

With one of his other arms, Patañjali reared back and threw his disc, which whizzed toward Bolster's head, a sinister Frisbee of death. Bolster ducked. The disc missed and thudded harmlessly into a tree. It lay there in the dust, ready for plucking. Bolster picked it up. One side was dull brushed steel, but the other was shinier, almost mirrored. Bolster had an idea. Maybe if he held up the mirrored surface to Patañjali, the deity would see his hideous reflection and would chill out a little. Generally, in myth, when there were a lot of snake heads involved, that sort of thing seemed to work.

The disc was surprisingly light. Bolster raised it over his head. He felt a little like Perseus. Only a little.

"Check it out, snaky!" he shouted.

Patañjali took a look at his reflection, hissed, and then a hundred more heads immediately sprouted from his neck. He raised his arm and roared. The disc flew out of Bolster's hand and back into the god's. Then Patañjali began to lurch toward Bolster, swinging the sword. This would be over soon.

Bolster took a breath, in for a count of four, and then out for a count of four. He immediately felt better, so he did it again. Then he did it in for a count of four, out for a count of six, and then a couple more times. He closed his eyes and kept breathing. Then he looked up. Patañjali had stopped and looked less enraged. In fact, the heads seemed to have shrunk a bit.

Suddenly, Bolster knew what he had to do.

He sat in the dirt, closed his eyes, and kept breathing, in four, out six. Then he extended his breath. He could hear Patañjali roaring, but he refused to let it bother him. It was just his mind acting unmindfully, tempting him with hallucinations and paranoid fantasies. He had to go deeper.

Bolster meditated. He listened to the sounds around him. Up close, of course, he heard the imaginary demon scream. But there were other sounds, too, chirping birds and rustling wind. This is what you did in meditation: you started close and went outward, extending your consciousness from the very close to the very distant, even imperceptible. Gradually, they merged.

Bolster breathed and meditated on the sounds and felt his mind relax. He was very present. He felt the earth beneath him. It was firm and supportive and loving. The air on him was cool, maybe a little too cool, but it had pleasant properties as well. He felt its dampness, its freshness, the way it made his skin feel slightly electric.

The surprisingly bitter smell of the leaves on the trees behind Bolster left an impression. He absorbed that sensation. Patañjali was still screaming, but it was starting to sound like background noise. Other sensations began to take its place. Bolster let them pass through his mind, observing them, not judging them. They flowed like mountain water.

The world, despite the foolish dance of external appearance, was actually part of one unified plane of reality—eternal, unchanging, joyful, and loving. All things, people, and places comprised its beautiful fabric. That plane extended out to the galaxy, to nearby galaxies, and onward to the beautiful, unknowable, undefined boundaries of the universe, of all space and time. Bolster didn't make this up. He also didn't feel it all the time; if he did, he'd probably go crazy. But he'd *studied* it. Personal experience had led him to conclude it was true.

Perhaps most importantly, Bolster understood that his *thoughts* were also part of this grand cosmic tapestry, not above or below it, not better than it or worse, but just organically intertwined. This was true of all the contents of his mind, the emotions and the memories, and it was true of all other people's as well. Those contents are important—in fact, they're vital, because they're so fun and easy to observe—and they're certainly real, but understanding that they're temporary matter, not something permanent and heavy, is the key to reducing human suffering in our time, and in all times. We are all part of something greater and unknowable.

Bolster opened his eyes. Patañjali was gone. He had beaten his mind. Apparently, he'd beaten Dr. Cohen as well, because he was there in the office, and the doctor had his hands tied with a stethoscope.

"How long was I out?" Bolster said.

"Five minutes, maybe ten," Lora said. She was standing behind Cohen, hands poised above his head.

"Really? It felt longer."

"The drug is not meant to be long-lasting," Cohen said. "I . . ."

"I didn't give you permission to talk," Lora said.

She'd been pulling his hair every time he whined. Bolster didn't know she'd had it in her, but she looked happy enough to help. She yanked and Cohen gave a little yelp.

"Didn't he knock you out, too?" Bolster said.

"I was playing possum," Lora said. "I could tell the dude was shifty from the minute I sat down. But you *had* to gulp down your water."

"I was thirsty," Bolster said.

"You looked like a stray dog," Lora said.

"In any case, I'm back now," Bolster said, getting to his feet. But he felt woozy and sat back down again. He put his head down on Cohen's desk and fell asleep for a minute or three, snoring loudly until Lora poked him with her foot. He woke up with a snort. *Now* he was feeling better and could enter cop mode. You always needed a transition, in yoga and in life.

"Has he been telling you anything?" Bolster asked.

"No, just whining," Lora said.

"All right, Cohen, listen. I want you to tell me who at the Hart Gathering had your drugs."

"Everyone!" Cohen said. "Tom had me cook up a batch of E for Saturday night."

"I don't give a shit about your party Ecstasy, doc. Were there other drugs?"

"There are always other drugs."

"What about the hallucinogen you just jabbed into me?"

"I gave those all to Hanuman."

"Did you give him a massive paralytic, too?"

"No."

"Who'd you give it to?"

Cohen looked afraid. He wouldn't answer.

"I . . . can't . . . tell . . . you . . ." he stammered.

Bolster had had enough. He reached across the desk, grabbed Cohen's head, and pressed it down, hard.

"Who was it? Tell me, goddammit!"

Cohen paused and then croaked out the answer.

"Barlow," he said.

Bolster let him go.

"I called the cops, Bolster," Lora said. "I figured they might want to break up this old hippie meth lab."

"Good call," Bolster said. "Leave his hands tied until they get here."

They walked out. The police were just coming in, many of them.

"The doctor will see you now," Bolster said.

Five minutes of explanation followed. Bolster gave them his number and e-mail. Then he and Lora went to her car.

"What's next, Bolster?" she said. "Let's have an adventure."

"I've got to fly solo on this one," he said, "or at least with someone else who knows how to use a gun. But I'm going to use you in the future. I promise. You're good."

"Don't I know it?" Lora said.

"Take me home," Bolster said. "You can stay with my cat."

"Why? Where are you going?"

"North," Bolster said.

CHAPTER TWENTY-TWO

Andrew Barlow read ten hours a day about yoga, from the original texts when possible. He didn't own a computer or a tablet. If he had to communicate electronically, he checked his phone (which, using great discipline, he kept turned off during most daylight hours). If he had to do some serious e-mail writing, he used his Gmail account on the computers at the Berkeley Public Library.

Every day, he woke up at five o'clock, scraped his tongue, drank a cup of hot water with lemon, did three hours of brutal *asana* practice, meditated for forty-five minutes followed by thirty minutes of *pranayama*, and then read until one o'clock, when he took a break for a cup of twig tea and a bowl of home-fermented kimchi. It kept him vital.

Then came three more hours of reading, after which he'd take a break, put on a leather jacket and a helmet, and ride his motorcycle around the Berkeley hills to clear his head. Every man needed a vice, and since Barlow generally abstained from sex, and even masturbation ("You should only eat when you're hungry," he always said), the bike was his. He'd jam the throttle and soar up into the NorCal glades, debating obscure points of yogic philosophy with himself since no one else cared to do so.

Then it was back home for a bowl of clear soup and three more hours of hard study before bed.

On Friday evenings, Barlow taught an *asana* class at a little studio on Telegraph Avenue to ten or twelve students. Two weeks a year, usually in September, he went to Taiwan. There, incongruously, was a studio owner who respected his scholarship and brought him over to teach workshops in which dozens of people sat raptly, in a large room, while he led them in obscure *mantras* and explained to them how chakra imagery had radically transformed between the late and early medieval Tantric periods. He went on all day about the true linguistic origins of the term *hatha* yoga, without using notes, and there were always at least an hour's worth of questions afterward. Yoga was different in Asia.

Barlow practiced hard, and with great fervency and faith. He'd done it for a lot of years. Lately, he'd begun receiving strange dividends. He'd developed various *siddhis*, extraordinary powers described in the Yoga Sutras. One morning, while meditating, he'd opened his eyes to realize he was levitating a couple of inches above the floor. Of course, at the moment of realization, he'd come crashing down, but it had definitely happened. The next day, it happened again.

Gradually, he began to realize that he could hold that levitation, even take it a little higher, just by breathing properly and practicing *prataharya*, or extreme concentration.

Other powers began to develop. Barlow realized that he could make himself invisible. Not *actually* invisible—he could still see himself in the mirror, and when he took a selfie, his image appeared—but he could walk through the world completely undisturbed, just by focusing his mind. He'd discovered this one day when he'd seen his neighbor coming down the hall with groceries, waved, and got no response. He'd waved again, still no response.

Finally, he'd said, "Good morning," and then the neighbor said, "Oh, hey, Andrew, I didn't see you standing there." There had been no way to miss him. Barlow needed to further test this power.

Ten minutes later, he walked into a Starbucks, went behind the counter, took a fat-free coffee cake out of the display case, walked out, walked back in again, and replaced the coffee cake. No one noticed him. It was the strangest thing, and it was happening to him. All those things that had been written about in the ancient books, he realized—matters to which he'd devoted his entire adult life—could actually happen if he practiced hard enough, and with enough devotion.

So he just kept going, even more fervently than before.

Barlow learned to slow his heart down so that it beat only every five minutes or so. He didn't do this a lot; it wasn't necessary under normal circumstances. Telekinesis was probably more useful. At first he was just scooting a hand-thrown, handleless ceramic cup (out of which he drank hot water with lemon every day before sunrise) across the table, but now when Barlow wanted a book, he'd merely think about it, and it would float across the room toward him. He could open windows with a finger-flick and could sometimes anticipate things minutes before they happened.

Like He-Man, he had the power.

Barlow had to keep practicing, even harder, both to keep his *siddhis* strong, but also to keep his ego in check. There were limits. He wasn't about to start generating earthquakes or tornados. He couldn't walk through walls. Barlow knew that he was a man, not a god, or even an X-Man.

But he was a *powerful* man, one who had broached a new level of mental possibility.

He hadn't told Tom Hart about this. Hart would have wanted the *siddhis* all for himself, because Hart wanted everything, all the knowledge, all the power. Everything had been owned in Hart's world, everything trademarked. But Barlow wasn't going to let Hart have access.

If Hart wanted to find it, he'd have to practice harder.

Maybe twenty years ago, before fame and money had found their way to Hart's door, he would have had a chance, but he'd fallen into decadence and greed. Hart's yoga had grown thin and shallow, full of ego. He'd been too silly, too buoyant. He used his power to manipulate people into superficial situations.

Barlow was the opposite. Even when he was hovering above the Earth in lotus pose—which he did now, every day, for a half hour or more—he stayed grounded. His yoga was private, so private that sometimes he felt like he needed to burst. Even when he taught, he kept it really basic. People weren't ready for extraordinary powers. He wasn't even sure that *he* was.

But he couldn't tell anyone, or at least not anyone other than the people he'd already told. People weren't ready to hear. The secrets he held were enough to make a man crazy.

One afternoon, Barlow was levitating a few inches when his phone buzzed. He'd forgotten to put it in airplane mode, which he usually did while practicing. The first time it went off, he was able to ignore it. The second time, he lost his concentration and plopped to the earth.

"Goddamn it," he said.

Well, that was sunk. It took him hours to warm up to the *siddhis*. Then once he'd achieved them, he had them for the rest of the day, sometimes even through to the next day. He wanted to make them permanent, but judging by the fact that he had to actually pick up his phone and not fly it straight to his hand, they weren't.

He looked at the unfamiliar number. It was generally best to ignore such calls, but he had a feeling. Barlow answered.

"What?" he said.

"It's Shell," said Chelsea Shell.

"I told you not to call me ever," Barlow said.

"I know I wasn't supposed to get in touch."

"Yeah? Well, maybe Bolster's putting you up to this."

"Don't worry, Bolster has no idea where I am."

"That's good," Barlow said, "because you get a little weak for him. And weak people talk."

There was a pause.

"I need a place to crash," Chelsea said.

"Well, you can't crash with me," said Barlow. "I don't have the space."

"I can sleep on a couch."

"I don't have a couch."

"Do you have a floor?"

"Yes."

"I can sleep there."

"Chelsea, I don't want you here. I don't need the temptation."

"What temptation? I won't tempt you."

"Right. Look, just get a hotel or something. Or call Kimberly."

"I don't have the money for a hotel. Not for more than a night or two. And Kimberly won't talk to me. She says I betrayed her trust."

"You did what was right."

"Did *you*?" Chelsea asked.

"I don't know."

"I don't either," she said, "which is why it would be a shame if I talked to someone."

Barlow rubbed his hand through his hair. He needed to think. But Chelsea Shell made it hard to do that. She also threatened his commitment to *bramacharya*, a commitment that he broke occasionally. He felt pretty hungry right now.

"Fine," he said. "You can stay with me. But not for long."

"I knew you'd want me."

"It's not about wanting," Barlow said. "It's a practical matter. When can you be here?"

"About two hours after you come pick me up," she said. "Three if there's traffic."

"You need a ride?"

"I'm not taking the bus, cowboy," Chelsea said. Reducing her voice to a purr, she added, "and if I like the vibrations on your bike, maybe I won't have to sleep on the floor."

Chelsea gave him an address in Big Sur. Barlow hung up and sighed. He went into his bedroom, put on jeans and a leather jacket, went to the bathroom, gargled with mouthwash, and picked his bike helmet off a little table by the front door. Barlow swiveled his head over his left shoulder and spat on the floor for luck.

With Chelsea around, he was going to need a lot more than that.

CHAPTER TWENTY-THREE

The morning after his epic hallucinated battle with the Lord of the Snakes, Bolster hauled Whitey up to see Slim. It was a brief stopover on the way up the coast, but Bolster felt like he owed Slim some time. He'd been calling him every day, but he had a question or two he wanted to ask him in person, to see if the cops had missed something in questioning Slim. And if they'd really questioned him at all.

Hopefully, he'd make it there.

Whitey didn't sound so good, really. It was whirring a lot. *Please don't be the timing belt*, Bolster prayed silently. Bolster always got Whitey's oil changed and had new tires put on every six years or so. He'd take it to get washed about once a month. But big-time repairs weren't in the budget. You kept a car like this because it was paid off, not to preserve it for future generations. Once Whitey broke, it would be scrap. At least it was old enough to be made of metal, and not molded plastic or carbon fiber or recycled juice boxes or whatever comprised the average Scion.

They were holding Slim in the Ventura County Jail, a depressing beige-and-concrete setup off the Santa Paula freeway, only twenty-five miles from the coast but leagues away for those inside. Bolster had made sure to keep all his marijuana implements buried deep in the trunk, under the spare. He had light supplies because he was going to San Francisco, where weed was easier to find than donuts.

Vijay Malik of the Ojai PD was waiting for Bolster at the entrance. He'd been there for a half hour. Bolster had called him and then had shown up late. He blamed the car.

"How's it going, Bolster?" Malik said.

"I mean, OK," Bolster said. "Considering."

"Find anything out?"

Bolster took off his sunglasses and squinted at Malik. Why was it that he always ended up doing all the work? The inland sun was broiling, cooking his brain.

"I got into a fight near Dodger Stadium with Hanuman Jones. Chased him into a ditch."

"Sounds productive." Vijay chuckled. "Heh," he said. "A white guy named Hanuman."

"Yeah, apparently he was in charge of the snake cult that gave Slim that pill the night Hart was murdered."

"Snake cult?"

"I'll explain that later."

"So he's our guy," Malik said.

"I don't think so," Bolster said. "I slapped him around pretty good. But he didn't confess and didn't really seem to be lying."

Bolster reached into his pocket as though here were moving for his pipe, but then he remembered where he was.

"OK," Vijay said. "Did he tell you anything useful?"

"Hanuman told me that he'd gotten the drugs from Dr. Cohen. So I went to his office in Pomona, where I got injected with a synthetic hallucinogen and fought an imaginary demon."

Malik laughed, shaking his head.

"You really know how to have a good time, Bolster," he said.

"Tell me about it," Bolster said.

"So did you beat the demon?"

"Sort of. I meditated him away."

"As one does."

"Right. And then afterward Dr. Cohen told me he'd given some sort of super-powered sedative to this guy named Barlow."

"The yoga scholar? Up in Berkeley?"

Bolster looked surprised.

"How'd you know?"

"I am, technically, the lead investigator on this case," Malik said. "Though my boss thinks it's solved, I'm not persuaded. Your friend is too good-natured to kill anyone."

"True," said Bolster, "though he does kick ass when threatened."

In particular, Bolster was remembering a walloping that Slim handed out with his didgeridoo a few months earlier, while they were on the Ajoy Chaterjee case. That had saved his ass. He could have used Slim on this case. Instead, he was dealing with makeshift assistance.

"I have a home address for Barlow if you're interested," Malik said.

"It's worth a look," said Bolster. "I was headed up there anyway."

As it turned out, Slim had made all kinds of friends in county jail. Not only did he know a half-dozen big-time pot growers, all of whom were protective and hands-off because they had access to excellent drugs, but Slim was also just a friendly guy. Even in jail, everyone wanted to party with him.

Bolster and Malik watched as Slim made his way through the room, shaking hands and giving high-fives to the other prisoners, and even a couple of guards. When he saw Bolster, he gave him a big hug.

"No touching!" the guard said.

Slim turned and gave a pouty face.

"All right, just a little," said the guard.

Slim hugged Bolster again.

"That guard is my buddy," he said.

He sat down and looked across the table, seriously.

"You've got to get me out of here, Matt," he said. "I'm *so* bored.*"

"I'm working on it, man," Bolster said. "You remember Detective Malik?"

Slim gave Vijay a little nod.

"It's important that you tell us things, Slim," Vijay said. "Do you have any idea how Tom Hart's blood got on your body?"

"No, I thought it was *my* blood."

"Some of it was. But there was more of his."

Slim looked puzzled.

"Well," he said, "I kind of remember having a dream. Someone was painting my face, like in a carnival."

Bolster leaned forward. The new information had arrived, certified mail.

"*Was* it a dream?" he said.

Slim looked excited.

"Maybe not?" he said.

"That's right," Bolster said. "Maybe not. Did you also dream that someone was painting your clothes?"

"Don't be a pervert," Slim said.

Bolster laughed, but Slim wasn't in the mood for that.

"I want you to figure it out, Bolster," Slim said, seriously. "That's some bad evidence against me. If I get found guilty, they're going to put me in a much worse prison than this."

"I know," Bolster said.

"At least here I can play poker with the guards. It's not so bad."

Slim looked sad, a puppy at a shelter. Bolster felt his heart melting. You couldn't exactly call Slim innocent, but he was good. Of course, the jails were full of good people who were getting screwed by the system. But most of them weren't accused of first-degree murder.

"How's Barbie doing?" Slim asked.

"Barbie?" said Vijay.

"That's his didgeridoo," Bolster said.

Malik smiled.

"Barbie is fine," he said. "She's in an evidence room in Ojai."

"Are you dusting her? She likes to be clean."

Vijay put a kindly hand on Slim's arm.

"She doesn't need to be dusted. She's in a bag."

"Oh, that's good."

Vijay patted Slim's arm.

"Dude, you don't have to treat me like I'm special-needs," Slim said.

"To be fair," Bolster said, "*you're* the one who's anthropo-morphizing musical instruments."

"Fuck off, Bolster," Slim said.

It was a nice visit. Bolster and Vijay left. Bolster was almost crying.

"We've got to help that poor schmuck," Vijay said.

Bolster's phone rang. He answered it. The voice on the other end said:

"I have to see you now."

Kimberly Wharton sat alone in her room with the shades drawn. She saw light only when she left the compound to drive to Whataburger, where she'd been punishing herself by eating twice a day. It had been five weeks since she'd had a yoga practice or eaten any vegetable matter other than limp burger lettuce.

This was what she felt she deserved.

Other than a couple of security guards and the occasional groundskeeper, Kimberly was the only person left at the Hart Center. Her job was now to see that it got sold to the highest bidder, with half the proceeds going to the Hart Foundation, which sponsored a few nebulous Yoga in Africa programs, and the other half going to Hart's mother. Kimberly intended to take a 10 percent cut, which would set her up financially for a long time.

But she hadn't been working at it very hard; at the moment, despite the prime location, there wasn't a ton of interest in a property at which a guru had recently been found with his heart stuffed into his mouth. Understandably.

The Hart Center was nothing but soft, warm winds and the sound of birds and insects, now that the piped-in "spiritual" music no longer filled the grounds. The setting couldn't have been better for quiet contemplation. But Kimberly had a troubled mind. She filled her room with TV noise. At night, she watched whatever, and by day, all the shows seemed to be people yelling at one another around tables about topics that didn't make any sense at all to Kimberly. Some of them were upset, some of them happy, but none of them *really* seemed to have any problems, and they all had really nice clothes.

Little more than a month before, she'd totally understood the world. Sure, her relationship with Tom had been confusing, occasionally brutal, and over-reliant on yellow crookneck squash for his sexual pleasure, but at least she'd known her place. She didn't take much pride in admitting that, and she certainly hadn't been happy, but her days had order. Then, in a moment of weakness, she'd opened up to Chelsea Shell, and it had all gone to shit. Kimberly had been looking for girl power but had chosen the wrong girl. Chelsea had a bad contract and a bad agenda.

"Leave the door unlocked," Chelsea had said. "We'll make sure that Tom gets embarrassed."

"What do you mean, 'we'?" Kimberly had said.

"I'm not sure yet."

Kimberly had sobbed and Chelsea had stroked her hair and told her that everything would be fine. The thing is, it *would have* been fine without Chelsea. Kimberly used to cry twenty minutes a day. Who didn't? Eventually she would have gotten out without Chelsea's help.

And now, instead, she cried twenty *hours* a day, and also had arms like hams.

She'd held it together until the cops had stopped coming around every day, and then she'd let it all dissolve. Her purple mat with the pink lotus flower sat rolled up in a corner of her room alongside two blocks, a blanket, and a strap. The usual props. She thought about the years she'd put into the practice, the endless hours of mental and physical effort. Pretty much every second of her adult life had been dedicated to unquestioning dedication toward yoga's innate goodness. And for what? Life was death, misery, and decay.

Fuck yoga, she thought. *It's all lies.* She'd never practice again.

Kimberly let out a disgusting Whataburger fart. Her gut begged for the punishment she was doling. A knock sounded at her door. She stood up and shuffled toward it, like a half-sentient troll.

It was time for Kimberly to tell what she knew.

CHAPTER TWENTY-FOUR

Bolster remembered reading as a kid about a bomb that would vaporize all the people but leave the buildings standing so an invading army could occupy a city without having to rebuild. That sort of weapon had never been used, as far as he knew. But it had really creeped him out, the idea that people could just *disappear*, like they'd never really mattered at all.

The Hart Center was like that now, not some sort of ruin, an abandoned hot springs resort sixty-five miles from Tahoe, but a place that, until very recently, had been the hub of life itself. It presented as modern, almost to the day. And yet it contained no sign of human life, other than the whirring of a distant maintenance cart.

Yoga would get done here no more.

Bolster and Malik walked through the wreckage, enjoying the quiet.

"Here was the church, here was the steeple, open the door, where are all the people?" Bolster said.

Vijay looked at him.

"Are you stoned, Bolster?"

"No, this is my natural state," Bolster said.

"Frightening."

Kimberly Wharton had given him a room number on the phone. She had her run of the place but seemed to have chosen an ordinary room to stay in, on the second floor of Building 3. The air smelled fresh and piney outside. Bolster inhaled deeply, as though he sensed what was coming.

He knocked. There was a shuffling, and then the door opened. Bolster almost gasped. The creature that stood before him barely resembled the Kimberly Wharton he'd met during the Gathering. Her face had splotches all over, like a slab of spoiled bologna. It looked like she had an egg sac hanging from her chin. That beautiful lustrous auburn hair had turned dry and wispy and hung from her scalp like an overused broom. Her eyes were red and exhausted.

As she opened the door more fully, it was clear that Kimberly Wharton was on her way to becoming very fat.

"Come in," she said.

Bolster and Vijay stepped into the room. It smelled like an abattoir. Pieces of crumpled-up wax paper were strewn about, greasy snowballs of unhealthiness. The TV was on, blaring a show where a group of people, not much larger than Kimberly, were eagerly tucking into perfect plates of pasta and blathering on and on about themselves.

This, Bolster thought, *is what happens to Americans when we don't practice yoga.*

Other than the TV, there was no light in the room. Kimberly had curtains drawn together and then had pressed a table against them so not even a crack of sun could get through. It was hermetic in there. Bolster didn't even want to *see* the bathroom.

"What happened to you?" Bolster said.

"This is what I deserve," said Kimberly.

"Did you kill Tom Hart?" Vijay said, not much for the softshoe.

"No," said Kimberly, "but I might as well have."

She moved into the room, over toward the table blocking the window, and cleared Whataburger bags off the chairs.

"Sit down," she said.

"Kimber, do you mind if we open the curtains a little?" asked Bolster, "and maybe open the windows a crack? It's nice outside."

"Fine," Kimberly said.

Vijay turned off the TV. Bolster did the curtains and windows. Kimberly recoiled a little, like a vampire. She may have even hissed. Darkness had descended upon the Hart Center™. She was the lone survivor of the apocalypse, with all the baggage that entailed.

Kimberly sat down on the bed.

"Tom had been fucking me for more than a year," she said.

Vijay hitched forward as though he were going to blow the contents of his sinuses out his nostrils.

"ERP!" he said.

"What?" said Kimberly.

"This sounds important. Can I record it?"

"Sure," she said.

Vijay got out his smartphone, fiddled with the appropriate app, and said, "Go ahead."

"OK," she said. "I liked it at first. I was lonely, and he was magnetic, and he'd given me so many gifts. It was a little weird, because we'd have these half-hour sessions, and then as soon as he'd roll off me, he'd start wanting to talk about the business. But I was able to compartmentalize.

"Then he started doing a lot of drugs. Not just the weed, but Dr. Cohen was giving him all these pills. Uppers, sedatives, a huge mix of stuff."

Again with Dr. Cohen, Bolster thought, making a reminder to tell the cops in Pomona about the extent of Captain Feelgood's operations.

"Sometimes Tom would call me at two, three in the morning, telling me to come over, begging, saying that he needed to see my face. I always did. Maybe I should have reserved some personal space, but I loved him. There was a tenderness in his eyes. But then he started doing weird things to me, telling me it was for my spiritual growth."

The narrative continued. Tom had taken Kimberly into the stockroom at Costco while they were shopping for coconut water and jammed two fingers into her crotch, whispering, "Come for me and the goddess Kali" until Kimberly had no choice but to fake an orgasm to get out of there.

He started using dog muzzles, and squash, all of which would have been fine if it had been consensual, but every encounter got weirder. Hart would mount her like a satyr, chanting wildly and incoherently in Sanskrit, the drugs flaming his ego out of control. He wouldn't leave her alone until she screamed "MAKE ME COME, LORD SHIVA!" When she did that, he'd go over the edge.

Five minutes later, or less, he'd say, "So let's look over the accounts."

Kimberly's eyes were getting teary as she said this, but not as much as Bolster might have thought. Her voice sounded flat, almost dead. Vijay's eyes bulged; he didn't hear this kind of thing much. Bolster looked a little less surprised. He knew the evil that yoga could do.

"I knew it was wrong," Kimberly said, "and I wanted it to stop. But I wanted it to stop on my own terms. I knew that I could control Tom. He was like a puppy. Scratch him behind the ear, and he'd follow you anywhere. It was a hard decision, but I decided to do it during the Gathering, when he wouldn't be able to exhibit so much drama.

"So on Saturday night, I was in the bathroom, crying, and someone came in. I told her everything, and she said she'd take care of it, even though I didn't want her to."

"Who?" said Bolster.

"Chelsea Shell," said Kimberly.

That was exactly the answer Bolster didn't want to hear, but he also somehow knew it was the only one possible.

"Keep going," he said.

"Chelsea was very comforting," Kimberly Wharton said. "She told me that what Tom was doing was appalling. I couldn't really disagree, but I wanted to take care of things my own way. Probably, I would have ended up doing nothing, but that was better than what happened.

"We talked for a while, and then she hugged me, and then she said she was going to go tell *you*."

Bolster looked surprised. Malik looked even *more* surprised. And then he looked at Bolster.

"Do you know something, Bolster?" he asked.

"Chelsea never told me *anything*," Bolster said. "She just showed up at Tom Hart's VIP suite and slapped him. And then after I got into a fight with Hanuman, I left with her."

"And she didn't say anything to you at all about this . . ." Vijay coughed, uncomfortably, ". . . quasi-consensual squash sex?"

"Not a word," Bolster said.

"So who *did* she tell?"

"I'm getting there," Kimberly said.

She paused a little, as though she were looking for breath, and then reached over to a side table to get a tissue.

"I'm sorry," she said, getting teary. "It gets difficult from here."

"Take your time," Bolster said.

Kimberly continued, "So after you left, everyone else left as well, except for Hanuman, who Tom also eventually let go. And then the bartender cleared out, too. So it was just me and Tom left in there. I knew how it was going to go then. We went into the bedroom. He took off his robe—he was naked underneath—got onto the bed in *virasana*. You know, hero's pose, the one where you're on your knees and sit between your ankles . . ."

"I *know* what *virasana* is," said Bolster, somewhat insulted.

"Sorry," said Kimberly. "We were alone in his bedroom, and Tom told me to lock the door. So I did. It's what Chelsea told me to do. When she came in the *first* time . . ."

Bolster felt a lump in his throat the size of a tennis ball. Chelsea had messed with him again.

"The time she left with you, Bolster . . ."

"I get it," Bolster said.

"She left her purse on the coffee table next to me. While she was outside, I slipped a room key in. And then when Tom told me to lock the door, I only turned it about three-quarters of the way until it made a clicking sound, and then I turned it back again. Tom was already playing with himself. He likes . . .

I'm sorry . . . *liked* to do that. So he didn't really know what was going on."

Kimberly stopped talking again. She seemed reluctant to get to the good stuff, or at least the relevant stuff. Bolster put a gentle hand on her arm.

"What happened next?" he said.

She took a deep breath.

"All right," she said. "We fooled around for a while. We were both naked and touching each other. Actually, Tom was quite tender, more tender than usual. He had that vulnerable quality in his eyes that I loved. He seemed almost sober, though his breath tasted a lot like wine."

This sounded a little bit too much like a romance novel for Bolster's taste. That didn't last long.

"Then he said, 'Get the squash,'" Kimberly said.

If Vijay had been a cartoon dog, he would have said "DERP!" Bolster felt close to saying "Zoiks!" himself.

"Those weren't words I liked to hear," Kimberly said.

"I can't imagine you would," said Bolster.

Kimberly narrated the scene like this:

"No," she said to Tom Hart. "It hurts me."

Hart said, "It's for me, not for you tonight."

"You want me to?" Kimberly said.

"It's OK, it's safe," Hart said. "I've been practicing."

Some master yogis develop their powers for good, others for nefarious purposes. For most, it's a mixed bag, but leaning slightly toward altruism. Tom Hart appeared to have reached the pinnacle of his art by developing his pelvic floor to such an extent that he could shove the top half of a yellow crookneck squash into his bunghole.

It was the most pathetic thing Bolster had ever heard, but it was certainly germane to his investigation.

Kimberly Wharton had Tom Hart on his hands and knees on the bed and was mechanically moving the squash in and out. It certainly wasn't love. She was a servant, nothing more. But Hart moaned victoriously. The door opened.

Chelsea Shell was standing there.

Wait, she was with me that night, Bolster thought. Or at least she'd been there when Bolster had woken up in the morning. He didn't really have a lot of memory of what had gone on after he'd gotten back to the room. Obviously, he'd passed out quickly, because judging from what Kimberly said, less than an hour had passed between the time they got back and the time she returned. Chelsea made his teeth hurt.

"But Chelsea wasn't alone," Kimberly said.

Bolster felt both relieved and worried to hear this.

"Who was she with?" he asked.

"Andy Barlow," she said.

Barlow again, Bolster thought. He hadn't even been aware that Chelsea *knew* Barlow. But it was starting to fit together, he guessed. All roads seemed to lead Barlow's way.

"What was he doing there?" Bolster said.

"I don't know," Kimberly said, "but I guess Chelsea had told him what was going on, because he looked pretty upset."

"Looks like you caught me in a bad spot," Hart had said, trying to be good-humored.

"Maybe you should save some of that energy for your next module," said Barlow.

"I've got energy to spare, pal," said Hart. "Maybe you should join us."

"Not interested," Barlow said. "I don't waste my yoga powers."

"It's not a waste," said Hart, "it's a party."

"How many other of your students have you 'partied' with, Tom?" Barlow asked, "and what have they gotten out of it?"

"Too many to count," Hart said. "But it's all divine energy, man."

"I'll show you energy," Barlow said.

He looked at Kimberly, who by now had wrapped herself in a sheet, looking humiliated. She held the round end of the squash away from herself, at a distance.

"Get rid of that fucking thing," Barlow had said. "Get it as far away from this room as you can."

"Why?" she'd said.

"I don't want to implicate you," Barlow said.

Kimberly put on a robe, went into the bathroom, washed her hands, and wrapped the squash in a plastic shower cap. She walked back in, and Hart was talking to Barlow, almost pleading, like a kid not wanting to be punished.

"Look, man," Hart said, "it was all just good fun. A thrill. Feelings. You know what I'm saying?"

"I know that you took a sacred, ancient teaching and distorted it," Barlow said.

Kimberly stopped in the middle of the room. Barlow looked at her, his demeanor growing much more intense.

"Ditch it," he said.

So Kimberly went outside onto the hot tub deck and pitched the squash as hard as she could into the night. It thudded into the chaparral some distance away.

Bolster asked, "Vijay, did any of your guys find a shit-stained squash wrapped in a shower cap in the vicinity of Hart's room?"

"I think that would have come up," Vijay said.

"Have them look again," Bolster said. Then, turning to Kimberly, he said, "All right. Tell me what happened when you went back to the room."

"It was bad," Kimberly said. "Chelsea was against the back wall. Her eyes were glassy, almost like she was in a trance. I said something to her, and she didn't respond. Tom was on his bed, in a robe now, open at the chest just a little bit, sitting back in *virasana*. He *definitely* seemed like he was in a trance. His eyes looked blank, maybe a little afraid. Something had struck at him deeply. Barlow was up close, in his face, breathing together. He opened Tom's mouth and slipped him a couple of pills."

"What are you doing?" Kimberly had said.

"He's not going to know anything," said Barlow, "but he's going to pay."

"Pay for what?"

"For what he did to you and to the others."

"But . . ."

Kimberly looked to Chelsea for help, but Chelsea's eyes were far away. Barlow walked away from Hart, who didn't move, sitting there like a wax dummy of himself, and went over to Kimberly. He placed his hand on her forehead and started saying a mantra that she didn't recognize. Once he touched her, though, she couldn't move. She stood there, frozen, and gradually felt the emotion draining from her heart. Suddenly, Kimberly Wharton was hypnotized, passive.

"The *siddhis*," Bolster said.

"The *what*?" said Vijay.

"Extraordinary powers," said Bolster. "It's in the *Sutras*. Barlow is a powerful yogi."

"Oh, come on," Vijay said.

"It's real," said Bolster. "Listen to the lady."

"I couldn't move," Kimberly told Matt Bolster and Vijay Malik. "I couldn't stop what came next. In fact, I couldn't even react. It was like a movie, but even more distant."

Here we go, thought Bolster. *The money shot.*

Barlow put on a pair of gloves. He placed his hand on Hart's chest, looking very serious, and began to mutter an incantation, over and over again. Hart's eyes widened. It was difficult to tell if he was feeling pain, or surprise, or if it was just some sort of undefined sensation. Regardless, Hart's flesh started to shimmer a bit, and then there was a pop sound. Kimberly and Chelsea stared on wordlessly as Barlow slid a perfectly formed cylinder of flesh and bone and muscle out of Hart's chest.

There were no screams in the room, just numbness.

"Oh, come *on*," Malik said as Kimberly described this to him. "That is ridiculous."

But Bolster believed. At least he believed enough. He knew what drugs could do, but more importantly, he knew what yoga could do. He'd met Ajoy Chaterjee's guru, seen what that man had done to the West's leading yoga teacher. Bolster wasn't there himself, but he'd heard yogis at the top of their games casting sinister spells. Yoga is powerful juju. Everyone thinks it's a force for good. But like in *The Wizard of Oz*, there are good witches, and bad witches.

"He has access to dark powers," Bolster said. "It's not good when someone channels their *kundalini* in that direction."

"It was horrible," Kimberly said. "Whatever Barlow took out of Hart's body, he put in a plastic bag. There was some blood, but maybe not as much as you might expect. Barlow gathered a little of that, too. And then he reached into Tom's body and grabbed his heart. Tom's mouth dropped open then. Barlow shoved the heart in. And then it was over, and Tom was dead."

"Wow," Vijay said. "That is *not* what I was expecting."

Kimberly finished the story.

She and Chelsea were standing there, frozen, stunned, and numb. Barlow went up to them.

"You won't tell anybody about this, and you'll feel nothing for weeks," he'd said. "Little by little, you'll remember it, little by little, but there won't be any guilt or any confessions. It won't bother you. This is exactly what Tom deserved, and we'll all be free because of it."

"I believed everything he told me," Kimberly said, "and I wandered back to my room in a daze, and slept really soundly. So when they found Tom the next morning, I wasn't surprised, but I also wasn't panicked. It just seemed natural. But Barlow was wrong. The spell *did* gradually start to wear off. I started to have little pangs, and now it's gotten really bad. I just wanted to tell someone what was going on. I didn't want Tom to die. Not that night. Not *ever*. And definitely not like that. He got *gutted*. And it's my fault."

Kimberly started to sob. Bolster put his arms around her, for a minute. She blubbered into his chest.

"It is *not* your fault," he said.

"I'm an accessory," she said. "I deserve to go to jail."

"You might be right," Bolster said. "But you and I both understand that this is an unusual situation. I'm pretty sure that Vijay does, too. Right, Vijay?"

"Pretty much," Vijay said.

"You have to believe us when we say that we don't want some of these strange details to get out, either. Now you have to tell us if you know where Barlow is."

"I just talked to him yesterday," she said. "He's at his apartment in Berkeley. He thinks I'm keeping quiet."

"We're going to head up there," Bolster said.

"We *are*?" Vijay said, looking like someone who just learned that he's going to be a first-time dad.

"Or at least I am," Bolster said. "I'm assuming you'd like to come."

"Do I have a choice?" Vijay said.

"Not particularly," said Bolster, and then, to Kimberly: "We're going to try to get him to confess to us and are going to try to get him to come quietly. We're going to try to make sure that you're not implicated here."

Kimberly snuffled.

"Also," Bolster said, "and this is the really important part: you have to start doing your yoga again. Don't blame the practice. Sometimes situations spiral in uncontrollably, but it's not yoga that does that. People fail to harness it in the right ways. To be able to exist, in the present moment, without judgment, is still the greatest gift that we have. Yoga may have gotten you into this situation, but it can get you out. It's waiting there for you, and it doesn't care who you are and what you've done."

"Thank you," she said. "But who's going to teach me?"

"I think you've had enough teaching for one life," Bolster said. "You can teach yourself from now on. And if you need advice, you've got my e-mail. I'll probably write you back stoned, but I'll always write you back."

They hugged, a little longer than was necessary, and then Bolster and Malik left.

Outside, Malik slid on his sunglasses and looked at Bolster like he was some sort of holy ghost.

"What the fuck was that?" Malik said.

"This is why you need a yoga detective," Bolster said.

"How can any of that be true?"

"There is more on heaven and earth than is dreamt of in your philosophy."

"But . . ."

"One moment at a time, Malik," Bolster said. "Stay in the present."

"OK," Vijay said. "By the way, that stuff you said to her at the end was very kind."

"And I meant it, too," said Bolster. "It's part of my training."

"It almost made *me* want to take up yoga," Malik said.

"You can start at any moment," said Bolster. "That's the beauty."

Inside her room, Kimberly Wharton kept the curtains open and stared into the late-afternoon sun. She felt the warmth on her skin, accompanied by a cool breeze. Kimberly breathed deeply. The air filled her lungs. It was fresh and new.

She sighed and walked over to the corner of the room where her yoga mat sat, rolled up and unused. Clearing out some of the month's detritus, she snapped it open and stood at the front. She took another deep breath. Bolster was right; she knew exactly what to do.

Kimberly went deep into her past and remembered the first time she'd practiced yoga, in the gym of her community college, how fresh she'd felt then, how young, how peaceful and uncorrupted by the business of the world. That was still available to her, if she could work with extreme patience. The healing began now.

She raised her arms over her head, turned her gaze up calmly, and began.

CHAPTER TWENTY-FIVE

Bolster and Malik had to take Bolster's car up to Berkeley. Malik's ride was department-issue, not authorized to go out of town. This made for an unpleasant few hours. It was a nice evening, but a little warm there on Interstate 5, the fastest way up north. Whitey's AC only blew lukewarm. You couldn't open the windows when you were going eighty (which made Whitey vibrate), and regardless, the driver's side window didn't work.

The suffering was mild, though it got a little more problematic when they arrived in the Bay Area proper. They had an address, but no way to find it. Bolster and Vijay's phones were out of juice, and Bolster not only didn't have a GPS device on his dash, he only had a cassette player. How did people get anywhere before technology? How did anything happen? Maps were useless.

But six hours after they'd left the Hart Center, there they were, two doors down from Barlow's apartment building in Berkeley. Bolster was dismayed to see that it looked a lot like *his* apartment building, maybe a little dingier. At the end of the day, despite the vast fortune of a few people at the top, most yoga people lived like burrowing animals, surrounded by whatever scraps they could gather, though admittedly with a decent array of new-media gadgets. It was pretty much like regular life.

The sun was low now, the sky a kind of smoky orange color. The air felt cool and damp. Bolster got out of Whitey and stretched. He wished he had a jacket.

Chelsea Shell was coming toward him on the sidewalk, carrying a bag of groceries.

"Hey!" Bolster shouted. "Hey!"

Chelsea saw Bolster, dropped the groceries, and started to run the other way, toward the main street.

"Uh-uh," Bolster said.

He charged after her, Vijay right behind. This was no time for niceties. Chelsea was in good shape, but she wasn't as fast as Bolster. He caught her and grabbed her arm.

"Hands off!" she said.

"Are you living in Berkeley now, Chelsea?" Bolster said.

"What's it to you?" she asked.

"It's everything to me."

"Maybe," she said.

"Just picking up groceries for dinner? Living your everyday life?"

"That's right?"

"Or are you crashing with Barlow now?"

Chelsea didn't say anything.

Vijay had caught up by now.

"We want to ask you some questions about Tom Hart's murder," he said.

"Who's your pony, Bolster?" Chelsea asked.

"Detective Vijay Malik of the Ojai Police Department."

"Ojai detective, huh?" Chelsea said. "You must work hard."

Bolster would have clocked her for a statement like that, but Vijay had a calm way.

"It pays the bills," he said.

Bolster pressed in close.

"Look," Bolster said. "We have testimony from Kimberly Wharton that puts you on the scene at the time of Tom Hart's murder."

"I knew she'd talk," Chelsea said. "But I didn't actually *do* anything."

"You were there and didn't stop it."

Chelsea winced a little.

"I was *hypnotized*," she said. "I couldn't have stopped it even if I'd wanted to."

There was a brief pause, and then she added, "And I did. I did want to."

"Why did you tell Barlow about this, and not me? We could have moved through normal channels."

"I don't know; I was stupid. Kimberly gave me that confession that night. It was good information, enough to bring Tom Hart down if I played it right. He had me under an exclusive contract to teach Hart Yoga for three more years and wouldn't let me deviate from his flow. Also, he was taking 30 to 40 percent of whatever I earned, which was fine at the beginning but it got old. I wanted to get out of my contract."

Bolster twisted a little more, which made Vijay draw back a little. But Bolster shot him a glance that said, *This woman and I have a history.* Vijay said nothing. Chelsea looked at them both, steely. She was used to being twisted.

"Who killed Hart?"

Chelsea shook her head.

"Just wait," she said. "That night I was walking back to the main hall. I ran into Barlow. And, I don't know, I just told him. He's kind of a dark, intense guy, but I didn't imagine this kind of reaction. He just listened, thought for a second, and said, 'Don't tell anyone else. I have a plan that will stop Hart permanently.'"

"And you listened?"

"He was very magnetic at that moment," Chelsea said. "I figured I'd still get what I want."

"And that's all that's important," Bolster said.

"Don't be harsh, Matt."

"You're going to take us into his apartment now," he said. "You're not going to announce our presence in any way. And you're going to help us arrest him for the murder of Tom Hart. We have an eyewitness. And you don't seem to be refuting her account. Maybe if you cooperate we can keep you out of jail."

To Chelsea's credit, she didn't try to play the seduction card. Bolster had found his way down Telegraph Avenue and had found his way to the killer.

"Fine," she said. "Let me get the groceries."

She had a key to the building.

"How long have you been staying here?" Bolster asked.

"A few days," Chelsea said.

"Are you fucking him?"

"He practices *bramacharya*," she said. "At least with me. It's very frustrating."

There was no elevator, just a short flight of dingy stairs up to the second floor, which had frayed red carpet and oak doors with rusted brass knockers. It was a nice place for an ascetic, and probably also the only place that Barlow could afford. Now that he wasn't being subsidized by Tom Hart, who knew how long that would last.

Chelsea opened the door. Barlow sat in the middle of the living room, meditating. More accurately, he hovered *above* the living room floor, levitated a few inches, wearing jeans and a leather biker jacket, looking cool and menacing. Barlow's eyes were closed. Bolster looked at Malik, whose eyes were bulging again, indicating that he needed to stay quiet.

"Did you get the kimchi?" Barlow asked. "It keeps you vital."

"Um," Chelsea said.

Barlow opened his eyes. He saw the cops, and his butt hit the floor with a thump.

"I didn't know we were having guests for tea," Barlow said.

"We're here to arrest you for the murder of Tom Hart," Vijay said.

"You don't have anything on me," Barlow said.

"Actually, Kimberly told them everything," said Chelsea.

Barlow huffed.

"Fuck," he said.

Bolster didn't trust what was behind those eyes.

"I have some questions," he said.

"OK, Bolster," said Barlow. "You usually do."

"First of all, how?"

Barlow smirked.

"Ancient Chinese secret," Barlow said.

Bolster was not amused.

"It's something I was working on for a long time. I practiced on a couple of dead birds. And on a couple of live cats."

Bolster didn't believe in cruelty toward any animals. But then he thought of his fat monster Charlemagne, hogging the sofa and the remote. Maybe it wouldn't be so bad . . . *No, he thought to himself. Barlow is filling your head with evil. Banish the thoughts.*

"OK," he said. "But, just as importantly, why?"

"Because I was tired of Hart manipulating yoga for his own purposes. Tired of the greed, and the abuse. He was an ego monster."

"But he wasn't a murderer," Bolster said.

"I've learned how to do . . . things," Barlow said. "Things you couldn't imagine, Bolster. Mysteries from before time."

Bolster rolled his eyes.

"You're not the first," Bolster said.

"He's not?" said Malik.

"Of course not," Bolster said, "but most people can control it, or are modest."

"It's not like I'm a mass murderer," Barlow said.

"Yet," said Bolster.

"Hart had to be sacrificed for the good of the overall practice."

Bolster took a step toward Barlow, who recoiled a little, back toward the window.

"And what about my friend who's in jail?" Bolster said. "Did he have to be sacrificed, too?"

"That's an unfortunate situation," Barlow said. "After I took care of Hart, I went for a walk so I could dispose of the evidence, bury it somewhere in the woods. There was a path, and your buddy was just lying there, out of sight. He seemed to be alive, just passed out. So I smeared a little blood on him and buried the remains nearby. It was a happy coincidence."

"For you," Bolster said angrily.

Bolster gestured toward Vijay.

"Get the cuffs," Bolster said.

"Hang on," said Barlow.

With frightening speed, he moved toward Bolster and put his hand on his chest. Bolster felt the pressure. Suddenly, he couldn't move.

"Andrew, no," Chelsea said.

Barlow leaned toward Bolster's right ear. He uttered a mantra. Bolster had never heard it before, but he instantly knew it was wicked. Then he uttered it again.

Bolster couldn't move. He couldn't talk. And he couldn't think. His feet felt numb, and his brain felt cloudy. He could look out through his eyes, but everything appeared gray and gauzy, like he was watching it from a distance, through a filter. The world was slow and colorless and abstract. He sensed that Chelsea was protesting and also sensed that Barlow was tossing her aside, somewhat violently, but Bolster couldn't move to stop it, or to stop anything.

Bolster had been controlled. Barlow went past him, and up to Vijay. He placed his hand on Vijay's chest.

"What is this, like the Vulcan death grip?" Vijay said.

"Sort of," Barlow said, "and it'll be less painful."

Vijay swatted Barlow's hand away.

"I don't think so," he said.

"It's hardest when you resist."

All this was happening just behind Bolster, so he couldn't turn to see what was going on. But he would have seen this:

Barlow moved in close, pinning Vijay's hands against the door. He leaned in and whispered a mantra.

"What did you say?" Vijay said.

Barlow whispered it again, and then a third time.

Vijay wrestled away and popped Barlow on the jaw.

"I'm not interested in your guru shit," Vijay said.

Barlow looked stunned. No one could resist his extraordinary powers. But it looked like Vijay Malik could. Barlow's eyes started darting for an exit. He looked like a scared first-time shoplifter. Vijay blocked the door. Barlow turned, ran across the room, flung open the rickety, old two-hinged window and launched himself out, feet first. Vijay ran over. He could see Barlow hitting the alley, feet first. Chelsea dashed past Vijay, out the door.

Bolster remained standing in the middle of the room, frozen. Vijay snapped his fingers in front of Bolster's face. Nothing. He slapped Bolster, hard, across the cheek. Still, Bolster didn't respond.

"Come on, Bolster!" he shouted. "We've got to motor!"

Bolster wasn't budging. Vijay saw a copy of *Light On Yoga* on the coffee table, hardback, original edition, probably pretty valuable. But he didn't know that. He just could see that the book was big and thick and useful in a way that its author, Mr. Iyengar, had probably never intended.

Vijay picked up the book, swung, and smacked it hard into Bolster's solar plexus.

Bolster let out a huge puff of air, and a pitiful groan, and then he put his hands on his knees.

"Fuck," he said.

Vijay yanked him out the door, leaving it open, all of Barlow's and Chelsea's possessions inside. Bolster felt woozy, but at least he could move. They got outside in time to see Barlow's motorcycle roaring out of the alleyway and onto the street, Chelsea holding on behind him. Barlow had a helmet,

Chelsea didn't, which seemed to Bolster to be a good metaphor for how recklessly she lived. But Bolster didn't have time to think.

"Can you drive?" Vijay said.

"Umm," Bolster said.

"DRIVE!" Vijay shouted.

Bolster got out the keys. Whitey's automatic locks hadn't worked since about 2004, when he'd accidentally gone swimming with the keys in his bathing suit. The manual lock-turn didn't always work, either.

"Jesus," Vijay said.

Bolster got the door open. He manually unlocked Vijay's door. Vijay got in. By the time Bolster started the car and buckled up, Barlow and Chelsea were three blocks up the hill.

"Gas it!" Vijay said.

Bolster did, but Whitey took a while to go, and Barlow was hardly using stop signs. Bolster could hear the skidding and honking from blocks away. Neither he nor Malik had a siren, and he could just hear his excuse to the local cops: "Officer, I'm a private yoga detective, and we're chasing this guy who used his *siddhis* to remove someone's heart and can hypnotize people into thinking it's no big deal."

Even in Berkeley, that excuse wouldn't fly far.

Bolster decided to risk the speeding ticket and cranked Whitey up to sixty-five. He could see the back of Barlow's motorcycle now and was definitely gaining. Chelsea's hair whipped behind her like solar coronae. Barlow hunched over the bars, squeezing the throttle, making his animal roar.

There was a stretch without stops, and Bolster got close. If this was Whitey's last run, then it would go down as honorable. He pressed the gas. The bumper touched Barlow's back tire, making the bike wobble. Barlow throttled hard and pulled ahead a little. Then he pulled into an intersection and braked. Chelsea grabbed his midsection as the bike went nearly horizontal, turned, and then righted itself around Bolster, heading the other direction.

That was more than Whitey could handle. Bolster hit the intersection, turned in a circle, slowly. He had to shift and reshift and position and reposition. It was a four-point turn. Bolster headed back downhill.

"This car is shitty," Vijay said.

"Tell me about it," said Bolster.

"Seriously, my mom turns faster than that in the supermarket parking lot."

"I'm poor," Bolster said. "Are you going to make me feel bad?"

Barlow was near the bottom of the hill now. He whipped around again, passing Bolster on the way up. Chelsea looked in the window, mouthed something that looked like *I'm sorry.* Then they were past.

Bolster had a narrow space to turn around. This was a crowded block, with cars parked up and down the hill on either side. It was going to take forever. In fact, Bolster wasn't even sure he could pull it off. It would take five or six discrete movements. Whitey had the turning radius of an oil tanker.

Barlow was long gone, roaring up into the Berkeley hills headed in God knows what direction. Vijay was plugging his phone into Whitey's cigarette lighter using an extension thing that Bolster had, but it was going to take several minutes before they could call the cops and several more minutes before they could actually get someone to start looking for Barlow, if they didn't immediately reject the call as being from a cranky weirdo. This was police work from the late '90s, at best, and it wasn't going to happen.

Bolster stopped the car. Whitey still had gas but didn't have the horses. There would be no epic chase. He double-parked.

"We'll catch them soon," Malik said.

"I doubt that," said Bolster.

Bolster really wasn't sure. For some reason, because he didn't believe, or didn't care, or some combination of the two, Vijay hadn't felt Barlow inside his mind. But Bolster did. That guy was *powerful*. And it wasn't the kind of power that dissipates. It only would increase with discipline, and Barlow wouldn't respond to stress. Barlow might not have any financial resources, but he could hide. Chelsea *certainly* knew how to hide. All they needed was a tank of gas and a cabin in the mountains.

Getting these two was going to be a long-term process, if Bolster could even get anyone else to care.

A bike cop pulled alongside him and started writing a ticket.

Bolster thought, *Now they show up.*

EPILOGUE

Ten days later, Bolster and Suzie Hahn drove back up to Ventura, to get Slim out of jail. Bolster hadn't wanted Suzie to come, but she seemed determined to continue to chronicle Bolster's dubious legend on her blog and podcast. On the way up, she interviewed him.

"So, Matt Bolster," she said, "how does it feel to have solved another epic yoga murder?"

"I haven't solved anything," Bolster said. "The suspect is still at large."

"Dangerous!" said Suzie. "What can you tell us about him?"

"I really don't want to comment."

"Understandable, understandable," Suzie said. "But maybe just a little bit?"

"Let's just say I used my extraordinary powers," Bolster said.

"Ooh!" Suzie said.

Bolster wished he knew more. The local, state, and federal cops had been combing California, looking for a leather-clad hippie and a hot yoga babe on a motorcycle, but they'd found nothing. Barlow probably had some kind of trick that made him blend into the trees. He was a dark yoga lord, a phrase that Bolster would never say out loud, out of fear of getting mocked. But it was true. The guy could have been hovering ten feet above the ground.

Chelsea, on the other hand, should have been easier to spot, with her penchant for bright colors and loud gestures. Then again, she always seemed to be able to persuade people to hide her, particularly men. She could easily be in Nosara for the duration, endlessly perfecting her warrior two under the Costa Rican sun. Bolster hated himself for wishing he could be there, too.

They arrived at noon, the hour of Slim's release. Vijay Malik was waiting for them.

"It was our fault he got held in the first place," Vijay said. "I wanted to see this through."

Vijay had worked hard, making sure that Kimberly Wharton had told her story several more times. He reiterated to his superiors, and anyone who'd listen, that Barlow had told him he'd planted Hart's bloodstains on Slim's body. It sounded like lunacy. And it was. But it added up to a story with a beginning, middle, and end, with multiple corroborating accounts. So finally the authorities had to relent.

Charles Slimberg belonged to the world once more.

Slim walked through the gate pumping his fist. Suzie took a cell-phone shot, which she'd later post to her blog, and it would get 390 hits, plus 23 likes on Facebook and an equal number on Instagram. Totally viral, it wouldn't go.

Slim shot up rock 'n' roll hands, stuck out his tongue, and shouted "FREEDOM! WHOOO!" Suzie didn't photograph that. She did take a picture when Bolster gave Slim a big hug and said, "Welcome back to the world, man."

"You got me out, Bolster," he said.

"I promised," Bolster said.

Vijay Malik said, "I have a present for you, Slim."

He walked back to his car and got out a long object in the type of plastic bag that people use when they're checking their skis at the airport. Slim took the bag, unzipped it, and howled with delight.

"Barbie!" he said, and hugged and kissed his didgeridoo like he thought the moment would never have come.

He paused, put the didge to his lips, and let out a long, celebratory blow. Bolster winced. Suzie recorded, but she wasn't going to use the audio. Freedom sounded kind of horrible.

"It's good to be alive, Bolster," Slim said. Bolster had to agree.

Suzie took Slim aside for an "interview," which she also wasn't going to be able to use, since he would use the phrase "cosmic malingering" three times, and that was at least two times more than her audience would find acceptable. While they did that, Malik slipped Bolster an envelope.

"What's this?" Bolster said.

"Your fee," said Vijay. "I pulled it together."

Bolster looked inside. There was a lot of cash, in big stacks.

"How much?" he said.

"Five grand," said Vijay.

That was about a tenth of what Bolster had gotten for solving the Ajoy murder. Solving the Hart murder had taken at least an equal amount of work, if not more. But he knew that Malik had tried. You got paid where you could in this business.

"I wanted to ask you," Bolster said. "Why didn't Barlow's mumbo-jumbo have any effect on you, back in the apartment?"

"I don't know, exactly," Malik said. "I don't believe in this yoga shit. Maybe belief is a requirement for it to work."

Bolster looked thoughtful. The idea that maybe people *shouldn't* do yoga hadn't occurred to him. He quickly perished the thought.

"I'll keep that in mind," he said. "But you really should practice. It's good for everyone."

"That's not in the plan right now," said Vijay. "But if I ever decide to, I know who I'll call for private lessons."

"Thanks, man," Bolster said. They shook hands, and then they parted, Vijay to return to his wife and kids and his fantasies of brunching with Fareed Zakaria, and Bolster to whatever the present moment had in store for him. It was usually something interesting.

He and Suzie and Slim got into Whitey. They left like a team, just like they'd driven up two months before.

"Let's cruise down to the beach," Slim said. "We can get high."

That sounded like a plan to Bolster.

Half an hour later, they were in Santa Barbara, parked forty feet away from a shallow bay, sucking on Bolster's portable pencil vape. Even Suzie was joining in the fun. They had something tangible to celebrate. Sometimes she'd play.

"This shit is strong!" she said.

"And stinky," Slim said.

Slim was in the backseat, as usual. He reached past Bolster's left arm, to the driver's side window controls.

"Let's get some air in here," he said, and pressed the button down.

Bolster was too stoned to stop him.

"No, wait!" Bolster protested feebly, as the window descended.

"What?" said Slim.

"It's broken," said Bolster. "It won't go back up."

"Damn, dude," said Slim, "I'm sorry."

"It's cool," Bolster said.

Of course, it wasn't cool, not really. Bolster didn't want to pay for the repair. But if it had to happen, this was a decent time.

Right now, he had the money.

ABOUT THE AUTHOR

A veteran crime and humor writer and a certified Ashtanga vinyasa instructor, Neal Pollack has emerged as America's most trenchant, and funniest, observer of New Age yoga culture. Pollack is the bestselling author of the memoirs *Alternadad* and *Stretch*; the novels *Never Mind the Pollacks*, *Jewball*, and *Downward Facing Death*; and *The Neal Pollack Anthology of American Literature*, a cult classic of satirical fiction. In addition to his books, he's also a regular contributor to *Wired*, *Vanity Fair*, *GQ*, and many other publications. When he's not writing or doing yoga, Neal is the front man for the rock and roll band The Neal Pollack Invasion and a ring announcer for the Texas Rollergirls. He lives in Austin, Texas, with his wife and son.

Kindle Serials

This book was originally released in episodes as a Kindle Serial. Kindle Serials launched in 2012 as a new way to experience serialized books. Kindle Serials allow readers to enjoy the story as the author creates it, purchasing once and receiving all existing episodes immediately, followed by future episodes as they are published. To find out more about Kindle Serials and to see the current selection of Serials titles, visit www.amazon.com/kindleserials.

11422536R00155

Printed in Great Britain
by Amazon.co.uk, Ltd.,
Marston Gate.